End.

"Dr. Dunham is a tremendously gifted writer, communicator, and leader. I have been blessed by his teaching and ministry for years and know you will too."

— Craig Groeschel, Pastor of LifeChurch.tv
Author of *Soul Detox, Clean Living in a Contaminated World*

"Drawing on thirty years building international relationships in Asian cultures, Dr. Dunham has created a background for a story with the intensity and thorough attention to details that parallels his professional service career in higher education. Dr. Dunham has the unique ability to see what lies within a society, what makes it tick, and then overlay an unfolding story that captures both suspense and sympathy. His depth of study and insight is unsurpassed.

— Glenn E. Short, architect, engineer, principal
FSB-Frankfurt-Short-Bruza-Architecture

"From the very first page, you enter into the heart and soul of a Korean orphan fighting for his life in a Korea that I remember as a middle school student. No American man understands the Korean heart like Dennis Dunham does. His book carries profound energy that is both funny and suspenseful."

— Seong Nam Lee,
President, Interstudy Korea

"A lot of people travel and experience the world, but few people will ever possess the diplomacy of this man. I've always admired his ability to connect with people everywhere he goes. No matter the language, culture, or given situation, he is always right on cue. He loves life and is always so careful to take in each little moment, often observing and deeply absorbing an instant that would otherwise go unnoticed by the rest of the world. Dennis is a success in his career, with his family, and as a friend. He is a true storyteller with great sensibility, a wonderful imagination, and a lifetime of memories are at the heart of it all."

— Kyle Dillingham,
Violinist Co-Creator of Symphonic Revival

The Good-Luck Side of the Rice-Paper Door

Kathryn,

You deserve "Good Luck" and now you have it.

Thanks for so many things, my best boss ever!

Denis Dunlap

The Good-Luck Side of the Rice-Paper Door

DENNIS DUNHAM

TATE PUBLISHING
AND ENTERPRISES, LLC

Published by Tate Publishing & Enterprises, LLC
127 E. Trade Center Terrace | Mustang, Oklahoma 73064 USA
1.888.361.9473 | www.tatepublishing.com

Tate Publishing is committed to excellence in the publishing industry. The company reflects the philosophy established by the founders, based on Psalm 68:11,
"The Lord gave the word and great was the company of those who published it."

Cover design by Chelsea Womble
Interior design by Errol Villamante

Published in the United States of America

ISBN: 978-1-62147-582-8
1. Fiction / Suspense
2. Fiction / Men's Adventure
12.10.22

Dedication

This book is dedicated to my three sons,
Brook, Joshua, and Casey.

Chapter One

Jason Young-Soo O'Leary
September 2, 1977
Kwangju, Korea

Some have said I should not feel shame in telling this story. I did not bring the shame on myself. That may be true, but innocent or not, in my people's way of thinking, shame has no conditions.

Koreans believe very much in *unmyung*. It is a kind of destiny. In my country, we say that destiny has four feet, eight hands, and sixteen eyes. It is therefore impossible for a two-legged human to escape. *Unmyung* changes our life, and it is neither good nor bad, although we hope it is good. We hope that *unmyung* will bring us good things.

But I told myself that I had no *unmyung*. I had luck, which is very different than *unmyung*. But I had the kind of luck that took things away from me, not the kind that brought good things to me. Sometimes, when I stood on the corner of my hometown, I saw the children riding in the back seat of cars. I never rode in cars. I never ate ice cream cones. I never had parents scold me. Luck took that away from me. Luck gave that to the children in the back seat. But I did not envy. The sun and the shade frequently change places. It could happen to them too. I did not wait for my luck. It is like waiting for death.

I always begged in the same spot in front of the only movie theater in town. My thirteen-year-old boss, who took all of the money I collected, assigned it to me. He said that I was cute and said if I was pitiful and cute, I could get a lot of money. Money for him. But he taught me to look pitiful. I quickly learned to hold my chin down and look up at the people who came. I practiced sad eyes with the other beggars until my boss was satisfied. He was right. I collected more money in a single day than some others in a week. As a result, my boss gave me an even busier spot. It didn't matter to me. No matter how much money I collected, my life never changed. I got a single bowl of ramen noodles at night and slept with the other beggars.

The man who later became my master for a while gave me a ten-won coin each day that he came by. He also said I was cute. He was tall for my people. Also very thin. He had very narrow eyes that stared down at me past large, round cheekbones. "Cute boy," he would say. "Maybe smart?"

I dared not stare at him long. But one day I followed him and watched him go into the most famous public bathhouse in Kwangju. Actually, it was the basement of a small hotel. The nearer he walked to the building, the more the people around him began to bow. By the time he reached the door, I knew he was its master. Then, somehow knowing I was there, he turned and looked at me.

I did not move. I did not want to anger him. I had followed him out of curiosity. Maybe now I would never again receive the ten-won coin from him. But he stared at me for a long time. "Maybe smart," he said. "Maybe work hard?" If it was a question, I never answered it. With a wave of his fingers, he ushered me into his house. And so on that day I had a new kind of luck. This luck took me out of the cold wind and hard streets. This luck took me into a warm house with food every day.

After I followed my master through the doors, I was amazed. I had never been in a bathhouse before. I was surprised to see a shiny, lacquered wooden floor with tiny lockers all around it. There was a glass wall, and through that were the baths, where I could clearly see marble tubs and showers of many sizes. No one was bathing, however, as the baths were closed for the night.

But I did not let happiness sleep with me that first night. This was only luck, not destiny. Luck was very temporary. Probably too short. I was only seven years old but knew better than to hold tightly to something good.

I was right about that. The warm bathhouse was not to be my destiny. My real destiny came to me through a man with many hairs.

It was the first day I had been given the great responsibility of opening the public bathhouse by myself, and I should have been proud, I suppose. Such a young person to have such important duties. But I was frightened. Bigger work could mean bigger mistakes. Big enough mistakes could make the master angry with me. Big enough anger, he could send me away.

I had not a single complaint. The wooden floor of the bathhouse had a charcoal brick burning under it all day and night. There was one very warm spot where the master let me sleep. It was so warm that I didn't even ask for a blanket. His wife made me breakfast and dinner, and the master generally gave me some of his rice and kimchi at lunch. The spicy, pickled cabbage was my favorite food, and when I was on the street, I rarely had even a bite of it.

I never asked for anything, but the master continued giving me a ten-won coin every day. He expected me to use it for candy, but I never did. I hid it in a plastic bag in a secret corner of the locker room. It would be there when luck took all of this away from me again.

I only went outside when my master sent me to buy something. The master never had to worry about me dawdling while on an errand. I ran to the store, and I ran back. I knew the streets would be waiting for me soon enough, and I wanted to stay away from them as long as I could. In addition, I knew my former street boss would be angry with me for deserting my corner. If he found me, I would be beaten. Only beaten, I hoped.

Sometimes I sat in the warm bathhouse and looked at the rice-paper door. The sturdy rice paper, framed with bamboo, was so thin that you see the shadows of the customers before they came in. But it was a great protectant, and I knew this was all that separated me from the sharp, frigid wind outside. As I look back, I knew that I was not bitter about such things. I knew that this was not a life I deserved, but it was the life that I had received.

Opening the public bathhouse was not nearly as difficult as the strenuous cleaning it required to close it. By morning, things had dried and merely needed to be put in their place. I pushed open the glass door to the bathing area and slipped inside. The tall showers were on the left, and I checked and refilled each shampoo container carefully. This was the first area for cleansing. Then in the center was the second bath. There was a large, square-shaped marble tub big enough for eight to ten men to squeeze into without accidentally touching each other. I stepped down into the deep tub and turned on the left nozzle. Scalding water immediately poured in, and I jumped back as the stinging drops bounced off my skin.

Along another wall behind the bath were the shorter showers, less than a meter from the floor. This is where the real cleaning took place. The previous night I had washed the little red plastic stools and placed them on the side of the tub to dry. Now I took them off, twenty-one in all, and placed them under each showerhead. There, each customer could sit on the stool, face his own private mirror, and shave, if he chose. A bucket was kept beside him if he preferred to pour it over himself and make the howling washing noises the men of my country like to make.

To my right was another smaller tub, the dreaded cold water one. There was only one nozzle, and this was the one I always had difficulty turning. Soon enough, the icy water was flowing solidly into the bottom of the bath. It surrounded my feet, and I jumped out of its way.

"Young-Soo!"

Startled, I turned around to see my master standing in the glass doorway. I did not greet him verbally but bowed low. "Young-Soo!" he called again, and this time I was certain. Somehow I had made him angry.

"You waste hot water." His voice was trembling. "Look at the hot tub. You foolish boy."

I heard the sound of my heart in my head. I looked. The tub should have had a few inches of water by now. But there was no water in the tub.

"Why did you not put the stopper in the tub?"

I looked bleakly at the empty hole where the water poured out. I had forgotten to pick up the stopper as I came into the room. Now it was in the master's hand. He threw it in my direction. I picked it up and then, needing to know the extent of the master's anger, I looked at his face.

"Do not look at me when I'm talking to you," he said angrily, and I jerked my eyes away.

I quickly took the stopper and jumped into the tub. The water was so hot that the pain shot up my arm. I fought the urge to jerk my hand back and kept it there until I had secured the stopper. When I pulled my hand back, it was red and throbbing and gave me some trouble for many days. But I deserved all this pain and more. He was right. I was a foolish boy.

"You waste expensive hot water." The master turned and walked away.

I finished my other duties and looked around the bathhouse several times. Everything was surely done. Once again my feet were on the warm wooden floor. *Will this be my last moment here?* I wondered, and I stole a look at the corner that hid my coins. Perhaps tonight I would sleep on the bad luck side of the rice-paper door.

The master sat down next to the door and was brushing his shoes. He looked up at me, and, once again, I silently bowed but this time kept my eyes at his feet. A moment passed, and then he grunted, "You need to learn how to clean shoes. This is a good job for you."

New job of cleaning shoes was the best sound for me to hear. "I can clean the shoes," I told him. "Teach me," I begged him. "I will learn quickly."

The first customer came in at six o'clock. He was dressed in a suit, but his tie hung out of his pocket. I bowed and welcomed him. He pulled his shoes off before he stepped onto the wooden floor. I opened his locker and gathered his shoes up to place them in the box beside the door.

The customer quickly stripped off his clothes and hung them loosely in the locker. I handed him the key on a rubber band. He took it from me and slipped it around his ankle. I handed him a small towel that he carried in front of him. Only then did I glance to see if my master was watching. He was, but he did not appear unpleased.

It is impolite to enter the tubs while dirty, so the customer showered first, and while he did, I stuck my fingers partway into the hot tub. It was still scalding, and I turned on the cold water, feeling it again and again until it was bearable. Still, the customer gasped when he stepped into the tub, but he did not complain.

Another customer came in and then another. Soon the public bath was full of businessmen. The bathing of the morning group was not pleasurable; it was hurried work before their day began. They did not chat, and they did not indulge in long soaking.

By nine o'clock, the morning group had fastened their ties, grabbed their briefcases, and with barely a word, gone off to their respective offices.

My master kept a clean bathhouse, and I followed his strict instructions to drain the water three times during the day. *This day has gone well*, I thought as I scrubbed the floors for the third time that day. I pictured myself once again sleeping on the warm spot of the wooden floor that night.

That evening, about an hour before my *unmyung*, my destiny, the customers began to arrive in scores. They were weary and threw their clothes off. They turned on the showers and leaned their foreheads against the wall while the hot showers flowed directly on their necks. They made loud, satisfied gasps and then fell, limply, into the hot tub.

Mr. Lee was a regular customer who had gray hair and a giant, round stomach. He was very rich, I had heard. But I would have known this without the telling of it. The rich have fat stomachs. The little red plastic stool protested as he squatted down on it. He turned and yelled, "Hey!"

"Hey" is what I was called here. Only the master used my name. If I had had a father, they could have called me by my father's name, but since I didn't, "Hey" had become a familiar sound to me.

"Hey!" he called again, although I was already rushing to his side. "Bring me the soap." He began to inspect his face in the little round mirror with his right hand and extended his left until I dropped the soap into it. "Wait," he said, and he thought for a moment while I waited at attention beside him, but then he commanded, "Bring me a towel." He then turned the shower on and aimed it at his face.

The stack of dry towels was very near him, but I reached the extra distance and handed him one. Again he reached for the towel and opened his fingers. I nudged his hand with the towel, but this time his fingers did not grasp it. His arm remained in the air. I nudged his fingers again, but his pudgy, short fingers remained dangling in the air. I looked at his face.

His eyes were wide open, and he was staring at a place beyond me. The room had become quiet. Only the sound of the showers could be heard. I slowly turned my head. All the customers had the same kind of transfixed expression. No one spoke. I followed their eyes until I saw the master. He was standing in the center of the locker area but was also staring raptly at the door. I continued my turn and moved forward slightly.

I dropped the towel.

I will not say the strange man standing in the door frightened me. Actually, I did not know how I should feel. I had never heard of such men. I had had no education then, and no one had ever explained things to me. I had no knowledge of any world other than my own. I did not know there was any place other than Korea, any city other than mine. I knew of no life better or worse than the one I had seen with my own eyes. And so I had not the slightest idea that such a man existed.

The first thing I remember was his height. Such a giant was he that he had to bow his head to stand under the door. His hair was longer than I had ever seen on a man so young, but it was the color that was the most shocking. I had seen such a color before—in the autumn, when the leaves turned from green to red to brown. His hair was the color of the leaves, just before turning brown.

The only thing after that I could see was nose. I wondered how he could get air through such a large nose. I could not take my eyes away from it.

The master was the first to speak, and he broke the silence with a well managed "Welcome," and then bowed, as he did to all his customers. Then the man bowed, smiled, slipped off his shoes, and stepped into the room.

He stood there awkwardly, as though he didn't know what to do next. His eyes turned toward the transfixed audience of customers who were staring at him through the glass partition from the tub. He smiled in their direction. Still no one spoke. He looked around again as if waiting for something.

"Young-Soo!"

My master was gesturing at me. "Come take care of the customer."

I take care of the customer? I take care of the giant standing in the middle of the locker room?

Now all eyes had turned toward me. Mr. Lee nudged me. "Go help the megook person."

That was the first time I had heard that word, *megook*. Later, I learned to use the English word that Americans call themselves by. But even today I never think of them as Americans, always megook.

"Young-Soo!" the master called loudly.

This time I ran. I opened the locker, bowed at the giant, and then went for his shoes. I stopped again. The shoes of the giant waited beside the door. They were so large, I found myself stifling a scream. I was actually afraid to touch them, but, more fearful of angering my master, I picked them up and placed them on the shoe rack. They stuck out so far that I waited for a moment to see if they would fall.

The megook was saying something to the master. I could not understand it, but the master nodded. The megook now fumbled with the buttons on his shirt. Again, no one moved. No one spoke. One by one the buttons came loose. I gradually became aware that what we were doing might have been considered rude. We never watched anyone undress. We never put our eyes where they should not be. The bathhouses were for cleansing, relaxing, and socializing. No one ever looked.

Then the shirt was off, and I could not stop the words that came out of my mouth.

"Oh, I'm going to die!"

The master hushed me, but even as he did, he too looked amazed.

With his shirt off, the megook made me think of pictures I had seen of monkeys.

He had hair on his arms and hair on some places of his chest. I could not resist the temptation to walk around to his back to see if he had hair there as well. But there was none.

At this point I sat on the floor, cross-legged, and rested my chin in my hands. The socks came off, and the pants came off. That was not too surprising, as I had seen many men who had hair on their legs before. But again, this hair was the color of the dark-red leaves.

Now the hairy giant with the leaf-colored hair and the excessive nose began to fumble with his underwear. Although I didn't think about it then, I am quite certain now we would not have moved had they announced an air raid from the North.

The underwear was gone, and the megook shoved it in the locker and closed the door. I think, at that moment, we all breathed a sigh of relief. Except for all that hair and nose, he was more like us than not like us.

In order to hand him his key and his little towel, I had to approach him. He leaned far down toward me to receive it and then quickly held the small towel in front of himself. I liked his smile, and he said something to me that I didn't understand. I was about to smile back when I received my next big shock. His eyes were not like our eyes at all. I jumped back, and he jumped a little too. But once again my curiosity was so great that I found myself leaning forward. He leaned forward too and then squatted slightly as though he was actually letting me get a better view of his face.

Before I did so, I looked up at my master. His face was friendly and calm. I looked back at the megook person. He seemed amused, as though I were the curiosity and not he. I moved closer.

Now I was sure. Part of his eyes was missing. Part of the center dark part. At first I felt sorry for him, that he was missing this important part of his eyes. But in the next moment I realized they had been replaced with something wonderful. And I laughed and clapped. It was the first time I remember being just a seven-year-old boy, laughing and clapping at seeing something so marvelous.

For in the center of his eyes were tiny round windows. And if you looked through the windows, you could see the sky.

Chapter Two

Charles Dickens

Sixteen Years Later (July 3, 1993)

Singapore

"So, they finally remodeled the blooming suite, did they?" I said to the porter as though he cared. "Well, it's about time."

The porter dropped my bag in the bedroom and followed me into the living area of this highly prized business-class suite located on the twenty-second floor of the Marina Mandarin Hotel.

First things first. I opened my bag and pulled out my laptop. "Now where did they move the blooming socket?"

The blooming socket was right in front of me. The porter raised a pointing finger and smiled. "Ah, there you are!" I said to the socket and began setting my computer up. I stood for a moment and admired the extra telephone line jack for the Internet connection. "Well," I said, as I stuffed five Singapore dollars into the porter's hand as he exited the room and closed the door, "it doesn't get much better than this, does it now?"

Blast! I glanced at my watch and saw I was already late for dinner with the client I had traveled ten thousand miles to see. I opened the mini cooler and pulled out a Coke. I held it under one arm as I rushed into my bedroom to at least open my suitcase and find my toothbrush.

When I popped open the Coke, it exploded in my face.

The doorbell rang.

"Just a minute!" I shouted at the closed door. Now the Coke had spilled on my shirt and soaked the top part of my pants. The doorbell rang again. I unlocked the door and rushed toward the toilet. "Come on in," I said. "I've spilled Coke all over myself." I grabbed the white towel and began mopping myself up. I heard an unfamiliar man's voice just outside the door.

"Uh, anything I can do to help?" he said. Still mopping myself, I stuck my head out the door.

A famous movie star was standing in the middle of the living room.

I stopped mopping myself.

Rod Chambers was the top box-office draw in America, actually the world. I had no idea that he was in Singapore. This guy, and his alleged scandals, was on the cover of all the magazines you stared at while waiting in line at the supermarket. My first thought, of course, was my pride. I was shaken and didn't want to appear it. He was, after all, I reminded myself, just another human being. But then there he was, the star of *The Argosy Initiative*—the latest one-hundred-million-dollar action movie.

Rod was dressed casually enough—dark-brown hiking shoes, tanned slacks with a burnt-orange golf shirt. His sunglasses were hooked over the front end of the collar. His hair was long, blond, combed evenly, and pulled back—right out of the movies. He extended his hand to me. "Sorry to have startled you."

Startled me, had he? No, of course, I'm quite used to famous people wandering into my suite. On the other hand, of course, I was all covered in Coke.

I managed to take his hand with my own slightly Coke dampened one. I was now ready to say something brilliant. "You're Rod Chambers, aren't you?" I said intelligently.

He smiled slightly. I'm sure he met stammering fools every day of his famous life. I refused to be one of them. I would even impress him with a glimpse of my originality, creativity, and famous Charles wit.

"I've seen all your movies," I said, and I hated myself.

He made no apparent acknowledgment of the compliment but continued to stand there.

Oddly enough, I found myself offering him a seat.

He sat. He sat, and he stared. He was staring at me.

"Let's try again. I'm Charles Dickens." I waited for the normal joke about my name. There was none. I stuck out my hand confidently this time. His handshake was loose.

We paused and looked at each other. *What the devil is Rod Chambers doing in my room?*

He said nothing, and so, as though we were at a reception, I found myself trying to fill the silence. "Is there anything I can do for you?"

Amazingly, he didn't answer. Those famous concave blue eyes remained focused in my direction. Many long seconds passed.

I considered the fact that he might have been ill and had just wandered into the first open door. "Are you okay?" I finally said, leaning forward.

"I'm fine," he said quickly and then sat up straight. "Perhaps we could just sit and talk a while," he offered.

Now it was my turn to stare. Sit and talk a while?

"Why don't you tell me about yourself?" he said.

I sat back in my chair. "You mean you want…" I was completely rattled. "Well, if you…well…why don't we talk about me?" I stuttered.

He nodded.

"Why?"

"Please," he said.

In all my thirty-seven years, I had had some pretty weird experiences, amazing adventures, but this… I looked around the room. My bag was there, the computer was there, and my heart was gladdened to see them. They made things seem almost normal until a memory of a young boy playing with a Rod Chambers's action figure flashed through my mind. "Well," I said, trying to think about where to begin.

Rod's eyebrows raised and leaned forward.

How very odd. And how very cool. What a good story this would be. I decided to follow its trail.

"I'm a businessman," I said. "Mostly, I act as a consultant, connecting international partners throughout the world."

Rod settled back in his chair. He seemed satisfied with how I had begun. His eyes were encouraging. Actually, they seemed downright intrigued. I was myself again and thought how much fun it was being fascinating to a young, famous movie star. I decided to amaze him with other details.

"I speak two European languages fluently and three Asian languages, although my reading level in Chinese is only about equal to an eighth-grader," I added modestly. "I've been in the international arena since I joined Peace Corp in Korea."

I paused for a moment. *What am I doing?* Then I continued, "Little by little I developed a large, extended network of friends and business associates around the world. Now, people call me. Someone needs a manufacturer to build a chip for their CD player. I know someone in China who can build it. I get them together for dinner, introduce them, and work out the differences," I said with satisfaction.

Rod crossed one leg on top of the other. He intertwined his two hands and placed them behind his head and leaned back.

Surreal. I almost said it out loud. *This is surreal.* He looked down; he opened his lips and then shut them. He looked at me, opened his mouth again, and then took a deep breath and sighed heavily. Amazingly, he jumped up suddenly and moved about the room, staying several feet away from me. He began to pace.

I can't stand gaps. If there are gaps, I try to fill them with whatever I can. Here was a gap, and for the moment I provided the best explanation that I could. Perhaps he was doing some research for a movie.

That made enough sense to allow me to gain confidence. I was not, therefore, especially overwhelmed by what he said to me next. He turned, stopped, and looked at me. "I know who you are," he said.

That had to be it. Research—perhaps about an international businessman. "What do you mean?" I asked without emotion.

He stopped and looked down at me. "I've been looking for you."

He paused, I suppose, to observe my expression. I had none. It all fit now and was tremendously flattering. I could not resist smiling and said, "Go on, please."

Now his face showed faint surprise. He almost spoke again. He froze for a moment and then slumped into the chair, letting his head roll back, eyes closed. "I thought I would know what to say, but I don't."

There was a stirring in the pit of my stomach. That didn't fit. A mechanical voice from somewhere inside spoke next. "Why don't you try?"

I realized then how very thick the walls of my hotel suite were. No sound whatsoever interrupted. He sat quietly and stared so long at the wall behind me that I turned my head to see if there was something I had missed earlier. There was nothing—not a single painting. A faint thought crossed my mind that I should be getting ready for my dinner meeting.

He rubbed his closed eyes. "You sound a little British, but I guess that's because your parents were born there."

My hands instantly became damp. "How did you know that?"

This time he looked straight at me. "You're a master at the art of the deal. And you have an MBA in international business. I guess your mom had a sense of humor to name you—"

A master at the art of the… "My mom, "I responded, as if it were none of his business, "was proud of English literature and wanted me to have a very famous author's name."

"You were editor of your high school paper." Not an ounce of emotion in his voice.

"What the blooming…?" I jumped up and walked to the other side of the room. I turned around. "Is this some kind of research for a movie?"

He quietly remained fixed on the chair where I had been sitting. Slowly he turned his head toward me. He spoke as though each word required a lot of air. "This is not research. I don't know any way to do this except how I'm doing it. Please be patient. It will all become clear to you."

Please be patient. It will all become clear to me.

Part of me wanted him to leave, to tell him to go on his way. Of course, I couldn't. I sat back in the chair. "All right," I said, beginning to feel perturbed for the first time. "Go ahead." And I folded my arms and waited.

He looked confused. His gaze lowered, and his eyes squinted as if he were trying to find something small on the carpet. He looked so sad. *Where have I seen those eyes before?* I thought, and then the answer that came to me. "In the movies" didn't feel quite right.

"But your interest in journalism was fueled during your freshman year, when you won the Schroeder award," he said evenly, as though he were reading from a speech.

A light went on. "We have a mutual acquaintance, don't we? This is what this is all about. I spoke with confidence. "Did you know my wife? Deborah never mentioned…"

"I didn't know your wife or your daughter," he said; his voice remained flat. "I was sorry to hear about your loss."

These words stunned me. "You know about the…accident?" There was something about that sentence, "I was sorry," that sounded like he had known it at the time.

A memory I always fought to repress suddenly raced into my mind. I felt the sudden heat as one of the jet's wheels collapsed on landing. I had held onto both of them as we began a fiery skid around the runway. The flames jumped up around us. I heard only Deborah's scream and felt her being pulled away from me as the smoke engulfed us. My next memory was waking up in the hospital—alone.

But that had been five years ago.

Another moment passed. He pulled his shades off his collar and laid them on the coffee table in front of us. "In any case, the scholarship paid for your attendance to a national journalism conference in Chicago."

The business dinner tonight would be held without me. I touched my top button, suddenly feeling a chill. "Yes, that's right."

I squinted at Rod now as though he were a bright light. If this were an exercise, a rehearsal for some kind of movie script, it was no longer interesting. I had now experienced pain. Ridiculous. "Why are you here? How do you know these things?"

Rod stuttered, and I could tell that he was on the verge of answering my question directly. Then he stopped. "The first night in your room, you played cards." He looked at me suddenly. "Do you remember that?"

I could see that this was a question, which, for some reason, I felt the need to answer. His eyes were searching my face. I began to think. I actually did not remember any such card game or who might have been there.

I tried to remember that night. I couldn't. I tried to remember anything that happened in Chicago. This was my first and only visit to the Playboy Club, false IDs in hand. There were the notable guest speakers. I almost had the nerve to talk to Walter Cronkite but didn't. Ann Landers was the funniest speaker, although she admitted she wasn't a real journalist. Then there was something about cards.

"The cards," I said, as though thinking aloud.

"I believe it was poker," he said quickly.

"Yes, that's right." He was leading me somewhere but was only taking me so far. I was on my own from here.

It was poker, and I was teaching it to two women in my hotel room. How I could have forgotten that? They were journalism freshmen at some junior college in Texas.

I remembered the blonde quite well. Her clear, honest eyes were the first things I noticed about her. She had grabbed my arm after one of the conferences.

"You look like a guy I can trust," she said, holding me close. "There are some real hit men out here, if you get my drift."

I could see why she needed protection. She was a long-waisted five-foot-three with dancing eyes. She was beautiful and laughed as though we were already friends.

"What makes me so trustable?" I asked, pretending to be offended.

"Have you looked in the mirror recently?" she had said.

Just from watching the expression on my face, Rod suddenly turned white. Perspiration appeared around the edges of his forehead.

I leaned forward, "Good heavens, man! You look like you're going to faint."

He jerked his hands up in front of his face as though I were about to hit him. I sat back in my chair. "Please," he said again. "There was a girl."

"Yes," I said, now breathing hard, and I tried to remember her name—perhaps Beverly.

She had refused to let go of my arm until I had invited her to dinner. There was a French restaurant in the hotel that sounded exotic. We arrived without a reservation, but the waiter found us a table. I pulled out the chair for her to sit down. She sat down lightly on the chair and began to smooth out her dress.

"So you're a Schroeder Scholarship winner?" I asked her as a stiff waiter handed us the menus. He made me nervous—I began to feel that I didn't belong.

"That's right," she said, as though the subject didn't interest her.

I found out she was from Wichita Falls, Kansas. *Not too far away from Oklahoma*, I thought. But she didn't press me for any details. She didn't even ask me the name of my school.

"So what do you want to be when you grow up?" she asked teasingly.

I paused until the waiter had poured the water and left. "I'd like to be an astronaut. I'd like to travel in space."

"No, really," she said.

"I'm serious. You asked me what I wanted to be. That's it." I shrugged. "But I know that is highly unlikely, so maybe I'll be a journalist who writes about astronauts."

She scrunched her nose. "Sounds dull for you."

"Dull? What could be more interesting than writing about space?"

"I don't know," she said simply. "I just think that whatever it is, you'll find it."

That evening we sat on the floor with her roommate and mine. I explained the difference between a full house, a flush, and three of a kind. We gambled with high-school silliness and pretended to bet our clothes off. After a quick trip to the bathroom, I returned to find that the roommates had left, and the blonde and I were alone.

The images of Beverly were still around me when I looked at Rod again. I could still feel her breath on my shoulder, smell her perfume.

My face must have betrayed my thoughts. Rod moaned.

I could feel the blood rushing to my head. "Was…" I began. "Was your mother in that room?"

He didn't answer me.

I reached over and picked up Rod's sunglasses. I opened them and closed them once. A voice, my voice, but from somewhere outside of me, asked the next question.

"Rod?"

"Yes?"

"Exactly how old are you?"

"How old do you think?"

I stood up and walked to the window that covered the western wall. The balcony was small but inviting. The Singapore bay was filled with large motionless ships, scattered around the giant docks in V shape, each waiting their turn to unload. Five thousand dollars an hour to dock, someone told me.

"You're twenty-one," I said.

I turned around and looked again. My son was still sitting in my living room. How could I have missed that hair? I combed it every morning.

He stood up suddenly. "I have to go," he said, and he moved quickly toward the door.

I stepped toward him. "How did you know all these things?"

"I've had someone check on you for some years now."

"A private detective?"

He was silent for a long moment. "I tried to meet with you in LA. I asked an attorney friend to contact you."

"That was you?" I had gotten a call as I was rushing to the airport. "I was already on my way to—"

"I know. I heard you would stay several weeks."

"That's right."

"I'm wondering if you could come to LA for just a day or so."

"Well…" I stammered. "I have an appointment July twelfth in Kuala Lumpur."

"You can be back by then, if you'll still want to."

If I'll still want to… "Why now?" I asked.

"I'd like to explain in LA. But it's quite urgent." He opened the door.

"Wait, please, stay a little longer."

"I really hope you can come. I'm sorry, but it must be there," he said firmly, and he looked me straight in the eyes. "I think it is a small thing to ask of you." Incredibly, there was bitterness in his voice. "Mom died two years ago," he said as he stood in the doorway.

"I'm sorry to hear that," I said.

"Do you remember her name?"

I took a deep breath. The lady or the tiger, no uncertainty allowed here. "Her name was Beverly," I said.

He nodded and shut the door behind him, but somewhere in this universe, where unseen things are seen, I hoped we had crossed a line.

Chapter Three

Brent Jackson
Seven Days Later (July 10, 1993)
Taipei, Taiwan

"You do like sea slug, don't you, Mr. Jackson?"

The question startled me into the present, as I had been trying to decide whether I was looking forward to, or dreading, my reunion in just a few days with Charles, who was waiting for me in Kuala Lumpur. I shifted my full attention to the group of Chinese circled about me in a private room of one of Taipei's most elegant restaurants.

The translator, the tallest Chinese man I had ever seen, was watching me, certain I was going to embarrass them all. The other seven Chinese at the table were straight faced and unconcerned. The businessman seated to my right had just offered the sea slug to me. To him, it was just another fish. Only the translator seemed aware that this might be a little problem for me. I imagined myself back in Oklahoma City, offering some of my friends sea slug for dinner: "Sea slug or mashed potatoes, Bob? How about a little catsup with your sea slug, Joyce?"

"I don't know," I said, turning my gaze toward Mr. Chang, the businessman I was courting. "Do you like sea slug?"

The translation flew across the table with the response back seconds later, "It's one of my favorites," Mr. Chang said.

"Well, then," I said. "I love sea slug too."

I was gratified by the warm laughter that circulated about the table. The joke successfully positioned our relationship—me, the needy and submissive guest, to Mr. Chang, the gracious provider and host. *Keep that thought alive*, I mentally reminded myself. *Leave him the opportunity to be generous.*

The sea slug was now on my saucer. I turned around and grinned madly at everyone. I only hoped that I appeared adequately grateful. I looked down at the gray, Jell-O like substance. *There's always room for sea slug*, I thought, and I strained to keep the laughter inside me.

There were only two other people in the world that would have appreciated my situation and laugh with me—Charles Dickens, whom I would soon meet in Kuala Lumpur, and Richard O'Leary, whose passing we were still mourning.

Charles, Richard, and I had met during a two-year Peace Corps experience in Korea. Charles was a first-generation American and had spent a lot of time with his parents and their family somewhere in Northern England. He had developed so many of their characteristics that many presumed him English. Richard and I had joined Peace Corps out of a need for adventure, but Charles had joined because it merely seemed the next logical step for him. He considered himself a global man—not completely American, not completely British. And I suppose that if there ever really were such a thing as a global citizen, that would be Charles.

The first time I had really talked to him was at Peace Corps training, some eighteen years earlier, during a cold January in the city of Choon Chun, Korea. Richard and I had met on the long plane ride from the United States to Korea and were already in the beginnings of the casual, teasing stage of friendship. All the trainees ate dinner in a large room of a hotel. I had saved a seat for Richard to my left. He was late.

Charles had chosen a seat to my right. I probably wouldn't have paid much attention to him that evening except that he was sitting quietly with his hands in his lap and pursing his lips.

"What are you doing?" I asked.

"There is a cockroach in my soup," he said, continuing to purse his lips.

His pronunciation was confusing. His vowels were rounded, like the British. But he pronounced his *R*s like an American. His habit of pointing with his lips, I gathered later, he had acquired in high school as an exchange student in Italy.

"Yes, I see it." I turned and continued eating my soup. It was tricky to eat soup with chopsticks, but I had learned to pick up a wad of noodles and suck them up fast enough so that a lot of the liquid came with them.

I heard the chair beside me scoot back. Long, lanky Richard fell into it and squirmed for a moment, trying to get comfortable. He was about to say something to me, which explains why he wasn't looking at his teacup as he reached for it and snagged it in the cuff of his sleeve. He tried to grab it with his other hand, but the effort just sent the cup spiraling across the table, soaking us all.

"*Pabo*," I said, using one of our favorite Korean words that most closely meant "dummy." "That's the third time. Why don't I just save you the trouble, Richard? Next time I see you coming, I'll just pour it on the table for you."

Richard flashed an apologetic smile, picked up his tiny napkin, and dabbed it around on the edges of the table.

I was attempting to help clean up his mess when Charles turned to me abruptly. "It doesn't seem to trouble you that I have a cockroach in my soup, does it now?"

With his blonde, curly locks and quarterback build, Charles could have been the poster boy for just about anything.

"Well?" he demanded.

I shrugged. "Nothing surprises me anymore. This is a new world here. We've had something that looks like fried minnows for breakfast, seaweed for lunch—"

"Octopus on salads," Richard joined in, "dried squid for snacks—"

"I am beyond being shocked by new food items," I concluded.

Charles turned back to his soup and stared down at it. "So Koreans eat cockroaches too, do they?"

"I suppose." This was our fourth week of training, and my mind was foggy after a day of eight straight hours of intensive Korean language study.

"I've got an uncle who said he ate chocolate-covered ants once," Richard said, "and that was in America."

"Well…" Charles picked up the cockroach with his chopsticks and stared at it. "Another of many firsts for me—be an interesting paragraph in a letter home, this will."

"Let me know how it tastes." In our third week in intensive Peace Corps training, I had discovered that expatriate topics of conversation were limited to three subjects: food, money, and bowel movements.

He peered into my bowl. "You haven't found one in your soup, have you?"

"Not so far."

Richard also shook his head. "I didn't get one either."

He placed the cockroach back in the bowl and stared again into his soup. "What if…what if it's not supposed to be there?"

"What do you mean?" I asked.

"What if it just fell in my soup and died. I mean, we can't be sure, can we?"

It wasn't a dumb question. "You're right. We should find out. I'll ask the waitress," I said, and I waved at her.

"What will you ask her?"

"If the cockroach is supposed to be there or not?"

We had both stopped eating by that time. "I'm Charles Dickens." He extended his hand.

"You're kidding, right?" But Charles just shrugged. "Brent Jackson here." A thought occurred to me. "Does anyone know how to say *cockroach* in Korean?"

Richard shook his head. “That’s not a word they teach in Korean 101. Why don’t you just ask if it is edible?”

“How do you say *edible*?”

Charles turned his head, cocked it to the side, and frowned. “I’ve decided something, Brent Jackson.”

“Perhaps I could say, ‘Are we supposed to eat this?’” I said. “Anyone know how to say ‘supposed to,’ in Korean?”

“Brent, all we’ve had so far even close to that was a lesson called ‘How to order in a Korean restaurant,’” Richard said. “I don’t recall a situation where we ask the waiter if we are ‘supposed to’ eat something.”

“I’ve decided I don’t care,” Charles said emphatically, dropping his chopsticks on the table and crossing his arms over his chest.

“I beg your pardon?”

“I don’t care if it’s supposed to be there or not.” He raised his voice, uncrossed his arms, and with one finger pointed defiantly down at the bowl of soup. “I’m not going to eat a cockroach.”

Richard leaned over me and spoke to him in a soft, soothing tone. “People are looking at you.”

Charles ignored him. “I don’t care if everybody here eats cockroaches. It’s still a cockroach.” He was flailing his arms around. “I’ll eat their guppies and their seaweed soup, but I draw the—”

The waitress had arrived and was staring at Charles.

“Excuse me,” I said in Korean. I was still searching around my sparse Korean vocabulary for an alternative way to get the same result. Finally, I just pointed to the cockroach and repeated a Korean utterance I had learned that very day.

“Is it delicious?”

She put her hand over her mouth and looked at me in horror. “Very sorry.” She grabbed the bowl and took it away, leaving us in silence.

Richard poked at his noodles while we considered what had just happened. "I guess," he finally said, "a cockroach is just a nasty bug in Korea too."

Charles was in deep thought. "Brent Jackson," he said after a moment. He looked at the place where his cockroach soup had been. "I almost ate a cockroach because I thought I was supposed to, didn't I?"

The three of us have referred to that incident about every three or four years with a customary burst of laughter and tears. We began to add to the story… Charles had, for all of us, drawn a line in the sand. We had almost missed it. But this was another one of Charles's moments that became a lesson we never forgot. Sometimes, we concluded, it doesn't matter what local people do or what they eat. Peace Corps wanted us to live as the natives did—fine. We tried our best and succeeded most of the time, but for the rest of our lives, when we were asked to cross a little too far over the line of what we were comfortable with in our culture—then it was a cockroach, and we had to say no.

Those were happy, exciting days. We developed the kind of friendship one can only find in some place foreign, or perhaps in military service. It is ironic, I have often thought, that the three of us all later became competitors in essentially the same court. Had we not had the close communication produced by our youthful bonding, we would very likely have been adversaries. Instead, we drew invisible boundaries over territories of the world that represented our greatest strengths. Each of us also became a specialist in our own area. I dominated the manufacturing, Charles, almost all electronics, except for computers, which became Richard's passion even before the home PC was popular.

Charles was funny, warm, and enthusiastic. Everybody liked him. Richard, Charles, and I met regularly throughout our two years in Korea. After our Peace Corps contract was complete, Charles followed me to Oklahoma, where we entered graduate school together. Richard secured a job with a multinational company in Boston and lived there with his son, but we stayed in touch.

Richard did not have Charles's looks for sure. Square jawed, with reddish hair and pink freckled skin, his strength was his honest blue eyes. Although his string of contacts was not as long as Charles's, the ones he had were fiercely loyal and would risk losing money before they would break their ties with him. Among the players in his circle, he had only to sit at the table to add credibility, even honor, to the deal. Among us, he was the rock.

But today in Taiwan, the sea slug was still waiting on my plate. The Chinese had virtually stopped all noticeable movement while they stared at me. I gained control. The sea slug, otherwise known as "sea cucumber," is a delicacy to over a billion people in Asia. It is not a cockroach. This lunch had gone remarkably well so far. The jet lag had gathered in the small of my back and was spreading fast, but my brain was clear, and the adrenaline was rushing. I was very close to settling an agreement for my clients.

Of course my client in Bulgaria was probably sleeping soundly. I decided that if the day continued as I expected, I would wake him with the good news the moment I got back to the hotel.

Mr. Chang was seated on the opposite side of a round table large enough for us all to dance on. He was small in stature and older than his shiny black hair portrayed. He was top gun in Taiwan, however. His companies made all kinds of little plastic cords, like the ones on telephones in half the developed world. With that money, he has bought a great deal of Taipei and a significant part, I was told, of Los Angeles. He also invested in new ventures, which is why I now had sea slug on my plate.

As he was my host for this trip, he had welcomed me enthusiastically when I'd first sat down and had constantly conferred with the translator to make certain I was comfortable. Mr. Chang's wife smoldered with power and large diamond rings. Her slightly crooked teeth accentuated her exotic beauty. She strategically chose not to sit beside her husband but rather to my left, where, I assumed, she could better scrutinize me. It didn't matter; I found her charming and only hoped she could tell.

Regrettably, my wife, Nicole, was back at the hotel, still recovering from the long flight over.

As the only American at the table, I had received the full focus of the Chang family, and whether or not the offer I was bringing Mr. Chang was attractive was immaterial to how I would be treated as a guest. They had been warm and complimentary. After the first course, shark fin soup, was consumed, they had toasted, all separately, my coming so far to see them in Taiwan. There was also the usual number of personal questions.

"You seem very young to have such an important job," the petite woman had said earlier as the translator whispered into Mr. Chang's ear. Mr. Chang was informed of every word, no matter how insignificant.

The comment was the cue for me to reveal my age. "I am thirty-eight," I offered.

Everyone gasped together. They spoke rapidly in Chinese, and others at the table nodded. Mr. Chang stared at me and spoke. "Mr. Chang says you have very smooth skin," the translator explained.

That was a new one. I guessed that it meant I looked young for my age. "Thank you," I said. My youth was relative to them. They were seasoned businessmen with adolescent grandchildren.

I thought of my sleeping client and his hoped-for twenty million dollars. I knew I needed to keep the meeting positive, but by now it was more than that. The Chang family was beginning to trust me, and I liked them. All the elements of a long, successful relationship were present.

I stared down at the waiting slug. It was much too large a piece to try to swallow without chewing. I would have to bite it. I grabbed my chopsticks.

Madam Chang spoke to the translator in her soft-spoken voice while gesturing toward me.

"You use the chopsticks very well." The translator smiled.

The compliment, at least for a moment, took my mind off the slippery feel. I managed a bite, chewed a couple of quick times, and swallowed. The texture was spongy and less than appealing but thankfully fairly tasteless. A little hot sauce on it might even make it palatable.

I smiled to my host as though it were buttered lobster. This must have encouraged Madam Chang to pile another portion onto my little plate. I smiled more. Mr. Chang's laugh told me that I had not fooled anybody.

Mrs. Leong raised her glass to me. "I toast to your knowing so well about Chinese customs."

I received her toast gratefully, bringing the small amount of stinging brew to my lips, tasting it, and showing her the bottom of my glass.

"And I toast to your smooth skin," Mr. Chang said. He seemed distracted by my youthful appearance. This worried me, but I tipped my glass back to him.

Mr. Chang raised his thimble-sized glass again. He spoke in Chinese, and the translator followed a few words behind him in English.

"We must all toast," the translator explained.

As if on cue, the waitress stepped from behind and filled his glass with the powerful local Chinese drink. She then quickly filled mine as well. We all held our glasses above the table.

Mr. Chang spoke in Chinese but looked directly at me. I looked directly back, as though I understood every word. "Mr. Brent Jackson," the translator said simultaneously, "we thank you for your coming. Although you are an American, you know the Chinese ways, and you make us feel very comfortable."

Everyone watched him as if he were addressing many nations. But he came to the conclusion quickly. "Today," he said, grinning widely, "we feel you are Chinese. Before, you were another businessman, but now, we are more friends than we are business."

Chinese wine-induced toasts can be a bit corny and sentimental, especially as the day and the wine goes on. But Mr. Chang controlled companies worth billions of dollars, received many foreign guests, and administered praise sparingly. His words and expression were sincere, and I responded to it.

I lifted my glass and mentally prepared a toast. Toasts to great leaders were tricky, as flattery was transparent and perceived as manipulation. "I have learned much from you," I said. "You are my first friend from Taiwan, and I hope you will continue to teach me."

Mr. Chang honored me by receiving my toast and then asked me to "Gan bei," one of the few Chinese expressions I knew—bottoms up. I tossed the thimble-sized drink down my throat and then held the glass upside down over my head to show that it was empty. There were smiles and nods all around the table that an American would demonstrate this simple local custom.

In the midst of the silence, Mr. Chang looked at me solemnly, shook his head slowly, and for the first time that day spoke in English. "You have very, very smooth face."

Impulsively, I responded to him. "I'm free Friday."

I gasped. It was a joke I would make to a pal my own age—not to someone at this distinguished table. The Chinese translation flew around the table; there was a moment of stunned silence as all grasped the fact that the billion-dollar, all-powerful Mr. Chang had been on the receiving end of a caustic joke.

Mr. Chang leaned back and laughed so hard that the translator reached behind him to steady his chair. The rest of the members at the table followed with relieved laughter.

Mr. Chang wiped his eyes with the napkin and spoke again in Chinese. "You have good humor," the translator said.

It was an important moment, and in that instant, I knew that we had established *Guanxi* "relationship." The deal was done. Mr. Chang's entire demeanor changed. He was not only concerned about my next dish; he was concerned about whether my hotel was satisfactory. Did I have plans for the following day? He and his wife were attending a concert—could I go? Madam Chang heaped more food on my plate and looked at me with a smile and a nod that I took for approval. I had passed into membership. We were friends. In Chinese tradition, that was like family.

Mr. Chang looked down at his lap, picked up the napkin, and laid it on the table. Talk around the table ceased at this signal that the luncheon had ended.

We toasted one more time and stood up. As we were gathering our things, Mr. Chang's assistant spoke to the translator, who turned to me and said simply, "Mr. Chang would like to have a signing ceremony for the agreement after the concert tomorrow."

That was the extent of the business discussions during this three-hour Saturday afternoon lunch. Details had been worked out between my client, Mr. Chang's assistant, and myself the past eight months. But all our efforts would have been in vain had not Mr. Chang and I shared that special, effusive moment.

We had bonded, and my client would get woken up.

"Mr. Chang will send a car for you at six p.m. tomorrow." The translator touched my arm. "He likes you very much," he said. Then he whispered, "And Madam Chang thinks you look like Tom Hanks." He patted me on the shoulder. It was clear he was also sharing the day's triumph. I patted him back.

Madam Chang moved closer and spoke into the translator's ear. "Madam Chang extends her regrets that Mrs. Jackson was not able to join us today," he said, "Madam Chang has also offered to send her physician to the hotel if necessary."

I thanked her but declined. "I believe it is some simple stomach distress," I explained. "She very much wanted to be here today and looks forward to being with you tomorrow." Not exactly a lie. I'm sure that Nicole would have agreed had she not been puking half the eighteen hours it took us to fly here.

Nicole had asked for one of the antacids I usually keep in my pocket as soon as we got on the plane—some mild acidity, she'd said. But then we ran into turbulence that I had not experienced in over a million miles of flight. When the plane finally landed at Chang Kai Shek Airport in Taipei, Nicole was still in the bathroom—worried flight attendants and resigned pilots all having conceded FAA landing regulations to a distraught and very cranky woman.

Mrs. Chang's personal driver took me home. I sat in the back seat of their maroon Mercedes and relished the day's victory. The hoards of motorcycles zigzagging through traffic seemed quieter. Even the kamikaze bus drivers seemed tamer than usual. When we arrived at the hotel, I fidgeted in the back seat as I waited for the Changs' chauffeur to walk around the front of the car and open my car door. I knew he would have lost face if I had sprung out of the door as I preferred to do.

The concierge stepped from behind his desk. "Welcome back, Mr. Jackson." He pushed the elevator button and waited beside me until I entered it.

"Will you be going out this evening, Mr. Jackson?" he said.

"I have had a wonderful day," I said, wishing I could remember his name. "And I am going to bed."

"Then have a good sleep, Mr. Jackson."

The elevator was excruciatingly slow. I hoped that Nicole was awake and feeling better. When I finally opened the door to our hotel room, I was pleased to see that although she was still in bed, her eyes were open and her color had improved.

I tossed my suit jacket on the bed at her feet. I was eager to tell her about Mr. Chang, about the lunch, but Nicole needed my sympathy now, and I gave it my best shot. "How are you doing, sweetie pie?" I rubbed her leg.

She moaned and looked at me. I knew I would never tire of those large brown eyes. Her ebony hair poured over the pillow and into the crevices of the sheets. Tall and long legged; her skin had the same golden glow as her Cherokee mother. Nicole's translucent beauty, perfect from every angle, often left me daydreaming about being an artist, just so that I could spend all my days painting her.

"Don't look at me." She groaned. "I must look like your precious seaweed soup."

"You're gorgeous—green, but gorgeous."

"Can we get home any other way than flying?" she said.

"Boat?"

She groaned louder and turned over. She stuck her lower lip out. "Did I just make a fool of myself on the plane?"

"They were a little uncomfortable when you asked if you could go outside."

"I just needed fresh, unrecycled air."

"We were at thirty-nine thousand feet."

She turned back suddenly and laid her wrist over her forehead. "What was that nasty stuff you kept sticking in my mouth?"

"They didn't have any nausea medicine on the plane," I said in defense. "I learned a few tricks about herbal medicine in Korea."

"Do I really want to know this?"

"The flight attendant had ginger in the refrigerator. It's an old trick for nausea."

"Ginger?" Her mouth fell open. "You put roots in my mouth."

"It's a natural treatment for stomach distress."

"You put roots in my mouth," she repeated, pretending to pout. "I thought you loved me."

"I do love you, dearest," I said and smiled.

She raised an eyebrow. "You're much too upbeat for being in a room with the dying. I suppose the meeting went well?"

"We sign the contract after the concert tomorrow." I could no longer suppress my excitement.

She managed to smile back, a weak but appreciated effort.

I sat down beside her. "Madam Chang wants to send you her personal physician."

"Suddenly I feel fine."

"For your information, he's a fine medical doctor."

"They stick pins in people over here."

I sighed. Nicole loved Asian people. She loved most Asian food, although I was glad she had missed out on the evening's sea slug surprise. However, Nicole was a traditionalist and felt that American ways, the way her mother did things, was good enough for anyone. "They are as trained as our doctors," I said. "But most have also studied the art of acupuncture."

"It's bad enough getting a needle for a shot."

"Your aunt Mannings had acupuncture for the pain in her back. She said it helped."

"That's strange. I remember her saying that the pain from the pins they stuck in her ears was so intense that it took her mind off the pain in her back."

"Relax." I unbuttoned my shirt and slipped it off. It was only 8:00 p.m., but I could put off sleep no longer. "I declined the offer."

She watched me silently while I finished undressing. "I guess my hair looks like an abandoned squirrel's nest."

I sat back on the bed. "Even if a squirrel was still nesting in your hair, you'd be beautiful."

She patted my arm. "Not exactly the way I wanted you to say it. But you're sweet for trying."

I checked my watch. "I was going to call my client, but now I'm too tired." My head was also pounding. "Can I get you anything?"

"We haven't called Daniel yet, Brent." She sat up weakly. "We promised him."

Until our son, Daniel, had surprised us with his birth eleven years ago, Nicole had traveled with me more frequently. Of course with Daniel it was harder for her, and she always felt guilty leaving him with my mother. This trip was the first time in two years she had come with me, and she had only agreed because it was a short one. In two days, when I headed for Malaysia, Nicole would return to Oklahoma.

"If we call now, we'll wake him up," I said.

"He won't care." Nicole sat up slightly. "He'll go right back to sleep."

I wanted to go to sleep and call Daniel in the morning, but I knew Nicole wouldn't rest until we placed the call. I found the long-distance dialing information directory, wrote the dozen or so numbers I needed to access the United States, and dialed the phone.

Daniel answered.

"Hello, son."

"Hi, Daddy." Daniel's voice was flat and monotone, an inflection he had not gotten from either his mother or myself.

"Well, we made it all right."

"What time is it now?" he asked.

I checked my watch again. "Eight fifteen. Saturday."

"Saturday?" Daniel was always amazed at how we could be talking and it would be a one-day difference.

"Yep. But we're getting ready to go to sleep."

"Wow," he said without surprise in his voice.

Daniel and I were not very much alike. He took his time getting to know people. I engaged them as quickly as I could. He was cautious and distrustful. I was impulsive and action oriented.

"Did Grandma buy you the Wars and Scores game for your computer?"

"No," he said with some disappointment. "She said we would go tomorrow."

"It's a good game." I lay down next to Nicole. "It teaches strategy."

"That's good," he said, and then, "Can I talk to Mom?"

Nicole took the phone. They were still talking after I had thrown my pants on the floor and my head finally hit the pillow. I closed my eyes.

All I have ever wanted for my family was peace and financial security, I thought. Although sometimes, I admit in those moments when I'm honest with myself, I would also like their admiration.

I lay there and listened to Nicole. The pitiful tones of motion sickness were now gone from her voice. She laughed and teased. Nicole was a wonderful mother.

"Brent." Nicole covered the phone with her hand. "The operator just interrupted and said that you have another call." She removed her hand and spoke softly again. "Sweetie, I have to hang up now. Your daddy has an important call.... Yes, I love you too."

She hung up the phone, and it rang immediately.

"Brent?"

"Hello, Charles," I said, "What's—"

"Brent," he interrupted; he sounded tired. "You're sure you're coming?"

"Of course, Charles," I said. "What is it?"

"It's my son."

"Your son... What..."

"We have to save him."

"You're making no sense, Charles. Save who?"

"My son. My son. For God's sake, Brent. Just be there."

He hung up.

I placed the phone down slowly.

Nicole saw the alarm on my face and put her arms around my shoulder. She waited for me to clear my head.

"Charles says his son is in trouble..."

"His son?" Nicole said.

"I don't know what he means." I leaned back against the pillow, exhausted. "Charles doesn't have a son."

Chapter Four

Brent Jackson

Two Days Later (July 12, 1993)

Kuala Lumpur, Malaysia

In Kuala Lumpur, Malaysia, the Royal Selangor Club operated in a massive colonial clubhouse surrounded by fifty acres of grass lawn with the texture and deep color of a putting green. The roofs of its six wings were pitched high, like an A-frame, and covered in black tile all the way to the ground. A large, white veranda, dotted with soft comfortable chairs and white round tables, encircled it. The club was a stark reminder of former days of British ownership, when sunburned Englishmen in white linen jackets and trousers strolled around on the grass carrying cricket clubs. Today it stood as a physical anomaly—in contrast to the rapid hustle of modern Kuala Lumpur life that buzzed around it and was now characterized by densely packed streets teeming with taxis, Mercedes, and Volvos.

I asked to be let out at the street rather than going around to the main entrance of the building, where the limousines dropped off the members to the exclusive club. Walking up to the Royal Selangor Club was the best part. The sidewalk was wide enough to encompass many groups of young men and women talking to each other in low voices while sitting on the many park benches that surrounded the pulsating fountains and eloquent statues. To my left sprawled the spacious lawn and, to the end of that, a seventy-five-foot, full-color television screen that was broadcasting a soccer game. Malaysia was not one of the players,

I surmised, as those that had gathered on the lawn to watch were few.

I had not yet reached the massive front entrance when I heard my name. "Brent!"

Dato rushed out of the doorways with his arms extended. Since we were still about three hundred feet apart, I hurried toward him to get the hug over with before his arms, raised high, would tire out.

His embrace was as enthusiastic as the tone of his voice. "I always forget how handsome you are. But I don't remember you being this tall. Are you still growing?"

"I don't think so," I said as he took my arm, a gesture of Malaysian friendship, as we walked slowly up the steps.

Had it not been for Dato's busy and expressive eyebrows, he would not have had a single hair on his head. He craned his head to look up at me. "You are the first to arrive."

"I wanted to spend a little time with you first," I said.

He laughed. "Dato" is actually not a name but a title given by a royal sultan of Malaysia. It can be loosely translated as the equivalent to the British "Sir." Dato was one of the top-five palm oil producers in Malaysia, a man worth millions who considered himself quite ordinary. I found myself feeling flattered that he was flattered. "Let's go in the club for a drink," he said, guiding me firmly. For all his humility, Dato was still a man whose habit of giving orders frequently showed itself.

"You don't have to tell me what you want." Dato sat down in front of me and gestured to the waitress. "Two mango juices," he called. He was right. The succulent, sweet mango in Malaysia was my weakness.

"You have an amazing memory," I said.

He began to chat. His optimism about Malaysia, its economy and growth, his viewpoint on its future and resounding place in the rising global economy were interesting. He chatted about local and world politics and then injected one of his notable golf stories. Apparently, on "hole number seven," a monkey who only wanted his ball had attacked him. He acted out the story, taking the roles of both himself and the monkey and even stood up beside our table to dramatically demonstrate how he had swung his golf club in front of him like it was a machete to defend his golf ball from the attacks.

We laughed ourselves to tears—I because of his story; he, because of my pleasure at his telling of it.

Dato checked his watch as though he had just remembered something. "They will be arriving soon," he said, and then I saw in his eyes that he realized his mistake. "I'm sorry. I meant he… Charles will be arriving soon."

I nodded. "It's hard to believe that Richard's gone."

He took a deep breath and smiled. "Shall I escort you to Somerset Maugham's table?"

When Charles, Richard, and I had had our first Peace Corps reunion ten years prior, it had not been in Korea, where we had met, but in Malaysia, where we discovered that we all had business at least a couple of times in a year.

Like many international American businessmen and women who had their foreign roots from Peace Corps, we were incurable romantics. We had set out to save the world and found out that the world would save us instead. Our Korean experiences had given us our toehold into the rest of Asia. We had not only learned the incredibly difficult Korean language but, more importantly, had received tools by which to read the hidden clues of foreign cultures. That was what we carried with us even today, and it was that art form that separated us from the struggling and puzzled Americans who tried to make their way into Asian business by applying American strategies.

Dato always paved the way for our reunions. He was, after all, a member of the Royal Selangor Club, and we were not. But he always made special arrangements for us to attend as his guests, every even year, on July 13.

Malaysia holds a special attraction for romantics. And the Royal Selangor Club offers special sanction to the incurable ones. On our first tour through the club, ten years ago, Dato had a titillating story about every room. He swept through the halls with tales of the rich and legendary people who had sat in this room, leaned against that wall, played on that piano. At one point he took us out to the sweeping veranda and approached a table that was on the very edge, near one of the large great columns by the front lawn. He paused and stared as though it were the Holy Grail.

"This is the table where Somerset Maugham wrote," he said, and he began to describe the gentle author who loved the Malaysian people and placed them prominently and magnificently in his stories and novels. As Dato spoke, we could visualize the large Englishman, always dressed in white from his hat to his shoes, sitting in that very chair. In my mind, he was sipping tea and looking past the lawn where the streets were filled with Malays, Chinese, and Indians.

"Can I sit here?" Charles had asked Dato in such a self-conscious tone that I wondered if he thought Dato would refuse him.

"Of course." Dato pulled the chair around for Charles, who sank into it slowly.

"I just finished reading *The Razor's Edge*," Charles said. "I still have it in my suitcase." While he looked around him, we became still. This was one of Charles's gifts—taking tiny moments and turning them into lifelong memories. "Incredible," he finally said, shaking his head slightly.

That first evening at Somerset Maugham's table, we sat there until 4:00 a.m. Dato went home whimpering at two. We drank green tea and told favorite Peace Corps stories. By the time we had to reluctantly admit that the evening was over, the Somerset Maugham's table tradition had begun.

Today, Richard was gone, but Charles and I had talked on the phone and decided it was critical we meet. It would give us some closure, Charles said. Although we didn't say so out loud, I think we both wondered if this might be our last meeting.

Dato and I approached the table.

"There, Brent, there!" Charles called, surprising me and sounding today more like a Manchester Englishman than an American. "It's good to see you, isn't it?"

He glanced at me quickly and then to Dato. I started to say something, but he put his finger to his lips. He smiled broadly, as though nothing were the matter. It had been two years, but Charles looked the same. His boyish face would no doubt linger on him well into his forties.

"Always good," I said as we sat down.

Now we were here for the first time without Richard and with new secrets that Charles was obviously going to keep for later.

"You must be hungry," Dato said. Charles shook his head and then swept the long blond locks out of his face. *He looks a bit thin*, I thought.

"Perhaps then some satay," Dato said gently, also apparently sensing something, and he ordered the spicy Malaysian chicken. The waiter, a tall East Indian, nodded and left.

"Should we be bowing to the waiter when he gets back?" Charles said to Dato, and then we all laughed.

Earlier, when the three of us had first met Dato, none of us really knew much about Malaysia, but like many beginning explorers, we felt we did. We had developed a quick friendship with Dato, who then became our guide and mentor. What we didn't know in the beginning was that Dato was also a devilish practical jokester.

"So you gentlemen are men of many cultures," Dato had said at our first dinner eight years earlier at the Royal Selangor Club restaurant. "What have you learned of Malaysia?"

"We all read the same book," Richard said.

"Malaysian culture isn't really so difficult." Charles nodded. "We already know about the yellow thing."

"The yellow thing?" Dato folded his napkin and laid it in his lap.

"You know." Richard picked up the fork and wiped it thoroughly with his napkin—an annoying habit he persisted on in even the nicest of restaurants. "That yellow is a color only worn by the sultans."

"We're very careful of that," I said. "Didn't even bring a yellow tie."

"Don't want to accidentally insult anybody." Richard's head nodded affirmatively.

"I think we've got the Malaysian culture pretty much under our belts," Charles said.

"But of course we'd love to have your advice." Richard, drinking from his water glass, dribbled at least half of it down his chin. Charles and I both rolled our eyes in chorus.

Dato looked doubtful. "Well…you didn't bow to the waitress," he said, speaking of the middle-aged Malay waitress who had earlier taken our order.

"Bow to the waitress?" Charles asked. "What does that mean?"

"Your book didn't tell you?" Dato shook his head. "In Malaysia, we believe that even the smallest in society must be treated like the greatest." He sipped his tea while we thought this over. "So we remind ourselves by this simple custom—we bow to the waiters."

"Lovely!" Charles said almost immediately.

"Beautiful custom," I added.

"We should do that in America." Richard nodded enthusiastically.

"Here she comes now." Dato said, "Why don't you try?"

As the tiny Malay woman brought our refreshments to us, we all stood in unison and bowed low to her. The poor startled woman set down our drinks and fled. Dato held onto his chair to keep from falling off in a fit of laughter.

We sat back down slowly. "Dato does like to have his fun with the foreigners, doesn't he now?" Charles said, a faint blush coloring his cheeks, but we soon joined in Dato's infectious laughter.

That had been eight years earlier, and as I turned to look at Charles, I saw he was looking at a place beyond me. At first I thought he was remembering as well, but when his gaze didn't waver, I realized he was staring at something.

Dato was also staring at the same place, and his face took on a rare look of annoyance and irritation. "Now, see here, young fellow," he said. "You know you're not supposed to be here." I followed his eyes and found a young man standing behind me.

At first I thought he was one of the Malaysian Chinese—a homeless waif who had wandered accidentally into this exclusively private club. He was leaning against the column near us. His large, almond-shaped eyes and pronounced cheekbones made me think he was Korean.

He looked like he had been in a fight. Although he apparently had started the day in a suit, the jacket and tie were gone. The white shirt remained, although it was torn and hung partly open. No iron would ever take the wrinkles out of those pants. It was not the kind of sight one was accustomed to seeing on the veranda of the Royal Selangor Club.

Charles leaned closer. "Jason?" he spoke, almost in a whisper.

Of course Charles was right. It was Richard's adopted son, Jason. And he was drunk.

"You could get all kinds of diseases," Dato scolded. "Don't they teach you about AIDS in America?"

Dato's wife and daughter scurried around the guest bedroom of Dato's home. Fresh sheets and pillowcases were flying about. They seemed to ignore the fact that Dato was standing in the midst of them. And their busy activity did not hinder Dato from lecturing to us all as though he were on a podium in front of the Rotary club. Jason was slowly sliding out of a thickly padded wicker chair he had been stuffed into. Charles had to get down on his knees and push up on his chest to keep him from tumbling onto the floor. I sat on another chair, breathing hard from the grueling task of dragging a limp Jason up the flight of stairs. Dato's house was big, and it had been kind of him to offer a room. It was clear that Jason was not only drunk but had been with a prostitute—something that Dato found disgraceful.

"If this weren't Richard's son, I'd have called the police." Dato sniffed. "I thought kids nowadays were better informed." He looked to me for concurrence.

"Mylsn wm ver bufiful."

I turned and looked. Jason's eyes were closed, but he was apparently trying to talk.

"Ver bufiful."

"What's he saying?" Dato kept his distance. Charles had already been vomited on, and Dato didn't want to be next.

Charles looked exhausted. "I think he said Malaysian women are very beautiful."

Dato gasped. "Good heavens! He's actually boasting about this. Hasn't he heard a word I said?" He looked at me again. I just shrugged.

Dato's wife touched her husband's arm. "Anything else?" she said, and she looked doubtfully at Jason.

Charles's eyes met mine in a look of disheartened consensus. We couldn't put vomit-stained, perfume-doused Jason into Dato's clean sheets. Charles's voice was filled with resignation. "Where's the bath?"

Had Jason not been filled with alcohol and weakened from the dry heaves, we would never have gotten his clothes off. He was strong, and for any man struggling to keep his clothes on, he put up a very respectable fight. "Yu gonnaadie!" he shouted.

His suit stank so badly that we just threw it in the trash. We would think about what he would wear tomorrow. Then boxers,

T-shirt and all, we dumped him into the bath water like one would drop a canoe into the river.

"Itakeknifekillyu!"

"How did he know to come here?" I squeezed the bottle of shampoo and sprayed it generally around on him and in the water. We washed him like one would a horse.

Charles held Jason's arms down and also tried to keep his nose out of the water. One foot appeared and nearly kicked him in the chin. "Right after I talked to you the other night, Jason contacted me…said he had traced me down through my office. He asked me where and what Somerset Maugham's table was." An arm got away, and Charles fought to catch it. "So I told him."

"Did you tell him when we meet?" I helped Charles turn him over. Jason was making this too difficult. We decided to just plunge him up and down in the water like one would the laundry.

"He said thank you and hung up," Charles said, now fully soaked. "I didn't have a chance to tell him anything."

"Imgonna keeel yu bofe!"

I pulled my hands away. "I think he's clean enough," I said, and Charles nodded gratefully.

I drained the water; Charles let go and dried his hands. Jason tried to stand up and immediately fell back into the tub. *This is Richard's son, the computer wizard he always bragged about*, I thought, warmness settling over me. "Believe it or not, Jason," I said, watching as he struggled to find a footing, "we're glad you came."

"Gonna keeel yu," Jason mumbled before passing out over the side of the tub.

Next Day (July 13, 1993)

When I checked on Jason in the morning, he hadn't moved from the position we had placed him in. He was breathing loudly, and I supposed he would sleep another few hours or so.

I started to move out, but he jerked suddenly, and I hesitated. His eyes twitched and then opened. He stared at the ceiling for a moment and then looked toward me. As I had been spotted, I moved closer.

He squinted. "I remember you."

"Good morning, Jason." I smiled as cheerfully as I could. "How are you feeling?"

He groaned. "I have things in my throat."

"I'll get you some water." I went into the bathroom and filled up a glass. He was sitting up when I turned back to him.

"Which one are you?"

I handed him the water. "I'm Brent."

He threw the water down his throat as though it were a shot glass. He handed the empty glass back to me. "Thanks."

"Would you like another?"

"No, thanks. Dad told me about you." Jason's English contained only a slight accent.

"Good things, I hope." I leaned against the bedpost at the foot of his bed.

"Good things, funny things," he said, looking at me. "He had a lot of Peace Corps stories." His eyes moved to the Persian carpet located near the door.

I paused. "We had some great times."

"So did we," he said, still looking at the carpet.

I shifted. "I knew you when you were little."

"You used to baby-sit me when Dad had to work at night."

"That's right," I said.

"You taught me to play fish."

"That's right," I repeated, pleased that he remembered.

There was a pause again.

"We're very glad you came, Jason."

He looked up at me and squinted. "Seems like I remember you saying that last night." Then he looked at the wall as though trying to remember. He did.

"Oh, no." He groaned and covered his face with his hands.

I changed the subject. "So how did you know to come yesterday? Did your dad tell you?"

He continued looking thoughtfully at the wall. "Yes, in a way, he did."

"When was that?'

"He left me a note to read after he died."

I didn't know what to say. "Your father was very thorough."

Jason nodded.

"May I ask what it said?"

He looked around the room. "Where are my pants?"

"Your pants, I'm afraid, were not reusable. We threw them away."

His dark, almond eyes widened while the scar over his eyebrow reddened. "My wallet was in my pants."

"Ah," I said. "It's over there." I pointed to the mother-of-pearl inlaid chest across the room. His wallet lay on top.

He looked relieved and then pointed. "It's inside. Please read it."

I opened the wallet. Inside was a dog-eared piece of paper that had been folded several times and placed neatly behind the bills. I opened it carefully and read.

Dear son,

Be at Somerset Maugham's Table: 4:00 p.m. July 13.

With all my love,
Dad

I wondered why Richard had written so cryptically.

Dato, his arms full of packages, bounced into the room. "I've been shopping," he said with great excitement.

"Shopping," I said, "Are stores open?"

Dato, eyes wide, ran to Jason's side. "My brother-in-law owns a clothing store. I called him this morning, and he opened it." He leaned closer to Jason. "Especially for you."

As Jason clearly had no idea who this man was, he shrank back slightly and pulled the covers up to his chest. But not fast enough. Dato grabbed Jason's bare foot with one hand and lifted it up. With the other hand, he pulled a brown loafer out of a bag. He crammed Jason's foot into it.

"There," he said with great triumph. "Perfect fit."

Jason looked skeptically at the shoe and at the same time pulled the covers tighter around his waist. Dato pulled out pants, shirts, and socks, even underwear, all perfectly coordinated colors, and all Jason's size.

"How did you...?" I started to ask.

"I measured him," Dato said simply, and Jason covered his face with the pillow.

Since Jason was hiding under the pillow, I spoke up. "We don't know how to thank you, Dato. You've been—"

"Not at all," Dato interrupted, and then he scurried out of the room.

I picked up the note again and looked at it. "You know what I think," I said. "I think that your father wanted you to take his place at the table. And that's what we should try to do again tonight." I moved the pillow aside but saw that Jason had, once again, fallen asleep.

Dato did not join us that night at Somerset's table. We tried to insist, but he felt that the boy needed to talk to us, his father's best friends, privately. He made all the arrangements for a preset Chinese-style dinner to be served and, amid our protests, put everything on his bill. Jason's new clothes fit perfectly, and he offered Dato many thanks, which were dismissed, and a few apologies, which were accepted.

"You've developed some bad habits, young man," Dato had said in a very serious tone just before taking his leave. "You get rid of them before they move in and make themselves at home."

Jason sighed and looked away.

As we sat down at the table, I caught Jason staring at the doll-faced Chinese waitress who was serving our table. She looked sideways at Jason, a quick glance, but the interest reflected in her dark eyes was easily noted. Jason stared hard, and I realized I was watching the opening scenario to a familiar pattern in Jason's life.

"So do you have a girlfriend back home?" I asked, attempting to start the conversation.

He smiled and sipped his tea. "They come and they go, Uncle Brent."

I was pleased to hear him use the name he had used so long ago when I sat with him in Korea. Jason was beginning to remember more.

"This is a pretty dramatic little venture you guys had, isn't it?" Jason leaned back in his chair and crossed his legs. "Meeting at the same table every two years? Very, how do you say? Cloak and dagger."

Charles spoke up. "We were all busy businessmen who started from the same place and time in Korea. The beginning was probably the most exciting to us, and we didn't want to lose that."

"Charles is right," I said. "Men like us don't stay in one place long enough to make deep friendships. It was important for us to keep the ones we had."

"So we decided to treat our friendship like we did any other project," Charles said. "We scheduled a definite time and a definite place. And we planned around that, didn't we, Brent?"

"Like Christmas or Thanksgiving," I said. "Except that we decided to be realistic. Once every other year would have to do."

"Jason," I said. "Tell us how you've been."

Jason's stirred his tea.

"One thing we do is tell what's on our minds," Charles said. "This is the place where we met, shared our lives, and, in a sense, rejuvenated ourselves."

"I know your father was worried about you. He called me after he found he had cancer. I think it's why your dad wanted you to come," I said, "so that we could talk."

"We're flattered that your father, in a way, entrusted you to us." Charles leaned forward. "You can tell us what is on your mind."

Jason shook his head. He didn't answer.

Charles nodded his head affirmatively. "Talk to us, Jason," he coaxed.

Jason sat up abruptly, wiped his eyes with the heel of his hand, glared at Charles, but said nothing.

I could stand it no longer. "Charles! What is it? What were you trying to tell me? You were talking crazy—"

"Okay." Charles looked at me and then back to Jason. "Jason, I don't know you very well. But now that you are here, you have to take Richard's place. You have to help. And, Jason, if you don't help, if you don't join us tonight"—Charles looked away, toward the front lawn, his voice calm—"someone is going to die."

We both froze and stared at him.

Charles continued. "Jason, I could count on your father for everything. I need your help. Will you do this?"

"Charles?" I had never heard him speak this way. "Who is going to die? What has happened?"

Charles didn't answer my question. He squinted and stared into Jason's face. "Five years ago I had a beautiful wife and a daughter. They died. Three weeks ago I had no one, and then I discovered…I discovered I have a son. Yes, it's true, Brent. It was almost wonderful. Strange but…well…it lasted just a moment. And then…and then I learned a terrible thing about him." He bowed his head. "Terrible. Had Richard been alive, I would have asked his help. Now I need to ask yours."

Charles looked at me. "I'm going to be asking you to use all your skills, all your unique connections for an end result that I will not reveal to you until the time is right. You will have to do what I tell you to do blindly. That means a lot of trust on both our parts." He looked back at Jason. "Are you up to it?"

Jason looked puzzled. Then the hardness crept back into his eyes. "So you lost someone too. I knew that. Dad spoke about her. Deborah, as I remember." Jason set his teacup so hard on the table I thought it might break. "There was a daughter?"

Charles flinched slightly. "Tell me about them." Jason's eyes were challenging. *Why the anger?* I thought.

"I'll tell you later," Charles said simply. "Take Richard's place, Jason. Talk to us."

Jason waited for Charles to go on, but when he didn't, Jason lowered his head and stared at his teacup for a long time. After a while, Jason took a deep breath and let it out slowly. "What do you want me to talk about?"

"Something easy." I leaned forward. "Richard told us you met at a bathhouse but not how he came to adopt you."

Jason took a sip of his tea. "That's not easy," he said. "As a matter of fact, that's probably the most shameful question you could ask me."

Chapter Five

Jason Young-Soo O'Leary
Sixteen Years Earlier (Winter, 1977)
Kwangju, Korea

The sunbeam will even peek into a mouse hole.

The next morning I woke up with that old saying on my lips, and as I sat up on my warm wooden floor, there was a strange certainty that I might indeed have *unmyung* after all—that it would somehow be connected to the hairy giant with the magic eyes. But unfortunately, for the first time in my life, I tried to create my own destiny. The mouse that goes out of the mouse hole can fall into a trap. But the trap I fell into, I fashioned as deliberately as if I had placed my head under its steel jaws.

Each day I waited for the megook. I tried not to show that I was anxious, but the master caught me staring at the door too many times and scolded me. Perhaps he understood my actions as curiosity to see the strange human again. I turned around at the sound of anyone coming in the door, trying to see if it was him.

When at last he came the next Saturday, I stared at him so wide eyed and ceaselessly that he laughed. This embarrassed me, and I hurried about my business but later turned to watch him as he entered the crowded tub, slowly sitting down in the steaming water with a loud sigh. He lay all the way down to where the water covered his shoulders. When he stuck his legs straight out, they almost reached to the other side. There were two old men with wrinkled chests—one on each side of him—who turned their heads toward him and watched with great interest. Across from him a father sat with his son. All were watching him as intensely as they would a soccer game, but after a few moments, the son gathered himself and stood straight up out of the water. A slender, light-skinned boy with knobby knees, he faced the megook and bowed fully. The megook nodded toward the son, and the son sat down again. That's how I knew that the boy was a student at the megook's school. All students must bow to their teachers, no matter where they see them.

This gesture was of great interest to the old men, who at once began to question the student. They talked among themselves about the megook as he sat quietly and stared ahead. The student explained that the megook was an English teacher at his school and spoke a little Korean. At the news that he spoke a little Korean, everyone became quiet. There was no movement, but all, except the megook, were watching the father of the student. He had apparently been chosen as the spokesperson for the bathtub group. He stared at the megook and then slowly began to move toward him. The megook turned his head, faced him, and smiled. The father smiled too and moved closer. The megook sat up a bit and waited.

When the father finally spoke, he pronounced each Korean word deliberately and slowly. "What do you think of Korea?"

The megook responded, but I could not understand him. I moved closer to the tub to hear better. The megook spoke again. But it was clear that none of the men understood him either. The father swallowed hard and spoke again. "What do you think of Korea?"

The megook again made the same strange sound. He sat even further up and leaned forward, speaking loudly into the father's ear. The old men came closer also. Again and again the megook made the same sound. Sometimes he spoke quickly, sometimes slowly, again quickly. No one understood him.

Even my master came close to the tub, trying to listen better to the megook's words. I crossed my legs and sat down on the tile floor. Later, after I came to America, I saw a movie about aliens coming to the earth. They tried to speak to the humans. Others in the theater ate popcorn and watched, but I understood. I had been there.

The megook had become flushed, either from the hot water or the attempts at communication. I did not know. But like the alien in the movie I saw later, he was determined to communicate. He spoke the same utterance again. I heard my master gasp. "I think I understand," he said, and he moved forward.

My master had on shorts and an undershirt but no shoes, so he slipped his feet into the water beside him. "Are you saying, 'Koreans are very friendly people'?"

The megook looked tremendously relieved and nodded his head many times. The men in the tub gasped and then began to laugh excitedly and repeat the megook's unusual Korean pronunciation: "Koreans are very friendly people… Koreans are very friendly people."

I laughed too but did not understand. I had never heard my language spoken by a foreigner before. The way he spoke my language was one more odd but intriguing quality about him. The bathhouse filled with gales of relieved laughter from the men.

The megook became very quiet. He stepped out of the tub, sat with his back to the men, and picked up the soap. He began to wash himself and did not look up.

It was as though everyone became aware of his leaving the group at the same moment. The laughter stopped so suddenly that I heard a hum in my ears. They looked at one other. The old man scolded the father of the student, and he stared down at his feet. The other old man leaned toward the megook, who was rubbing the bottom of his foot with a washcloth. He rubbed it so hard I thought it must surely hurt.

The old man spoke very slowly and very loudly. "You speak Korean very well!"

The megook turned his head and looked at the man, and then he looked at the group of men who were now staring at him with serious faces. "No," he said softly, in words that I was now able to understand, "I don't speak Korean well at all."

"Excellent Korean," the men said, and the room was filled with that phrase, "Excellent Korean. Excellent Korean." The men nodded and smiled approvingly to him and to each other lest there be any doubt. "Excellent Korean!"

The megook looked at them one by one, and his face slowly filled with the same smile I had seen earlier. He picked up a bucket, dunked it into the tub, and held it above his head where he turned it upside down. The soap now off him, he returned to the tub, and the men gathered around him. They spoke slowly and listened carefully and spent so much time there that when they finally dried off later, their skin was pink and shriveled.

I had wanted to stay and listen to the stories, but my master put me to work folding the little white towels the men used after their bath. After the megook finally dressed and slipped on his socks, he stood up and faced me, examining me for a moment.

He slipped his hand into his front pocket and pulled out a packet of gum that he offered to me. I loved gum and rarely had it, but I was shy and refused. He insisted and finally took my hand and placed it in my palm. I watched him as his giant fingers closed my small ones over the bright-green package.

Then he pointed to his chest and said the word *Richard*. He looked at me expectantly.

I had no idea what he was saying, but he repeated the word again. *Richard*. And he waited.

I got the idea he was teaching me a word in his language and he wanted me to say it. "Lee Chad," I said, and this time it was his turn to laugh. He repeated again, "Richard."

"Lee Chad."

He nodded, approving. "Very good," he said, and he patted my head, a gesture I did not understand. And then he said in Korean,

"My name is Richard." He then turned, slipped into his massive shoes, bent down, and walked out the door. I rubbed the package in my hand.

I didn't know why he had told me his name. I only knew the names of children my age. All others I called by their position, or if I didn't know, they were "Uncle" or "Auntie." In any case, I found myself practicing the word over and over again: "Lee Chad… Lee Chad."

His visits were a highlight of a life that had previously had no highlights. I listened and learned all that I could about Lee Chad. From the conversations between the other bathhouse guests, I learned that he had just moved to our city and that he was a teacher in the neighborhood boy's middle school. He was sent by the Beautiful Country to the East. I also learned more about English, that it was another language, that there were many languages in the world, and that Lee Chad spoke that language very well.

I also learned that although America was a rich country, he lived in a small room with a poor family only five minutes walking from our bathhouse. Like most houses in our city at that time, there was no indoor washing. And in the winter it was very cold to wash outside.

Lee Chad once told the master that he took a bath every week "whether he needed it or not." This must have been a joke because Lee Chad laughed a long time after that. My master just smiled. After about two months of his regular visits, the neighborhood men had become so accustomed to him that he could enter the bathhouse without causing interruption.

It was a very cold, wintry Saturday in January when the money fell out of his wallet.

Lee Chad had finished his bath and was paying my master, who was asking him if there were bathhouses like this in America. He explained that houses in America had their own baths, although, he added quickly, they were much smaller and not nearly so nice.

As he slipped the wallet into his back pocket, a large bundle of money fell on the floor behind him. I almost reached to give it to him, but it was such a large amount of money that I froze.

Lee Chad bowed at the master, who returned his bow. He stepped out of the building. The master moved into his office, counting the coins that Lee Chad had given him.

The money lay there three feet away from my toes.

I looked up slowly through the glass doors into the bath. Only four or five men remained, and they were in the last stages of showering. Their eyes were even shut.

This was certainly my destiny.

Without another thought, I picked up the money and carried it into the toilet room where I could shut the door.

The master had taught me to count, and I quickly found that I had fifty thousand won in my hand—a month's salary for an educated man!

I stuffed the money in the front of my white undershirt and stepped out of the toilet. The master had not come out yet, but two of the men had stopped their showers and were drying. I looked at my secret spot and moved slowly in that direction, anxious to hide it.

It was strange that at that time I felt no shame. I somehow knew that the megook was my *unmyung*, but I did not know how it would happen. It was suddenly clear to me that this money was meant for me, that Lee Chad, even though he didn't know it, was destined to help me out of my mouse hole. I had no purpose for this money. I knew that I would not be rich. Mostly, I felt I would not be hungry again for a long, long time.

I had heard it said by my people that when good fortune comes to visit, it is accompanied by a devil. I saw no devils, only the chance for a new kind of freedom. I felt no sorrow or even pity for Lee Chad. He was from a rich country, after all. I could not allow myself to feel anything but a driving need to hide the money.

The front door opened, and Lee Chad walked back into the room. He looked around and knocked on the office door. The master came out.

For a moment, I lost the feeling in my legs, but I looked again at my secret spot, took a deep breath, and slowly moved toward it.

Lee Chad was explaining that he was buying milk at the store next to the bathhouse when he discovered his wallet was empty. He was very embarrassed, he explained, but he had lost his monthly salary and hoped he had dropped it here in the bathhouse.

I bowed my head. I did not want them to see my face.

"Young-Soo!" The master looked in my direction.

I could not speak. My experience in lying had been limited. I tried to control my breathing and slowly looked up.

They were both staring at me, amazed. I followed their eyes down to the bundle of money that was bulging in my undershirt. *How ridiculous I must look*, I thought, and I felt the redness flush through my body.

I still had not moved. The master walked toward me, bent down, and without a word, pulled up my T-shirt. Some of the money fell down on the floor. He picked it up slowly but did not look at my face. I put my head down again and then heard him address Lee Chad, "I'm very sorry. Please count it."

"I'm sure it is all here," Lee Chad said.

"Please count it."

A few moments passed with the sound of rustling money. I saw the glass door open, and two men stepped out. They looked at me; they looked at the money; they looked again at me.

I was ashamed.

I heard the door open. Lee Chad left.

I saw my clothes now thrown at my feet and heard the master's voice. "Foolish boy," he said. "Thought you were smart."

I would not shame myself further by crying. I put my clothes on slowly. The master opened the door and waited. "Work hard, but can't have a thief in bathhouse," he said.

I looked at my secret place.

"Go," he said quietly.

I pointed toward my secret place and looked at him and waited. After a moment, he nodded sadly. "Take what is yours and go."

I ran to my secret place, opened the box, and took the money. I did not look at the master as I ran out of the bathhouse. I ran into the street and kept running until I was blocks away. I ran to a small alley that led to some of the simple but nicer roofed houses in Kwangju. The narrow alley was lined with the concrete walls of the houses and extended several blocks up a large hill. No one was there, and I stopped to catch my breath. I sat down.

After a few minutes, I began to wonder what I would do next. I heard the women in the market peddling their vegetables.

"Buy my tomatoes."

"Buy my garlic"

"Buy my onions."

It began to snow.

I asked myself where I should go now, but the answer came too quickly—I had nowhere to go. Once again I was on the bad side of the rice-paper doors, except that this time it was not bad luck but my own foolishness that put me there. *Bad luck is better*, I thought.

I leaned against the cement wall that protected the house beside me. I thought of my warm wooden floor and the many times I had been burned by the stinging hot water. I thought of my master's stern face and remembered him putting the ten-won coin in my hand every day.

I put my hand in my pocket and felt the coins. There was enough to feed me for a few weeks.

I slept and tried not to dream.

Heavy feet woke me as they pierced my side with sharp kicks.

"Wake up, you little thief!" a voice above me shouted.

I looked into the eyes of my thirteen-year-old boss, a look of triumphant anger alive in his eyes. "Someone told me they saw you run in here." He kicked me hard in the stomach this time.

I folded over, trying to protect myself.

"Nobody leaves me!" he shouted. "I told you that." Two other young boys and one girl about my age were watching. He turned to them and placed his heavy shoe on my face.

"Watch! This is what happens to you if you try to leave without my permission." He screamed the word *permission*. He kicked me once in the face—hard—and then stepped away and pointed at me. "Check his pockets."

"No!" I protested, but hands were all over me.

"This pocket," said the little girl as she pulled out two of my master's coins.

"It's all I have. I'll starve," I pleaded, and I shamelessly grabbed the boss's shoe. "Take the money, but take me back too," I begged.

"Just lie there and die," he said. "And be a lesson to the beggars who would leave me." He pulled his shoe out of my grip.

Then his voice became quiet. "And if I catch you begging, I'll kill you next time."

I lay on my side, gasping for breath, and watched him briskly walk away until he turned the corner and disappeared. Blood dripped from a place over my eye. The snow turned into large white puffs that settled on my face. I closed my eyes.

When I opened them again, I looked straight at two white, plastic upturned shoes only inches away.

"You can't stay here." The auntie nudged me on my shoulder with her toe.

Obediently, I tried to stand.

She stepped back. "You sick? Why are you sleeping here? You got a home?"

I ignored her questions and staggered to my feet. She reached into her purse and stuck a ten-won coin in my hand. I looked guiltily into the street, fearful that I would see the beggar boss standing there, waiting for me to take a coin. The streets were empty.

"Can't stay here," she repeated, and then she opened the small gate into her house, ducked under the low doorframe, and entered.

Leaning against the wall, I moved ahead. As soon as I stepped into the street, I was blown back by the strong, frigid wind.

I looked to the left and to the right. There was no place to go, and a ten-won coin would only buy a single candy or a pack of gum.

Like the green gum pack that Lee Chad used to give me, I thought.

I sat down on the street. No one around seemed to see me. I lay down and closed my eyes.

I felt the snow cover my eyelashes, then my lips. The voices of the market aunties were all about me, laughing, arguing, calling toward customers. "Buy my garlic." "Buy my onions."

At some point, darkness fell, and the numbness began to be replaced by a new warmth deep within me. That's when I knew I was dying. And I was grateful for it. I felt the arms of death around me, lifting me up. I was flying, floating, suspended above the ground. Death pressed me closer. I became warmer and then colder—numbness and my clothes being pulled off—yanked, torn from my body; stinging pain deluged my legs, my hands—someone rubbing me—warm towels on my feet, on my head—choking as hot barley tea passed over my lips, a soft, soothing voice in my ear. I began to cry, and Lee Chad wiped my eyes.

Brent Jackson

Sixteen Years Later (July 13, 1993)

The Selangor Club

Charles and I were both smiling. Jason had stopped and was looking thoughtfully in the air.

"Go on," Charles encouraged him.

Jason's eyes lowered and focused on Charles. He looked startled and then grimaced, his mouth pulling down in anger. He covered his mouth and looked away.

"You're still mourning," Charles said. "It's understandable."

Jason looked at Charles blankly. "What is mourning?"

"Mourning?" Charles blinked and looked at me. "It's the process of…well—"

"Healing." I interrupted. "The healing of the heart."

Jason spoke softly, evenly. "One must still have a heart for it to heal."

Charles leaned forward, started to say something, paused, and then sat back in his chair silently.

Jason shook his head, as if in disgust. "Well, thanks, Uncles, for the little talk. Now where is that cute waitress?"

The waitress appeared again, and Jason turned to her. "Hello again, Shu Ling," he said, and he took one of the white orchids out of the vase on the table and handed it to her. "This orchid will look more beautiful on you."

Charles and I exchanged looks.

She held the orchid in her hand and, without a word, slowly tucked it inside her apron. She cast a longing look at him and spoke in a low voice.

"Sorry," he said, "I don't speak Chinese."

"Okay, Brent." Charles turned toward me. "Will you be the second?"

"Charles, enough! Stop with the game," I said. "If this is a life-and-death situation, you have to tell us more. What can we do to help?"

Charles looked at Jason and then me. "Not just yet," he said firmly.

"I want to hear about Deborah," Jason said, still staring at the waitress. "And then I want to hear something about Uncle Brent." He turned and looked at me. "I kind of like this, Uncle.

You have to tell me something hard—really hard. I'll know if you're cheating."

"And then?" Charles would not give up.

"I'll tell…more," Jason said.

Charles smiled. "You could tell him about the flying alligators, Brent."

Immediately my mouth felt dry, and I took a sip of water. Outside of Nicole and Mom, no one knew the whole story. Charles knew just one embarrassing part of it."

"I thought we would focus on Jason tonight." I swallowed and took a sip of my tea.

The waitress filled Jason's tea again. "Flying alligators, Uncle Brent?" Jason asked.

"It's a long story," I said.

"All right, Jason," Charles interrupted. "We'll give Brent a chance to gather his thoughts while I tell you about Deborah."

"Then this isn't the 'life-and-death' thing?" Jason asked, disappointed. "I did my part."

"Not quite, Jason," Charles said.

Chapter Six

Charles Dickens

Fourteen Years Earlier (March 12, 1979)

Memphis International Airport

The flights just can't be on time, can they? Oklahoma City to LA…late! LA to Memphis…late! I'm left to run the obstacle course through the LA airport to catch the next flight to Hong Kong then to stand at Gate 22, clearly marked on my boarding pass. But they changed the gate, didn't they? Five minutes to go as I stood searching for the correct gate in front of the long row of TV monitors.

"Excuse me. Excuse me."

It was a woman's voice, and I ignored it. She was speaking to someone else, I thought.

"Sir? You with the laptop."

Still panting from the long run, I turned around and looked down at a young woman in a dark business suit. I smiled expectantly.

"Oh my goodness." She stepped back as though she had seen something scary.

"Yes?" I asked. It is annoying for someone to become frightened after looking at you.

"You don't know me," she said. "Well, actually, I don't know you either. Not really."

I looked at her hands to see if she were carrying something she wanted me to sign or a can for me to put money in. Her hands were holding on to each other; she was wringing them. I looked up at the clock on the TV monitor. *Probably selling something*, I thought.

She took a deep breath. "I know this is crazy, sounds crazy. Honest, I'm not a crazy person."

I looked down at her again. It was true she didn't appear daft. Her business suit was tapered professionally to mask a larger-than-average waist. She had a roundish face, a small mouth that formed a pixie smile, and a large dimple on her right cheek. I could think of nothing to say.

She stepped back and looked at me and appraised me, as if I were a little boy she hadn't seen in a long time. "My, my," she said. "It's just that you are so much…well, prettier than I thought you'd be." She shook her head for a moment and looked at me all over.

It occurred to me that she was looking for an airport romance. "I'm sorry," I said. "I've got to catch a plane, don't I now?"

"Oh." Her face turned pink. "You're not English, are you?"

"I'm not English the way you mean it, but I am in a terrible hurry."

"Well, yes, me too."

I turned back to the monitor. I located the flight number, gate 12, about a twenty-minute walk. I could just make it.

She stepped forward and snagged the outside pocket of my jacket with her fingers. I realized that I had just been grabbed and looked down at her. "Now see here…" I started.

"Let me just say this and get it over with," she said, still holding on to my pocket.

"I'm really going to have to run, love," I said. "This is an airport, isn't it? And I'm just the spitting image of a man in a hurry, aren't I now?"

She didn't let go of my coat. There was urgency in her eyes and a softness that made me hesitate. I hadn't remembered anybody ever looking at me quite like that.

"Well, you sometimes, you have a hunch, you know." She looked down at her feet for a moment and then back again, as though retrieving some lost courage. "Actually more than a hunch. I couldn't do this for a hunch. And so well, I have it…and uh…I just wanted to tell you…"

"Yes?" I looked away from her for a moment—perhaps a security officer was about. I looked back again. She didn't appear mad.

She let go of my sleeve, stepped backward, and put her hands on her hips. "Well. I'm the one." She looked over at the clock and shook her head rapidly as though she were perturbed about something. "I'm pretty sure anyway. That you're the—"

"What? I'm the what?"

"One." She smiled and sighed. "There, I've said it. I will have no regrets. Now I've got to catch a plane."

To my astonishment, she turned and walked away.

I found myself following her. "This is quite extraordinary. You can't say something like that and just walk away. I've got a plane to catch. The one what?"

She kept walking briskly through the airport and spoke over her shoulder. "The one! You know."

I stopped completely. She sped up.

"I don't blame you!" she called. "You're much prettier than me. I hadn't expected that."

I nearly knocked down a tall middle-aged man who was standing still, reading the departure schedule. "Sorry." I mumbled at him as I whisked by.

She had stopped at gate twenty-seven and was handing the flight attendant her boarding pass.

"Where are you going?" I said.

"Overseas," she said, tucking her pass into the side pocket of her purse.

"Are you absolutely sure you're not daft?" I stopped at the gate and watched her.

She walked a few feet down the gate to the plane, stopped, and turned around. "I love your accent." She giggled.

I began to notice more things about her. Her long brown hair was pulled just behind her ears—it was an elegant touch. Everything about her was ample, but without exaggerations. Her shape was harmonious and symmetrical. We were far enough away from each other that I was aware of the magnitude of her eyes for the first time.

"Maybe I am a little daft," she said, and she turned and walked away.

"At least tell me your name," I called to her.

"No," she said. "If I'm right, we'll see each other with no help. If I'm wrong, we'll never meet again."

She disappeared around the corner, and I stared at the spot where she had been for a long minute. I looked at my watch, gasped out loud, and ran to my gate. The stewardess frowned at me when I shoved my boarding pass into her hand, but they opened the door. I stuffed my laptop under the seat in front of me and slumped into my own.

I thought of her, off and on, mostly off actually, until the time we met again in Korea, eighteen months later.

I was at a congratulatory party for Samsung Company's top two hundred employees of the year. I had connected the billion-dollar, high-tech corporation with half a dozen or so contacts by that time, and they insisted that I attend the party as an honored guest. We were all flown to Cheju, Korea's resort island, and gathered in the ballroom of a luxurious hotel for a formal congratulatory party.

Even in the five years since I had left Korea as a Peace Corps volunteer, Korea had burst into the twentieth century with supersonic speed. There seemed to be a new fifty-story office building and a five-star hotel rising in every direction you looked. The ten million population of Seoul was rapidly spreading south and had developed an entirely new city south of the Han River, an area that only six years earlier had been an array of rice paddies.

The vice president of Samsung was the master of ceremonies for the evening's events that had included some traditional Korean dancers; a couple of bluegrass fiddle players, who, like me, had also been flown in from America; and a lavish, Korean-style buffet, with four types of kimchi.

Mr. Han, the director of human resources, had been placed in charge of me and was keeping me appraised of the evening's schedule. We all sat in our formal wear at the round VIP table, just inches away from the entertainment. There were three hundred people in the room, and outside of the entertainers, it seemed that I was the only American there.

Mr. Han's English was minimal, but when I switched to the Korean language, he looked nervously at the vice president. From that, I determined that he was afraid the vice president might assume that he didn't speak English and therefore Mr. Han would lose lots of valuable face. We did English.

"We're getting ready to have a decoration director," Mr. Han leaned over me and whispered.

"What will we be decorating?" I leaned over the table and reached for a few of the crisps that had been placed there for us.

Mr. Han looked worried, took his pen out, wrote something on a napkin, and stared at it.

I was stuffed from the inexhaustible amount of food at the Korean buffet and had laid my chopsticks down, resolved never to eat again in my life.

"We will have a decoration director soon," Mr. Han said again, looking at his napkin and speaking a little slower than before.

"So…we will be decorating something?" I said again, also speaking a little slower.

Mr. Han frowned, wadded up the napkin, threw it on the table, picked up his chopsticks, and devoured a single clove of raw garlic. He chewed furiously.

"I think he means recreation director, silly."

I turned and looked behind me to see who had spoken. She was sitting at the table behind me, crammed into a table of about fifteen or so Korean women.

I couldn't believe it. "It's the mystery lady," I said. "I didn't see you come in."

"You've been sitting at the VIP table and haven't bothered to look back at us peons," she said, smiling. "But I've been watching you."

"When were you planning on saying something?"

"I've been having a lot of fun not saying anything."

I stood up to approach her table. "You've been stalking me, haven't you?"

She frowned. "I have not," she said, and she pressed her finger to her lips "Shh." She waved at me to sit down. "Here comes the recreation director."

I sat back down at my original seat and reluctantly turned toward the stage. *If she hadn't found me, how could this be?* I wondered, and I needed to know more. A Korean man dressed in a white dinner jacket had stepped to the front. He grabbed the microphone and called out to us as though he were calling from center ring of a Barnum and Bailey Circus. "Everybody, stand to your feet. We're going to begin the fun!" he shouted. "Grab the hand of the person next to you, and give it a squeeze."

"Oh, hello," I heard her say to someone behind me as both the vice president and Mr. Han grabbed my hands and squeezed them.

"What is he saying? I don't speak Korean," she called out to me in a loud whisper.

I didn't have time to respond.

"Now tell the person to your right how happy you are to be here," the recreation director shouted in Korean.

The person to my right was the vice president. I told him how happy I was to be here.

"Excuse me?" Her voice rose about the chatter. "I can't really understand anything, and people are doing some strange things."

"I'm sorry!" I called back. "He's talking too fast to translate. Just do what everyone else is doing."

The vice president of Samsung, following another order, leaned over and kissed me on the cheek. "Well, you've kissed me now, haven't you?" I said.

"All part of the fun," he said without conviction and pointed to the recreation director, who had just ordered us to find three people and tickle them.

"Excuse me? Anybody got a clue why I'm being tickled by total strangers?" she called out again.

I bowed to the vice president and pointed to the men's bathroom. "I'll be right back," I said. But he was occupied with trying to balance a chopstick on his nose. I walked past the mystery lady, grabbed her hand, and pulled her out the door into the hallway.

A small red sofa was backed up against the wall, and we both fell into it, laughing. "What were they doing?" she asked after we caught our breath.

"Must be a new kind of fad," I said. "Planned fun. Koreans are the Irish of the Orient, you know. They work hard, and they play hard."

"I always thought they were very reserved."

"You're thinking of the Japanese," I said.

We sat back and leaned against the sofa. She was dressed in a loose, beige evening gown, one arm rested easily on the sofa. Her hands were round, soft looking; her eyes measuring me again. *It's my turn*, I thought. So I measured her, studied her from her long, brown hair to the dark, strapped shoes on her tiny feet.

She frowned, sat up, and looked away. A roar of laughter came from the other room. The recreation director shouted muffled orders. She laughed and looked back to me. I didn't smile, being busily occupied with my visual examination.

A group of Korean Samsung staff members walked by and into the ballroom we had just escaped from. She stood and looked down at me. She wasn't much taller standing than I was sitting down. "People are staring at us," she said.

"No, they aren't," I said. "Koreans respect privacy."

"So they just don't look."

"It depends. Have you ever seen a man pee outside?"

"Not lately," she said, and she raised one eyebrow.

"Well, men in some countries used to pee just about anywhere there was grass," I said, "at least in the countryside."

"How convenient for them."

"I always thought so."

"I thought Koreans were very private people."

"Oh, they are," I said. "There's no contradiction."

"I sense something insightful coming." She raised her eyebrows and moved closer.

I took her hand. She stopped, looked down at it, and lifted my hand up to her face. I thought she was going to kiss it. But instead, she looked it over carefully, turned it, and ran a single finger over the center of my palm. I felt the hair on my arm rise to attention. I felt warm, retrieved my hand, slipped off my jacket, and laid it on the sofa. I rolled the sleeves up on my starched tuxedo shirt.

"Deborah," she said, finally introducing herself.

"Hello, Deborah. I'm Charles."

"I'm still waiting for something insightful, Charles."

"Yes," I continued. "It's like when a woman has to breastfeed in public. The conventions of nudity are disregarded. People simply do not look. She becomes invisible."

"So no one will see me if I do this?" She stepped forward, bent over slightly, and untied my black bow tie. She lifted the collar slightly, pulling the tie forward until it came free.

I swallowed. "Absolutely—especially in high-population countries. The blanket of privacy, however artificial, is essential to the preservation of the culture."

She played with my tie, stretching it out and then winding it around her fingers. "So if I see a guy pull down his zipper and take a—"

"Well, they don't do that so much anymore. Korea is quite developed now with sufficient public toilets. The development of their civilization no longer has to depend on—"

"But before that," she said. "He would just disappear?"

"Incredibly so." I folded my arms in front of me. "I remember reading how a couple of police constables were chasing a thief on the streets. They had nearly caught him when he suddenly stopped to pee. The police stopped as well, of course, and looked in other directions. By the time, they looked back, he had gotten away."

She studied my face for a long moment. Finally she shook her head. "That's pitiful. It wouldn't even get you an honorable mention in the Liars' Club."

"I had actually hoped for the championship."

She didn't respond but laid my tie gently over my coat. That gesture brought her lips close to mine, and I kissed her.

Her lips were softer than I had expected. I felt the hair on my arms rise again. She pulled away.

"I'm an English teacher for Samsung executives," she said.

"I wondered."

I laid my arms over the top of the sofa. She leaned over and kissed me again. Her mouth was closed, but she took turns, first kissing my upper lip, then the lower one. I kept my head back and followed her moves. Finally she pulled away again and straightened up.

"Oklahoma," I said.

"My favorite musical."

I leaned into her stomach and wrapped my arms easily around her waist. She stroked my hair. I felt the softness of her back and pressed my fingers into the grooves between her ribs. She took a deep breath, and it was as though her body ignited the robust smell of a wildflower garden, mixed, indistinct—the crisp odor of things dried in the sun. The strangest thing was that it seemed so familiar to me.

"Are we still invisible?" she asked.

"As if we were in Paris."

She wrapped her arms around my shoulders. I could hear her heart, beating strongly with the systematic cadence of the wheels of a slow train.

"Psychic?" I said finally.

"Absolutely not!"

What extraordinary beauty, I thought. And with one quick tug, I pulled her next to me.

THE SELANGOR CLUB

FOURTEEN YEARS LATER (JULY 13, 1993)

BRENT JACKSON

Directly across the way of the Royal Selangor Club was the Kuala Lumpur Royal Police Station. It was a recently painted solid-white structure of pure nineteenth-century colonialism. As Charles came to the conclusion of the story, I turned and faced it. I had a rare urge for a cigar. Not because I smoked—had never—but because it seemed the right thing to do sometimes at Somerset Maugham's table. Smoke a cigar and sip brandy. I could easily imagine the rich cigar smoke flowing smoothly down my throat and puffing out again in rings that circled the air above the table for a moment.

There was no escaping the fact that I would be the next storyteller.

"When did you marry?" Jason still wanted more details.

"Three months later." Charles leaned back. The waitress had refilled his tea, and it was warm. He cupped it in his hands.

"And you had a daughter"

"Yes," Charles said. He lifted the cup to his mouth, sniffed at it twice, and then took two quick sips.

"Her name…?"

"Petra," Charles said.

Jason sat back and clasped his hands in front of him. "Petra for rock."

"She was mine," Charles said.

"And…?" Jason wouldn't stop.

"And now we hear about flying alligators." Charles turned toward me. He nodded affirmatively.

"Well," I said, "there's something I have to explain first."

Jason leaned forward. "I would imagine so."

"I need to tell you what happened to me." I looked at Jason. "It is truly humiliating. It was the other night…the day before I left from Taiwan."

Chapter Seven

Brent Jackson
Two Days Earlier (July 11, 1993)
Taipei, Taiwan

When I let myself think about it—and I try not to—I wince when I hear people say they like to listen to music. I suppose it's a trained way of describing one's action. We hear others say that, and so we say that. We listen to music. Nicole says I overanalyze things. I agree. I told her once that I had no idea what people meant when they talked about listening to music. Nicole frowned at me. She was right. I also often exaggerate slightly to make a point. The truth is I do know, sort of, what they mean. I just don't agree with the way they say it.

Of course I believe we have souls. The soul is what is left of us after it is all said and done. We can affect the soul. We can also infect it. But I don't want to get into all that. Let me put it this way. I've never heard anyone say that they tasted their meal last night. They would say that they ate it. Food is tasted before it passes to the stomach, and that is eating. Music is listened to before it passes to the soul, and that is—well, I don't know what that is. But I know we don't sit quietly in an auditorium and listen to music. It just can't be done.

I have watched other people's response to music, and I try to imagine what they must be thinking…experiencing. By the smiles on their faces, the tears in their eyes, it must certainly be something wonderful. It lifts them. It calms them…at least for most people—for normal people.

For those who are broken, music becomes something else. I remember when one of my many roommates during my college days lost the love of his life to his best friend. My roommate stayed in his room, missed lots of classes, and clamped headphones on, singing loudly and badly with the Rolling Stones for the next two and a half weeks. For him, music was an aspirin, lulling him through the bad times.

But there is a deeper pain than a broken heart, and for those, music is something quite terrible.

Yes, this sounds very philosophical but necessary as an introduction as to what happened next and to what has happened before. It began comfortably enough. I remember that the Taiwanese conductor was moving his baton slowly, apparently lost in his own pleasure, as though he were the only one in the auditorium. It all seemed so innocent, so nonintrusive.

Nicole sat to my right, and Madam Chang beside her. Nicole speaks no language other than English but is a master at the "nonverbal." Through gestures, animated eyebrows, and plenty of affirming nods, she is an impressive communicator and had formed a remarkable friendship with Madam Chang, who spoke no language other than Mandarin Chinese. Madam Chang was pointing to perhaps the youngest violinist in the orchestra—this was Madam Chang's niece, and the reason we were all present that night. Nicole cooed and clucked to show how impressed she was.

Had I heard Shostakovich's Fifth Symphony prior to this evening, I would never have risked coming. I would have made an excuse—jet lag, stomach distress, anything to avoid facing what someone told me later is the most arousing composition of the twentieth century.

Arousing? He should have been with me that night.

But I had no idea it would be playing. I watched with interest while the conductor raised his left hand toward the brass and whispered something to them. They began to silence, one by one.

Unexpectedly, only the sounds of the strings hung in the air.

I felt a slight tingling sensation in my right hand. I rubbed my fingers together and tried to look at them. It was dark, but I saw just enough to fear what might be coming. My hands were trembling.

I tucked my right hand under my leg and looked about me. The petite woman and her husband were to my left. Mr. Chang to the far right. All were perfectly seated according to formality, except that it made for poor communication. The interpreter was behind us, which made his occasional attempts at facilitation awkward and noisy. During the first movement, we had nodded toward each other in appreciative smiles, but now we sat in silence.

I tried not to pay attention. I thought again of my cleverly negotiated triumph just the night before. I did not feel like smiling, yet I smiled; nevertheless, just in case the act of doing so would make me forget…help me not to listen.

Just a few violinists remained, playing together just on the edge of a harmony that I had never heard before—to my uninitiated ear it was almost out of key. *Not beautiful*, I thought, *actually terrible. Perhaps I can get through this.*

The brass joined in a triumphant entry, and I began to panic.

Distract myself. Think of something. Anything. I turned to examine Mr. Chang and tried to catch a smile, but he was deeply enraptured by his wife's niece, who sat at alert readiness with her bow poised. The conductor, his arm still moving as though the entire orchestra was engaged, finally pointed at her section, and fifteen-second violins began to affirm a defiant cascade of… what was Shostakovich describing—rebirth perhaps? It was brutally beautiful, and I knew I had little time but could not stop myself from giving in completely. I took out my shaking hands, gripped them, and pressed them across me.

I gasped as the brass disappeared suddenly. The violins dominated. They carried us, all of us, through their long sojourn until finally even they slowly faded away and the entire symphonic cacophony was hushed.

It might have been an oboe that spoke next. There wasn't a cough or rustle of clothes. Mrs. Chang began to cry, as she received into her heart one of the most intensely beautiful themes that I had ever heard.

The oboe was mourning for me, and I let it in. For just a moment, I felt washed in love and physically swayed my head from side to side with its hypnotic rhythm.

Then it attacked.

It's the only way to explain it.

I felt heaviness against the back part of my head as the sounds of the music began to swirl around me, as though they were physical manifestations probing directly for some hidden part of my soul. They pushed firmly, and though I resisted, they were able, in an instant, to find the inner door that I myself had been searching for all my life.

The door was locked, but that angered the force, and it seemed as though parts of my body were enlarging from its strength. The music became louder, and with it, its energy became stronger. I felt it circling me, like a lion circles a gazelle, waiting for the right moment. I remained frozen, waiting for the inevitable.

Then I did the absolute worst thing that I could. I somehow found the strength to turn my head and look at my wife.

The light from the stage accentuated my Nicole's Athenian profile. Her hair was pulled back over her swanlike neck. Six perfectly shaped pearls dangled from her ears where the sharp lines of her jaw ended, blending softly, like the touch of an artists' brush on silk. She turned and looked at me. I wanted so badly to be able to just continue staring. Just sit there and look at her for the rest of my life. Her raven eyes were reminiscent of the figures drawn on the Saturday morning cartoons, too big for a real person; they both explored and implored. I wanted to reach out, but I knew any attempt to do so would be foolishness.

This had, after all, happened to me too many times before.

The heaviness left in such a rush that had I been standing, I'm sure I would have staggered. This also was familiar. I should point out that psychotherapy is not without its reward. I knew—constantly told myself—that none of this was real. I had had many such attacks, and so as it left me suddenly, I knew that there had not been anything there at all to actually leave. And when it returned as gentle fingers on my shoulder, I knew there were no fingers really there. Yet I felt the relieving massage on my neck. I felt the fingers pass softly over my back, sending a tingling through my body that stopped at my fingers and toes. They seemed tender, almost loving. I was tempted, as always, to reach for the hands. But I resisted, the terror of feeling them on my shoulders was somehow not as horrible as the terror of reaching for them and them not being there. I sat quietly and waited; the end of this was never quite the same. The persistence of the music was now inconsequential. There was no conductor's cord that would stop this train.

Nicole was still looking at me. Perhaps by now she was at least able to sense its arrival. She watched me for a moment, frowning. My mouth was open, gasping for breath, and I felt dampness on my forehead. She smiled and took my hand as though my behavior was the most ordinary thing in the world. She did not know how far along I was, how really near the edge. So she took my hand, turned her head back to the conductor, and waited. We both waited. It might pass.

But its hands had become heavier and began to press its fingers deep into the creases of my neck. He was becoming rougher. I felt my head move forward as I resisted its force. I reminded myself dutifully that this was my imagination, that it couldn't be real. But that gave me no comfort, for my imagination had become a beast of tremendous physical strength that now had me firmly in its grasp. A determined but quiet shudder surged through me. I jerked again, and this time felt a sudden flush of embarrassment.

In the midst of all of this, I did not want to make a spectacle. I did not want people to know.

Fortunately neither the Changs nor the Leongs moved—also hypnotized by the conductor's baton, they were unaware of the battle that was now raging within me. Only my lovely Nicole, with her all-seeing eyes, could sense it, feel my despair. She acted quietly and quickly.

She stood and gave my arm a firm, commanding tug. I rose obediently and followed her, like a prisoner would follow his guard. I felt hot breath on the back of my neck. Its hatred engulfed me. Sweat poured from my forehead, but except for that, my long practice to retain my composure appeared to be working.

A woman in front of me, who had insisted on wearing a ridiculously high brimmed hat to this event, turned and looked up at me as I rose. She probably thought I had developed a fever and instinctually leaned forward as though she were afraid of catching something. The thing beside her, the sharp-nosed beast with buckteeth turned also. He glared at me, and I was repulsed by him, suppressing the desire to tell him to turn around.

I blinked, and in the next moment, I saw him again, a curious and perfectly formed smile on his lip. His eyes radiated kindness and willingness to help. "You don't have my soul yet," I whispered to my tormentor.

I had evidently whispered louder than I thought because Nicole turned and looked at me sharply and then pressed forward with more urgency.

Mr. Chang looked up toward me, back at the stage, and then quickly back to me again. Perhaps the beast that tortured me was making himself visible to them. It seemed so. Mr. Chang's eyes widened and seemed to look beyond me. The conductor's baton rose higher and higher.

The gentle hand on my arm pressed harder. She was pulling me now into the aisle. The music deepened into bass; the violins dropped out. Only the cellos and the bassoons remained. Did

Shostakovich himself have a demon? How was he able to do this to me?

The doors to the lobby opened. A woman wearing a too short and too red dress stood near the bathroom, smoking. The whole lobby was filled with redness…red carpet, red drapes, and red doors. Why would a woman wear a red dress to a theatre like this?

Beautiful Nicole appeared in front of me. I felt such bitter shame. Her loving eyes, her smile, only showed approval at how fiercely I was resisting him. She didn't realize that I had, after all, won. My door was still locked; I knew the demon was not real, and it knew that I knew, making its last frustrated attempts even more violent. The thick, hard fingers metamorphosed into razor sharp claws and began to slash at me. I grabbed the back of my head for protection, and then they slashed at the back of my knee. I screamed in anguish and fell forward, with the cowardly sobs of one who is being taken where he does not want to go. My wife's arms now struggling to catch me, the soundless bounce of my head on the carpet. A male voice now, offering assistance. Nicole's controlled, calming response…redness everywhere and then blackness. And it began to leave.

Brent Jackson

The Selangor Club

When I had begun telling Jason and Charles the story, both of them were leaning on their elbows with their jaws thrust forward. When I finished, they were leaning back far into their chairs and staring blank faced at me.

Jason smiled broadly and leaned forward. "That's a very interesting story, Uncle Brent." He stretched his right arm over the table and unfolded my napkin. "I'll be taking care of your knife for a little while, Uncle Brent. Any other sharp objects on you I should know about?"

"Very amusing," I said.

Charles laughed and spread his hands. "Well, Jason, you see now, don't you? We can talk about anything, can't we? Even if it makes you look like a fool." His eyebrows pointed toward me.

"Or a crazy person." Jason raised his eyebrows and dramatically stuffed the knife in his pocket. They both laughed.

"I'm so glad I could be a source of amusement for you both."

"Sorry, Uncle Brent." Jason controlled his laughter. "But we really are interested in knowing what the back-biting thing is that appears when you listen to music."

"Okay, Jason," I said. "That's quite enough."

"And we haven't even heard the part about the flying alligator." Jason doubled over.

It was good to see Jason laugh again. Even if was at my expense.

"Richard was very proud of you. He spoke of you constantly," I said.

"He liked to tell of your aptitude for computers," Charles said.

"I've heard the same about both of you—high-tech travelers, Dad used to say."

"Brent is the gadget king." Charles punched me.

"So"—Jason raised his eyebrows—"Uncle Charles. My people say that it takes two hands to make the sound of a clap."

Charles stared at Jason vacantly.

"I think that means, Charles," I said, "that we have done our part. We need more information from you."

Charles nodded, surprising us both. "You're right. You've done well. I think I can tell you at least part of it," he said. "I've had something quite extraordinary happen to me." His eyes had the peculiar expression I had noticed the day before. "As I explained, I need your help. But, Jason, from here on, these things are totally secret between us. Can you promise me this?"

Jason nodded, took his eyes off the waitress, and leaned forward. Charles leaned forward too. "This will remain secret between us, won't it? I have told no one." This time he looked at me.

"Charles!" I said in protest.

Then without further hesitation, Charles began to tell us his incredible story in minute detail. He explained how he had found out that he had a son and the strange circumstances in which he had met him.

When he had finished, as if on cue, Shu Ling brought us some crackers and light vegetable soup, setting them down lightly in front of us.

"Rod Chambers," Jason said. "Awesome!"

"But what is the terrible thing that you spoke of?" I was impatient for the answers

"There is obviously more to the story," Charles said, "and after you know it all, you are going to understand."

Jason waved his hand in the air, and Shu Ling reappeared instantly. "What can I bring you?" she said.

"How about finding a little whiskey? Come on. You know there's got to be something to drink in this club somewhere." He slapped her on the bottom.

Shu Ling gasped. She searched Jason's eyes…waited, I think, for an apology, an explanation. When he offered nothing, merely stared, without expression, at his bowl of soup, she turned and sadly walked away.

Jason glanced up as she left. "She'll be back." He shrugged and then looked at Charles. "Now don't you have some advice for me, Uncle Charles? Something about time…?"

I was confused by Jason's behavior. I sat back and listened. Charles did the same.

"Oh, yes. Why don't you say it?" Jason picked up a cracker and buttered it. "Time is going to help me forget that I not only lost my father. I lost my whole family."

As soon as the words were out of his mouth, Jason gasped and looked at Charles. "Uncle Charles," Jason said. "I'm so sorry."

It had been a stupid, self-obsessed thing to say, and Jason was instantly aware of it. Charles's entire family had disappeared in a moment.

I waited for Charles to say something, and when he didn't, I wondered if I should. "Charles?" I prompted, but his quick and firm glance in my direction shut me up.

Not more that fifteen seconds later, Jason sat up straight, took a deep breath, and turned toward me.

"Lest the moment of my complete impertinence linger even longer," he said as though he were now talking about the weather, "you could go on with your story."

I swallowed. "Okay," I said. "Where was I?"

"You were being eaten by a thing on your back," Jason said evenly.

"Yes, that was the end of that," I said. "Was there something else?"

"Right," Charles said. "You were going to explain how you weren't crazy."

"Right."

Chapter Eight

Brent Jackson
Twenty-Six Years Earlier
July 1967

I am not mad—at least not in the sense that I accept and control my madness. I know that it is going to come and go. I know that the only injury suffered is to myself. I've heard that the truly mad think they are not mad, and I know that to an extent I have some madness. Therefore, because of my acceptance of this, I am not really mad. Dr. Andrew, my therapist, actually agreed with me. He said I had spells, anxiety attacks, that a lot of people have them, and as long as I didn't hurt anybody, I could live my life outside bars. We talked a lot about the locked door and are both still as clueless as ever. He said I was a "wounded" child. But many of us are, he said, especially men like me who grew up without fathers. I probably felt a lot of anger mixed with curiosity, he said, and the best thing would be for me to reestablish a relationship with my father.

I told him that would be difficult, since he was never married to my mother and dumped her before I was born and that he disappeared like a stray cat, never to be seen again.

I suppose I thought about cats a lot when I was with my therapist. He reminded me of the Persian species. Dr. Andrew had a flat face that sprouted hair all the way up to his cheeks. He had half-opened, tired eyes and bored stares. He accepted the revelation about my father with the same slight nod, as if I had said that it might rain.

I suppose, though, I was fortunate to have him. He truly wanted to help others, and as my mother was poor, he gave sessions for a fraction of his fee. I believe he devoted himself to my case, and I understand that he pored over journals with articles about psychosomatic apparitions found in fatherless boys. After reading one of those articles, he decided to try a therapy technique whereby he assumed a father-like role model for me. I endured a few awkward and unappreciated hugs and finally thanked him for his efforts but felt like this treatment wasn't for me. I'm sure he was relieved, and we talked instead about my spells, which had begun when I was seven and increased in intensity and frequency until my fourteenth year—the year of my "empowerment," as Dr. Andrew called it.

After that, the spells did not come so often.

In September of my fourteenth year, I told Dr. Andrew about the strange thing that happened at my YMCA camp experience (I'll get to that), and he stroked his beard thoughtfully for a long time. This was the first time he used the term *empowerment* and said that this was a good thing. That term rang true, and I have accepted that as the best explanation to date.

One thing we never agreed upon, however, was the flying alligators. Dreams can be very real, he said. Less TV, he recommended.

My first alligator visited me when I was about seven. My mother let me sleep in a small room that was just off her own bedroom. There was much too large a window over my bed, and the curtain was always open. In the dark, the trees took different shapes. They frightened me and yet so compelled me that I would not take my eyes away. I stared transfixed at the shadows that eventually assumed the shapes of motionless witches, lions, and alligators. When I reported such sightings to my mother, her eyebrows crumpled, but she explained calmly that I had been dreaming. I knew differently.

One night, one of the alligators moved, rose silently above the tree limbs, past the day lilies, and right through my window above me, and landed on the floor not two feet from the bed. I did as any seven-year-old would when confronted in the dark with a living creature. I put my head under the covers.

I listened for a long time and heard nothing but the sound of my own rapid breathing. After some time, my breathing slowed, and I dismissed it all as my overactive imagination. I ventured my head out for another peek. There were two alligators this time.

I dropped back under the covers and decided to stay there until morning. My heart beat loudly, and the air became stale while I thought furiously about what I might do. I would hurtle myself out of bed, shout in an attempt to stun them, and jump while trying to look as frightening as possible onto the bed of my mother. When I had at last run out of air, I executed my plan, screamed loudly at the alligators, and leaped to my mother's bed with wild, scary gyrations in only two bounces.

Mom took all my candy away from me after that. Nevertheless, two sugarless weeks later, the alligators returned, this time in pairs, floating over my bed and landing on the floor beside me. As Mom had reacted so unreasonably to the first visitation, I endured this silently for several nights. But after falling asleep during a reading session in class, I finally confessed to my second-grade teacher. Within minutes, she had called my mother. My therapy sessions began shortly afterward.

Dr. Andrew's first statement was to look steadily at me and say, "You know there really aren't flying alligators."

I wondered for a moment if Dr. Andrew might be crazy too. "Of course there aren't flying alligators," I said.

I was shocked at their relief when they realized that I understood that my apparitions were not real. Of course, I knew that alligators didn't fly through windows. But I saw them. So whether they were real or not, while my friend Danny used to go to sleep staring at little florescent stars on his ceiling, I learned to go to sleep with my bedroom floor teeming with crawling, snapping, snarling alligators. And they all came, like Peter Pan, flying through my window.

I grew up with a mother who placed me before all things, including herself. I took this for granted and never imagined that it could be any other way. We were somewhat poor, but in that she catered to me. I knew what it was like to be spoiled. But she worried because I never seemed to fit in with anyone.

Mom worried a lot about this. Being a half orphan, as she called it, had left me crippled, I needed more exposure, she reasoned. So, at fourteen years of age—poor as we were and as much as I resisted—she sent me off to a YMCA summer camp.

I was still pouting when I arrived at the camp in Southern Arkansas. I was the last to get off the bus and slowly moved down the steps. The sounds of laughter, the screams of boys, and the shriek of whistles were everywhere around me. It was both exciting and scary.

There were about fifteen tents, with each having ten boys and a "leader." The leader was usually a college student who was doing this for summer work. One of the tents was designated as the "outpost." It was located about half a mile from the others and was supposed to be tougher. Partially, I had chosen it so that I could get as far away from the main group as possible, but I think another reason was that I was already feeling the thirst for adventure, no matter how small.

The outpost was generally available only to older boys. And as I was fourteen, I barely qualified.

"Brent Jackson?"

I turned and looked up at a green-eyed, dark-haired young man who, except for the extra weight, could have passed as my older brother. "Yes," I answered.

He extended his hand and shook it vigorously. "I'm Joe Hackett, your tent leader. Stand over there with the other boys of the outpost."

The other boys were herded under a tree. I would now have to go stand in that unfamiliar group. I walked forward, hating it, but quickly found that life could still get worse. There under the tree was Billy Schmidt, a red-haired, freckle-faced bully from my school who was so stocky his arms couldn't hang down straight beside him. He noticed me almost immediately, so while I paused and stared in stunned resignation, he began to smile. It was easy to see that he had just figured out that camp was going to be fun after all. In front of my eyes, while I stood there, he poked the guy next to him and pointed at me. After he talked for a minute, the other boy laughed with him. The torture had begun. Thanks, Mom.

I stepped down to our leader, who was escorting the last three boys up the hill. "Uh, sir," I said.

"Call me Joe, and carry this. We've got a lot to take to the outpost with us. No cafeteria there, you know. We have to cook our own meals."

I grabbed the bag full of dishes he gave me. "I think I've changed my mind. I think I'd rather stay in the main camp."

"Change your mind? Impossible." He was passing out sacks and tent poles to the other three new members. "All the assignments have been made." He paused and looked at me. "Don't worry. It's not that rough. We'll all have fun."

I nodded. I almost relaxed, having adopted the philosophy much too early in life that if you can't avoid the speeding train, why worry about it? I walked forward toward my misery with the solitary comfort that in one hundred years, we would all be dead.

We had the usual difficulties getting the tent up. It was massive, and although there was only one right way for the tent poles to go, there were thousands of possible combinations. Joe had left the directions at home.

Of course Joe assigned me to sleep in the tent of the evil Billy. I fed the campfire as long as I could until Joe shouted to me that we all needed to get to bed. I crawled into the tent and received my first insult.

"What are you doing in here, Jackson?" Billy called in a voice loud enough to wake the raccoons. "Only studs allowed in here."

I dealt with Billy like my science teacher had told us to deal with a wild bear should one ever cross our path. Don't make eye contact. Don't run from it. Never, never feed it.

"Hey! Are you listening to me?" Billy had found a cohort, a jock nicknamed "Surprise" who had also taken an interest in the festivities. Surprise, I quickly found, was not able to utter original sentences.

"Yeah. Only studs allowed," Surprise echoed.

There was one other boy in the tent—on my side. He had short, curly hair and deep-set eyes with a welcome look of intelligence. He was one of a half dozen black campers who I had noticed at the whole camp. He was squinting at Billy and Surprise as if trying to figure them out. I was tempted to introduce myself but knew that speaking to him, in front of Billy, could associate him with me and make him a fresh target of their torture.

I reached over for the round knob at the base of the kerosene lantern that was between us. "Everyone ready for the light out?" I said to no one in particular.

Billy sat straight up, his bloated belly hanging over his small white briefs. "Are you deaf? I told you to get out of here."

"You must be deaf," Surprise mumbled from the other side of him.

The sequence of events was becoming clear. I was afraid of Billy but still had a remnant of pride. There was no way I would leave the tent. If Billy touched me, I would hit him. Then he and Surprise would beat me up. Joe would intervene, lecture us all, and then leave us. Billy and Joe, satisfied, would go to sleep. I would be left with my bruises, but I would finally be left alone. It had happened before.

"Joe told us to turn out the light," I said, breaking my "wild bear rules" and looking directly at Billy.

"Touch that light, and I'll put out yours," Billy growled.

I just couldn't help myself. "Billy, a metaphor—I didn't know you were capable."

The boy on my side of the tent laughed. "Good one," he sat up and extended his hand. "Lenny's my name."

I shook his hand and introduced myself. "Thanks," I said. "I really did mean it—being impressed, that is. It seems like just yesterday that Billy began using compound sentences."

Lenny's laughter squealed. He fell over, dramatically.

The happy moment was quickly over. "You're dead meat!" Billy screamed, and he lurched toward me. I hopped to the side as Billy's shoulder hit the burning kerosene lamp. He yelped and boxed it. The lamp fell on its side, pouring oil and what looked like burning lava onto the plastic tent floor.

My sleeping bag ignited like dry leaves, but fortunately I was not in it. Flames climbed to the pointed ceiling of the tent, where they refracted and spewed like a sparkler down its sloping sides. The first gust of heat was warm, not searing, but as the flames fell back toward the floor, I felt pain and withdrew my leg.

Billy and Surprise pushed the flap and were out the tent door in a moment, but the fire had consumed our exit.

I had pushed up against Lenny, who now shouted, "Throw my blanket on it. Snuff it out."

I pulled his blanket out from under us, but before I had a chance to throw it, another figure had stepped inside. Joe had a fire extinguisher and was spraying everything in sight, including us.

The fire quickly surrendered, and we were left with white powder all over our bodies.

Outside, we waited for Joe's fury, which never came. He never even asked for an explanation. I was the only one burned, although mildly, but Joe took out the first aid kit and nursed my leg. He checked us all, made us wash, and then miraculously found space and sleeping bags for us in the other tents.

Billy said nothing to Joe, but when we passed, he whispered, "Dead meat," to me. I ignored him, falling back on the "wild bear rules."

In spite of a miserable beginning, I slept well the rest of that night and woke up slowly with the sun. One night down, thirteen more to go.

I was glad that I was already awake when Joe began his loud and annoying wake-up call—slapping his hands together and shout-singing, "Oh, What a Beautiful Morning."

"Today we're going to do something very special." Joe stood like a drill sergeant beside the clear running stream as most of the members of the outpost kneeled and washed the dishes. "I'm going to a place where only a few have been."

Billy was not enthralled. "What is it?"

"It's a surprise."

"How long is it going to take us?"

"It's in that direction, "Joe said, not answering Billy's question and pointing out toward the north where the water oaks thickened.

So before the sun was even in its midmorning position, we gathered canteens of water, our knives, and little else. "What food are we bringing?" Surprise asked, and I noticed that although he remained respectful to Billy, he was walking a healthy distance away from him.

"Nothing," our tent leader shouted almost joyfully. "This is a survival hike."

The other boys groaned, but my heart quickened with anticipation. A survival hike wasn't a safari, but it was the closest thing I had ever come to it.

Billy pushed his hair up off his forehead and scowled. "Survival hike! What is that?" He made it sound as if Joe had just asked us to put on girls' dresses and run through the campsite.

Joe ignored his tone, slipped his knapsack over one shoulder, and responded cheerfully, "It means we have to find our own food."

Billy kicked his knapsack hard, and I smiled.

"What's so funny?" Billy yelled at me. I became occupied with the task of tying my shoe and then followed the now-departing Joe in the direction of the "special place."

Joe pranced before us like a hunting dog, quivering with excitement, turning down one trail then down another. We blazed new trails and were repeatedly stung by overgrown oak saplings that lay in front of us. It was hot, and by the time the sun was overhead, our canteens were half the weight they'd been when we started. Billy and his friends grumbled in such a consistent pattern that if a bird watcher had been listening nearby, he would have declared the discovery of a new species called "Nowhowfar?"

Finally, as we neared an area where the stream widened and began to pool a bit, Joe turned to us and said, "We're going to break here for lunch."

Billy looked at him incredulously. "Lunch? What are we going to eat?" Joe leaned over and let his backpack slip off his shoulders. He reached into the back and pulled out a wad of papers. He began to pass them out.

"You need to study these handouts and decide for yourself what you want." Billy's jaw hung open, and he accepted the papers from Joe as though they were his quarterly grades. I squatted down and leaned on a deformed root of a large cottonwood tree. The possible grocery list included pictures of cattail root, a cactus called prickly pear, various berries, and fish. "I leave it to you to decide what you want to eat," Joe said. "There are a few fish in that stream but not many. Also, you must not drink the water."

I had never had luck at fishing, so after analyzing the list and its probable outcomes, I made a dash for the river.

"Come on." I waved at Lenny. "There are cattail roots all around the river."

Lenny hesitated. "How do they taste?"

"I don't know," I said. "But they have to taste better than the nothing that Billy is going to catch in the stream."

Lenny nodded and joined me. The cattails were just a few feet into the river, and we found that it took only a mild tug to pull them up. Only the bottom three or four inches were edible, according to our manual. While Billy was grumbling about turning rocks over looking for worms, Lenny and I, assured of our dinner, enjoyed the moment.

Billy complained mightily. "I'm starving," he said, and I wondered for a moment if we were going to have to wrestle over our bag of roots. But instead he demanded, "Where'd you get them?" I pointed to the river. Billy got up, grunting like an old man, and marched toward the river. We were at a higher plain, and the banks along the river were very steep. Billy had to hold on to the sparse bushes as he slid down the banks to the water where the cattails were. There he stopped.

I bit off a piece of a cattail and chewed it. Hunger made it almost tasty. Billy chose a different spot on the river than I had, which immediately put him in a precarious situation. He needed both hands to pull up the cattails, but if he let go of the bush, he would fall into the water.

He stood motionless, like Pavlov's dog, and scrunched up his face as he tried to decide what to do next. He moved his right foot onto a half-submerged log. He put a little weight on it, and it immediately splashed out from under him. Jerking his foot back on the bank, our eyes met. He was trapped. I sighed. I would have to help him.

I slowly moved toward him, my intentions apparent. I grabbed hold of one of the many oak saplings at the top of the steep embankment and held it as long as I could while sliding down next to him. I placed one foot against the exposed root of an elm tree in front of me and let the branch go. First, I grabbed a bush with my left hand and motioned for Billy to do the same. We did this without actually speaking to each other.

He followed my example, let go of the one bush he held with his right hand only, and leaned down to the water, where he grabbed a single reed. He tugged on it but did not have enough leverage to pull it out. I found that my bush could swing around so that I was able to move closer to Billy. I leaned out and grasped the upper part of the cattail, whereas Billy had the lower part. We pulled together, and it popped out easily. We repeated this twice again.

Three roots were not nearly enough for Billy's growling stomach, and there were four more cattails, but they were farther out in the water. Billy would have to either wade into the water or depend on me to support him while he leaned out.

He decided to depend on me.

Joe and the others had come to the side of the bank to watch. They first peered down and then settled into the grassy shade above us. Our task had become an exhibition sport.

"You're going to have to get wet, Billy," Joe prompted.

"Maybe not." Lenny squatted next to Joe. "Brent, how strong is his belt?"

I could see Lenny's idea. Billy's belt was thick leather, so I decided to give it a try. I held on to the back of the belt with my left hand and also curled a couple of fingers into his belt loops to add extra security. I located a small but well-rooted oak sapling and held it with my right hand. Again without comment, Billy grasped the idea, leaned forward, and picked two more roots. He turned around to me and grinned. He was clearly surprised by the personal satisfaction he had found in accomplishing this simple task. Since the memory of him setting me on fire was still quite fresh, I was not able to return the grin.

He spoke for the first time, "There are two more. That's all I'm gonna mess with."

I nodded but was already trying to figure out how I was going to assist in this new exercise. Billy obviously did not want to get wet, but it was necessary for him to dangle two additional feet over the water. The members of the audience seated comfortably on the soft grass above began to offer varied types of advice.

"Brent needs a firmer hold!" Joe called down.

Joe was right, and so I prompted Billy to back up. This time I grabbed the oak with both hands while Billy carefully moved around to the other side of me.

Joe was now shouting at us like we were on the last seconds of a playoff. "Get a better hold of the tree. Have Billy use your arms to balance on, and then reach out for the cattails."

He gave Joe a concerned backward glance, but this he did. He leaned forward on my arms, causing them some stress, and instinctively hooked his right calf around the oak tree and stretched out toward the cattail roots. He began to tug.

There was a rustling noise and the sounds of new activity above me. I could hear my tent mates moving.

"Over there!" I heard Lenny shout.

And then, Joe's loud clear warning...

"Snake!"

Billy jerked his body to the left, and his right foot slipped into the water. "It's a rattlesnake, Brent!" Joe shouted. "Look out!"

I had no time to look. Billy's calf had slipped from behind the tree. For some unclear and aggravating reason, I recollected later, I was still determined not to get him wet. So, in order to support us both, I thrust my left leg in the water, and as he fell forward, I freed my right arm so that I could support him around his abdomen. His chest now hung over my shoulder, but he was still squirming to turn around and see. We both turned and looked at the same time.

The large rattlesnake, coiled and active, was about seven feet above our heads. Obviously disturbed at all the commotion, it was now striking out repeatedly in the direction of Joe and the others. After one terrifyingly swift strike, it backed up to the cliff and then turned around and fled...straight down toward us.

Billy was now leaning dumbly on my shoulder, and I halfway expected him to try to climb me. *Perhaps*, I thought, *if we stay perfectly still, it will go right past us, either into the water or turn away*. I caught the glimpse of metal above me, and I looked up as Joe pulled out his knife. Was the knife for the snake or for the unlucky one of us who got bit?

"Freeze!" I commanded. But the snake, in its own panic to escape, lost its balance and began to fall in an out-of-control spin.

I glanced at Billy. His face registered what I now foresaw. The rolling, spitting, angry snake was on a collision course with our feet.

I realize now that there were a number of events that happened in that single moment. In my memory, my thoughts slowed down; the action slowed down. I remember everything in crisp detail.

Astonishingly enough, I was not so afraid of being bitten as I was concerned with being at least four hours away from the nearest clinic. The idea of snakebite didn't please me, but my rational mind knew that a leg bite wasn't normally fatal if you could get help quickly.

I knew there was no quick help.

Running away was also impossible on the muddy bank. We could throw ourselves in the water and swim. But then we risked a deadlier bite to our neck or face—places where you couldn't put a tourniquet.

Billy, mercifully, was frozen in fear. That was better than struggling, which would have complicated the situation. I glanced at the rattlesnake. It was now rolling like a rope straight toward us. Only our feet stood in the way of the snake's tumble into the river. All of us, Joe, Lenny, Billy, were quiet, like the hush of passengers on a jet taking a gliding dive to the ground.

It was almost at my ankle.

The next sound I heard was the snake plopping into the water.

But we had moved.

We were now six feet above the cattail site hanging onto the side of the cliff.

The face I was now staring into was Joe's. He was looking at me like I had, well, just carried a 130-pound boy six feet straight up a cliff in a single bounce. He caught his breath and managed to grab my hand that was tenuously gripping a bush. Billy was still clinging to my shoulder. He pried himself loose from my grip and then stared absently at the smashed cattail root in his clinched fist.

Joe explained to us that evening that he had read about things like that before. I had been able to jump six feet straight up the cliff because of the sudden release of adrenaline in my body. By that evening, we were telling the story over and over again, rolling on the ground and laughing louder each time. It was a great moment.

Billy never actually verbalized any gratitude for saving him from the snake. But he stopped beating up on me, and so I figured that was his little way of saying thank you. We never became friends, but I associate him with one very good memory. He was with me when I became empowered.

That night, as we slept under the sky, it began to rain. While the others groaned and escaped deep within their sleeping bags, I rose and greeted this midnight surprise as a new friend. As I looked about the world with my new eyes, every tree I looked at, every star, every animal brought a new quickening in my soul. Life had become exciting.

I had never liked myself very much before, so now I took new faith that I had the courage to become something that I would be proud of someday. I reached out my arms to the rain and told God that I was ready. Somehow, at fourteen, even without a father to guide me, I could picture myself someday being some sort of a man. At the same time, I had been bitten by the call of adventure and now knew that somehow, some way, the new and the untrodden would be my life's work

My troubled childhood, I reasoned, could now be put in the past, in its perspective.

Or so I hoped.

The Selangor Club

Twenty-Six Years Later (July 13, 1993)

Brent Jackson

Charles was shaking his head as I finished. "So you jumped six feet up a ledge with a boy on your back, and you became a man."

Charles's tone had a totally unexpected harsh edge to it. I became instantly defensive. "In a nutshell, yes. So what? I discovered that I had something important inside me that didn't need a father to make happen."

"It's blooming nonsense," Charles said bluntly.

"It's not nonsense. It was a healing moment."

"Oh, you're healed, are you? I have an idea. Let's talk again about the back-biting, flying, invisible thing that attack you during a symphony. Every healed man ought to have one of those."

I found myself shaking my finger in Charles's face. "It is not exactly conducive for our 'free sharing' if you are going to be so critical, Charles."

"This isn't about just sharing."

Jason put up his hands. "Uncles!" he said.

I tried to change the subject. "Jason, it's your turn again." And I could not resist adding, "Charles, let's please not be so critical of Jason."

"I don't have any intention of being critical," Charles shot back. "But I believe he could take it if I did."

"He needs a little special consideration."

"You don't give him enough credit!"

"Well, I know it's my turn, Uncles, but I have nothing left to tell you," Jason said.

We crossed our arms and looked at each other.

"Uncle Charles? Do you trust me yet?"

Charles breathed deeply. "There is one more thing I want to know from you, Jason. But that can come later. For now, I want you to know that I do trust you. Listen carefully. I'm going to tell you more. I woke up the next day after Rod came into my room thinking it was a dream. But if it was a dream, then it became a nightmare, and I'm still living it. Rod is going to die if I don't—we don't—do something.

Chapter Nine

Charles Dickens

Five Days Earlier (July 8, 1993)

Los Angeles, California

As I said, I had fallen into a deep sleep. I was dreaming, wasn't I? I was dreaming that it had all been a dream, and I had woken up. Rod was a face on a magazine. There had been no mysterious encounter in my hotel. I had actually met with my client, and all had gone well. But then I heard the phone ringing, and that was what woke me from my waking. I picked up the phone confused…trying to remember. But Rod's voice on the other end was unmistakable, and I sat straight up in bed. His voice was relaxed, but he wanted to know how quickly I could get to Los Angeles. I was almost shaking with curiosity, but I calmly said I could be on my way the following morning. He asked if I would mind taking a cab and gave me the address.

Getting a flight on such short notice was not only expensive but also indirect. I had to fly through San Francisco and then to LA. Business class was full, so by the time I arrived, my long legs ached from the cramped coach seats.

Our appointment was at 6:00 p.m. When I arrived in LA at 11:30 a.m., I still had time to check into my hotel, take a much longed-for steaming hot shower, and have a pair of pants pressed. By the time my taxi driver was driving around Beverly Hills looking for Rod's address at five forty-five, I smelled of hotel shampoo.

It was a Los Angeles cab, but I could tell the driver had been born elsewhere. "How long did you live in Mumbai?" I asked him.

His head whirled around. He looked me up and down briefly and then returned his direction to the road. "How did you know I was from Bombay?" he asked.

"I've always liked the unique Mumbai accent," I said.

We drove silently for a while. The driver had the radio on, and I heard the announcer mention Rod Chambers.

"Could you turn up the radio please?" I asked him.

"Are you from England?" the driver said.

"My parents," I said. "Please…" And I pointed to the radio.

"Al Renfield is known in Hollywood circles as one of the leading agents," the newswoman said. "Rod Chambers being his most famous creation."

"Besides Rod Chambers," she continued, "Al Renfield was known as the 'man with the Hollywood famous touch.' Whoever he touched became a star, and he represented the biggest and the best."

"I didn't catch all of that." I leaned forward. "Did something happen to Rod Chambers's agent?"

"They don't know," the driver said. "He's turned up missing. His wife is on the phone with the cops every day begging for the continued investigation. Thinks he may have been kidnapped."

The driver recognized the house as we drew closer.

"This is Rod Chambers's house."

"It's as big as I thought it would be," I said.

It was an artfully decorated fortress with blazing white brick walls framed by a stair-stepped landscaping. Each step was surrounded by red and yellow flowers. The tops of the walls were laced with black wrought iron that folded dramatically at the gated entrance area. Rod had given me instructions on how to ring him from the entrance—but the gate was open.

"You know Rod Chambers?" The driver had twisted his head around to get another look at me.

I felt the temptation to say, for the first time, "Yes, he's my son." But instead I said, "I know him," reached into my wallet, and took out thirty dollars.

"Shall I park here or drive in?"

"Drive in, I guess."

Very impressive, I thought. Hedges that looked as if they had been squared by a carpenter's level surrounded the driveway. A police constable's car was in the driveway ahead of us.

"Let you out here?" The driver pulled to the right, just behind the constable's car, which, I observed, was empty.

"Thanks." I handed him the money and stepped out.

"You sure look like him," the driver called to me.

I stopped at the front door and looked around. The rich and famous in Asia have amazingly simple homes in comparison to Americans. Even the rich in Asia usually live with an extended family, and this is rarely conducive to entertaining. As a result, most Asians entertain in restaurants that abound in private rooms designed especially for such occasions.

However, this was a Beverly Hills movie star's home, complete with fountains and a lavish swimming pool. Its lush landscaping and tall white walls were designed to be both impressive and intimidating. The effect was successful. I was both impressed and intimidated.

One of the front doors was wide open. I looked around and didn't see a doorbell button, so I knocked on the doorframe and then stuck my head in.

The glistening entryway could have been built out of the same translucent marble as the Taj Mahal. A crystal chandelier with hundreds of prisms dangled to the left of a large six-paned skylight. A circular staircase rose from the center to a white balcony on the second level.

I saw no one but stepped inside.

Voices were coming from the second entryway to the left. The voices were still muffled, and I crept closer.

A man turned the corner rapidly and ran right into me.

I jumped back, saying, "Sorry, sorry, sorry."

"Do you know this man?" The gentleman I had bumped into was very stocky, five-foot-ten-ish. His eyebrows matched the thickness of the mustache that covered his upper lip.

A frowning Rod turned the corner as well and looked at me. He didn't seem pleased. "Yes, I know him, Detective Ryder."

"I'm very sorry," I was still muttering.

Detective Ryder ignored me. "You won't be leaving town to go to Singapore again, will you?" His sentence was filled with gruff, sharp, staccato-like words.

"I don't think so," Rod said.

"That's good," he barked. "Because I don't want you going anywhere unless you talk to me about it."

"I don't plan to."

"And you'll let me know if your agent contacts you?"

"You'll be the first to know."

The detective left, and we stood in the hallway facing each other.

I swallowed hard, once again grappling for words. "Nice home."

"How much did you hear?" he responded.

As he stood only about two feet from me, I realized that this was the closest view I had had of Rod: deep-set eyes, pronounced cheekbones, dimpled chin—perfect face.

"I didn't hear anything," I said.

His eyebrows arched. "Too bad. It might help you understand some things."

"What things?"

He shrugged. "Later. Would you like a drink?"

"Just water with lime, if you've got it." I followed him into the next room. I thought he would take me into the den, but this was...well, I didn't know what it was. Many men had had to work a long time in the quarry to chip out all the marble this room contained. My eyes fell on the fairly authentic-looking Persian rug. There were glass tables, a large ebony bar surrounded by no less than eight bar stools, and a marble statue of a horse pressed up against the wall. Disconnected and unrelated pictures hung in odd places around the room.

Rod moved behind the bar and chopped a small piece of lime. "What do you think of my house?"

A brothel came to mind, but it didn't seem the appropriate moment for directness. "Beautiful carpet," I said.

"Thanks," he said. "You've identified one of the few things in this house that I actually bought myself."

"Who owns the other stuff?"

"It came with the house. It's all leased."

"You've leased this house," I repeated

"Yes. Now why don't we cut out the crap?"

In front of Rod, the garish, over adorned interior with odd angles screamed, "Notice me!" Visible through the giant glass window behind Rod were low-cut shrubs laced with red geraniums introducing a small grove of stunted fruit trees. Behind them lay a body of water so skillfully designed that the only things missing were the ducks. The inside of the house could have been designed by a set decorator for a Broadway musical; the outside, by an artist.

He was breathing hard.

"All right," I said in as normal a voice as possible. "Is there something you'd like to talk about?"

"You surely don't think I have asked you here so that we can have a father-son reunion, do you?"

I was beginning to realize that Rod loved to be outrageous, loved to shock. *An attention-getting device*, I thought. "I didn't know what to think," I said.

"Talk about each other's lives? Ha!" He poured another drink into his glass and slammed the glass on the table. "Drink cocktails until morning and then fall into each other's arms and cry?" The veins in the side of his neck bubbled up into thick, red welts that matched the growing color of his face. His voice grew louder. "Perhaps by the time you left I would be calling you 'Daddy'? And I'd send you a necktie for Father's Day?" His eyes were now red, and the lines in his forehead I had observed earlier had deepened dramatically.

He was screaming. "Is that what you thought?"

I froze, stunned by his outburst. For a few seconds, he took loud, gasping breaths as though he had just returned from a long jog; then his face began to relax. He picked up his glass and slowly sipped his gin. Within moments, he was again the face on the magazine cover, the boy next door, every woman's dream.

"Sorry," he said flatly, looking not so much regretful as contemplative, like it was an action he could now reflect upon. "That's not what I intended." He looked wistfully into his glass. "But then it never is."

I could think of nothing to say, and so I didn't. While he sipped his drink, I tried not to stare, so I shifted my gaze to the pool that looked like a pond. My heart was beating fast, and to slow it down, I allowed myself a moment to stare at the sunset. *A strange phenomena*, I thought, for perhaps the hundredth time in my life—the more the sun slipped away, the warmer and more authentic the colors seemed to be. I began to relax a bit.

Rod took a small brown leather case from behind the bar and placed it on top, next to his drink. "I don't know if you've heard or not, but my agent has been missing."

"I had heard that." I didn't know if I was relieved or not at this change of subject. "My taxi driver said he might be kidnapped."

"Oh, the great Detective John Ryder doesn't think he was kidnapped," Rod said. "He feels pretty certain it was foul play."

"Is that what you think?"

Rod offered me another drink, which I declined. When he poured himself another one, I knew then that it was true that all in Hollywood did not glitter. "People think Al discovered me, but he didn't," he said.

"Who did?"

"There wasn't just one."

"Where'd you start?"

"Mom helped me get in a dog food commercial when I was six."

"I don't remember seeing that."

"It wasn't much. Stood around with a dog in front of a dozen grown people with their bright lights. I don't even remember where the cameras were."

"I see. Were you nervous?"

"Nervous? Hell no. I was just a kid." His barstool swiveled around. He turned his back to me and looked out at the landscape for a moment. Without turning around, he continued to talk. "I got a little part in a TV show and then a few little parts in movies."

"What movies?"

"Little movies, movies you probably never saw."

"What was your first important movie?"

"On my sixteenth birthday, I had a bit part in *For Love of Abbie*."

"A bit part?" The Rod I was getting to know would not be so modest. "That was one of your biggest movies. It was the first time I remembered seeing you."

"I had a bit part until Al Renfield walked onto the set and changed my life. He told me, didn't ask me, that he would take care of me from then on. Mom signed the papers, and the next thing I knew I had the lead role."

"And you became famous."

"Famous and rich." Rod stared for a moment at the brown case. "He said I was his favorite. I believed him."

I waited to see if he would say anything else, but after a few moments of silence, I spoke up. "So does the detective have any leads?"

"Yes, he does," Rod said. "He suspects me."

"Suspects you? Suspects you of what?"

"Of foul play. He says that I was the last person to see him."

"Oh?" I could think of nothing else to say.

Rod read my thoughts. "If you're wondering…I do know where Al is."

"I was wondering." I couldn't sit in that chair any longer. I got up and walked to the glass wall.

Rod never moved. "You like my garden, don't you?"

"It's beautiful."

I heard the tinkle and splash of another ice cube into Rod's glass. "You see the pink Caladiums?"

"The ones to the side?"

"Those are the ones."

They didn't seem to fit perfectly with the rest of the garden. "Did you plant them?"

"You might say that," Rod said. "I replanted them on top of Al."

I stared at the Caladiums and tried to think of other possible meanings to what he just said, besides the one that first came to my mind.

"You don't seem surprised." Rod was leaning over the bar with a strange smile on his face.

I didn't know why he was smiling, so I smiled a little too, as though I had gotten the joke. Finally, though, I said, "Sorry. I don't get it."

"Don't get what?"

"What you mean."

"I mean exactly what I said."

I must have gotten quite a look on my face because Rod laughed. I stepped back away from the window. Ever since the first day Rod had appeared in my hotel room, he had thrown me shock after shock, and I was beginning to find them tiresome. "You're enjoying my distress, aren't you?"

"Somewhat," he said evenly.

"Is this a joke?"

"Hardly."

"Did you have something to do with Al's death?" I needed to sit down and found the only soft chair in the room.

"I had everything to do with Al's death." He opened a drawer and quietly took out an envelope.

I remembered napping on the sofa, some ten years earlier, when my wife, Deborah, brought my new baby girl to me. She laid my freshly diapered daughter on my bare stomach. Deborah's pregnancy had been a surprise, and, although I never relayed that to her, I was not pleased. The timing was wrong. I was too busy with my career. There were lots of bills.

But when I felt the warmth of my daughter's tingling live body on me, I was flushed with shame that I had ever felt anything but love for her.

"So you killed him." I knew he wanted to tell me this.

"Yes." He stared at the envelope, rubbing it between his thumb and forefinger.

"How?"

"I hit him."

I looked out again at the pool that looked like a pond. "You killed him, and you buried him," I said, more to myself than him.

"Yes."

The shadows of the garden no longer hid cute, little, imaginary ducklings. Rod walked slowly over to me. "This is for you." He paused. "I spent a long time writing it."

"It's a letter to you," he explained, and he held it toward me, not taking his eyes off it. I took it gently from his hand, opened it, and read the first line.

"Dear Charles. I have killed, and now you must pay."

The Selangor Club

July 13, 1993

Brent Jackson

"Good Lord, Charles."

Charles reached into his satchel and pulled out an envelope. He tossed it on the table in front of Jason. "I can't," he said. "Here, read it."

Jason unfolded the wrinkled sheets of paper carefully.

"Read it out loud, Jason," I said. "Hurry."

Jason took a deep breath and began to read.

Chapter Ten

Rod's Letter

Written June 24, 1993

(One Month Earlier)

Los Angeles, California

Dear Charles:

I have killed, and now you must pay.

Not that I meant to—kill, that is. Of course I knew that I was going to hurt him. I wanted to hurt him badly. I didn't know he would die. Never imagined I would now be a killer and find myself doing these things killers do, like burying my only friend in the back yard of my estate.

That's right. Buried him. Though it's not really my estate. That's one of the problems, as I will explain. Actually, I don't know why I'm bothering with any kind of explanation for you, except that it suits my present mood. This is, after all, a kind of suicide note. Such messages are typically short, I would imagine. But it is important for me that you know everything, that you understand everything I have experienced so you feel, in so much as it is possible, what you have done to me.

Al, the friend I killed, didn't want me to buy a home. He wanted me to rent this fashionable mansion. He thought it was close enough to him that he could drop by often during those difficult last months of my mom's cancer. When he wasn't being my agent, I think, at least for a while, Al fancied himself a kind of father to me.

Al had never prepared me for the role of murderer. The worst I had played was a twelve-year-old pirate, a year before Al took charge of my career. He's the one who taught me how to be charming and amusing in front of the camera. Once I was established as the boy who always got the girl, my career and my fame soared. I never played a bad guy. Never a killer.

That's the only reason I can give as to why I did so many stupid things right after I realized he was dead. Why I took him by the arms and dragged him out back. Why I shut off all the lights and searched over thirty minutes looking for the place where the gardener kept the shovel. Why I threw dirt, rocks, and Caladiums in the air like a madman and dug a hole four feet deep in just over three hours.

I could barely see his face in the dim moonlight and was glad of it. He had looked so shocked when I came at him. He didn't even have time to raise his fist before I hit him. The loud snap let me know that my fist, powered by the years of karate and tae kwon do lessons—Al himself had forced me to take—had just broken his jaw. Blood burst from his mouth.

Al's arms flew above his head. His feet, for a moment, seemed to leave the floor. Al was caught in a backward fall and yanked his arms down behind him in an attempt to lessen its impact. His feet kicked forward—trying to gain some advantage of friction on the floor. His left heel met the surface, but the marble was too slippery.

That white marble horse monstrosity was waiting behind him. Al fell backward on its square foundation. There was a dull thud, and blood spattered as high as the horse's girth.

He looked so scared. He looked right at me and knew. I stepped forward, and with every step, there was something in his eyes that began to lessen. By the time I reached him and put his hand in mine, that look in his eyes had totally disappeared. The bleeding stopped promptly. Al Renfield was dead.

My first impulse had been right; you have to give me that. I ran to the phone, picked up the receiver, and held it in my hands for a few moments. I dialed nine and then one.

I thought of the police—the reporters. I had no one to help me through this. I hadn't made a movie since Mom died. That's why Al had gotten upset with me.

"You haven't made a picture in two years!" Al had stood in front of me, trying to get me to look him in the eyes.

I'd tried to be patient, had tried to hold back that temper of mine that had been written about twice in *People Magazine*. "You know I haven't been able to think about movies since—"

"I know. I know." Al had lowered his voice almost to a whisper. "Your mom was the only family you had." He had grasped me around the shoulders. "She's been gone two years now. You need to—"

"Why do I need to, Al?" I'd pushed his hands away. "We've had this conversation before. Why do I need to get on with my life? I have plenty of money…"

Al had dropped his hands and stood back. "Do you think the Rod Chambers frenzy is going to continue forever? You think someday you're just going to start right back up again and—"

"I haven't noticed a drop in the tons of fan mail you dump over here. I don't think I've been forgotten." I had taken a deep breath…still trying to hold it in. "Have you been to a magazine stand lately?"

"Then think of me, for once, Rod." Al had thumped himself on the chest. "I'm under a lot of pressure from the producers."

I'd turned my back on Al. I had tried to walk away. "I can't think about that now. Leave me alone."

Al had reached in his back pocket and pulled out a folded sheet of paper. "I didn't want to pull contract on you, but have you looked at this lately?"

If Al had just let me keep on walking. "I don't want to look at it. Just leave me alone."

Al had shouted with the full force of his 250 pounds. "Well, you'd better take a look at it."

"Get it away!"

He'd grabbed my shoulder. "They're going to sue us, Rod. You'll be ruined. I can't help you anymore!"

I could still hear those ironic last words as though they had just been spoken. *No, Al,* I thought. *You can't help me anymore.*

The phone I was holding began that *beep*, *beep*, *beep* it does when it's been on the line too long. I hung up and stood there thinking that this had been one of those "moments of truth" I had heard others talk about. There was the man who I might have been—the one who would have called the police and worked it out step by step. And then there was the coward, the man I turned out to be. The man that you made me!

Hide the body. Hide the evidence. Hide. Hide. Hide...

I pulled black garbage sacks out of the kitchen drawer, wrapped them around Al, and lowered him as gently as I could into the grave. I hesitated, ran back in the house, and found a blanket in the guest bedroom, a gray woolen one, carried it outside, and placed it over him, tucking it carefully around his sides.

I pushed soil into the grave with my shovel and got down on my knees, smoothing the top as best I could. The last thing I had to do was replant the Caladiums over him. I stood up and tried to imagine what it would look like in the daytime. The gardener was sure to notice. I would need to think of a story.

I returned the shovel to its spot, entered the house, and slipped my shoes off. Mom had taught me well. No sense tracking more mud through the house. I felt a deep aching in the pit of my stomach and put my hand over it. The blood on the floor was still waiting. One thing at a time. I walked into the laundry room, where I dumped my stinking clothes into the washer.

There was a shower off the entryway. It felt strange to shower with the lights out, but the darkness gave me some feeling of security. As the warm water flowed over my back, I felt the release of tension that comes with having a little time to plan. I allowed myself to think of the next step.

I knew I could clean up the blood well enough that no casual observer would notice. But that wouldn't hide a serious police investigation, certainly not one that included DNA testing.

The lease on the house would be up in four months. I had always hated this house and had never planned to stay here this long. It had just been easier to stay than go. But now the owners were ready to move back. I knew I could hardly spend the rest of my life wondering if they would dig under the Caladiums someday and build a gazebo.

Perhaps I could buy the house, offer them twice what it was worth.

But no. The police would be looking for Al. I would be questioned soon, and after all other options failed, the police would begin searching. A sudden purchase of this home, especially at an inflated price, was bound to create suspicion.

Yes, I know. I should have called the police right away, when Al first fell. It's hard to explain my instinct for running, actually. Now, unburying the body is really not an option, is it?

My thoughts shifted to my last birthday. Al had insisted on giving me a party since it was the big twenty-one. It had only been his family and me. He knew I didn't want to be around a lot of people. Al's four-year-old son, named after me, had just been given a Nintendo game. I spent most of the evening teaching him how to play.

Little Rod. Little four-year-old Rod. Now fatherless. I want you to know that, Charles. I need for you to know that.

I turned the water several degrees hotter and turned my face into the shower. I held it there, feeling the stinging pain until I could feel my skin throbbing. When I turned my face away, I began, for the first time, to consider the other option. It had always been there, I guess—one of those little thoughts that lurks. That's the word: *lurks*. It lurks around and behind the other thoughts. Never very clear…always there. But it was becoming clearer by the moment. And then it was standing directly in front of me. Clear. Clear.

Option two was consistent with my character. It was for cowards but had the advantage of permanence. Complete escape. It was weirdly, strangely alluring…

I put my hands on the faucets and immediately had one of those out-of-body experiences, like I was watching myself take my last shower. I turned the water off, stepped out, patted myself dry, and slipped on a robe.

I felt lighthearted, an unexpected exhilaration that comes from being clean and still having choices. Going to prison, I had decided for sure, was not one of them. I stood in the marble entryway and tried to see the boundaries of the blood pool.

I decided to turn on a light, if for only a moment, to see the extent of the damage. I went to the window and pulled the curtains aside. A deep-green Jaguar was parked at the entryway, under the covered part of the circle driveway.

I slumped and leaned against the cold wall. Al's car. How could I have forgotten? Stupid. Stupid. Stupid. The leased house, the DNA, the car—it was impossible. Option one disintegrated in front of me. My legs gave way, and I collapsed on the floor.

I don't know how long I lay there. Maybe thirty minutes. Maybe an hour. I know that I stood up with a burning desire for lights. I walked around from switch to switch and snapped on every one of them, engulfed the house with lights. Darkness didn't matter anymore. Hiding didn't matter anymore.

I just needed to be dead before they found the body.

I climbed the stairs to my bedroom, my thoughts flowing in as many streams as the blood that had run down Al's face. One stream of thought was just focusing on every step of the carpeted red stairs that I was taking. The other thought was my escape plan. I also thought about who would find me. It would be poor Rita, the housekeeper, who single-handedly tidied up the few rooms of the mansion that I used.

I entered the bedroom suite, keeping my eyes away from the balcony that overlooked the garden. I pulled open the double doors to my mammoth closet and perused the hundreds of clothes hung neatly on wooden hangers. *Rita should find me dressed*, I thought, and I picked out blue jeans and a soft white T-shirt emblazoned with the words *Behind Closed Eyes*, my first blockbuster movie, which put me on the cover of every teenage magazine in the country. I slipped my favorite leather sandals on and turned out the closet light.

The gun was in the drawer beside my bed. I had purchased it once on a whim because it looked just like the one I had used in a movie. I picked it up and remembered how its weight used to feel so good in my hand. Never had fired it. Not once. I don't think I ever even loaded it. There was a box of brass bullets in the same drawer. I picked up a few and stuffed them inside my front jeans pocket.

I combed my hair again and tucked in my T-shirt. That's when I thought of you. I leaned against the counter and watched my face in the mirror redden as the familiar anger that focused around you flushed through me. *Al is dead because of you*, I thought, and I slammed the comb on the counter, snapping it with a satisfying crack. What a shame that you could not be here to see what you have done. That you didn't have to lay Al into his grave. That you could not sit across the table and, at the very least, watch while I blow out my brains.

The Selangor Club

July 13, 1993

Jason Young-Soo O'Leary

I slammed the letter onto the table. "This is crazy. Is he crazy?"

Charles had a difficult time speaking. He cleared his throat and took a deep breath. "Perhaps, he is. But I don't think so."

"Don't think so?" I picked up the letter again slowly. "Why he is blaming you, Uncle Charles? Why does he hate you so much?"

Charles swallowed and paused. "Just keep reading, Jason. Please go on."

I took a deep breath and continued to read aloud, "Everything felt different...."

Rod's Letter Continued

Everything felt different. The house was filled with a strange kind of silence that included spooky snaps and creaks from rooms I had rarely visited. I touched the pistol. It felt cold, but the hard, steel nozzle was smooth and round, like the Venetian angels my mother used to love.

I heard a loud fluttering of wings behind me and ducked as Gabe, my green cockatiel, flew out of nowhere. He landed like a hawk directly on the nose of my Magnum, wrapping his tiny feet around it and holding his wings outstretched until his balance was secured. Gabe glanced down at his new perch and bent over for a quick taste. With furrowed brows, he jerked his head to the side and rapidly moved his eyes up and down, examining me for any sign of treats. His eyes finally focused steadily on my left hand, resting on the table. Gabe hopped off his perch and strolled directly over to the fingers, looking only out of his right eye, cocked to the left and then to the right, methodically, like a general inspecting the troops. He found a suitable one, my forefinger, and bowed his head low.

"Gabe," I whispered as I began to scratch him gently on the head, just behind the tall, feathered crown that rose up from between his eyes. Gabe pulled his head back, exposed his yellow throat, and pressed it against the end of my finger. I moved it back and forth, ruffling the feathers and sending Gabe into such rapture that he had to close his eyes.

My rage.

I had hurt many. I struck a director. I smashed the nose of a reporter. I never touched the exotic dancer, Elena, the only one I almost loved. But I had shouted and screamed at her until she had fled, shoeless, from my home. I had spent the rest of that night with a bottle of Russian vodka and my regrets.

I withdrew my finger from Gabe and took out one brass bullet. I held it in the soft part of my palm and stared at it. Strange to see the instrument of your death. I slipped it in the cylinder—one single bullet—cocked the hammer and held it in my hand, the barrel facing away from me for the moment. I had no knowledge of suicide outside of what I had seen in the movies, read in the scripts. A familiar movie scene reeled in my mind—the man pointed the gun at himself…it went off slowly, plenty of time to see the brains exit through the back of the head. Lots of blood.

I shuddered.

Gabe, his feathers rumpled from the sudden interruption of his petting, had hopped to one of the armchairs and was turning his head back and forth, getting a good view of me with the left eye, then with the right. I reached over and pushed my finger under Gabe's fat stomach; he climbed on, one foot at a time, and with wings raised rode with me while I headed toward the den. "Don't worry, Gabe," I told him. "Rita has always wanted to have you."

I lifted up the door to the large square cage, big enough for a flock of Gabes, and pushed him inside. His feathered crown low in submission, Gabe hopped onto his feeder. He whistled the first three notes of the chorus of the *Andy Griffith Show* song.

I had spent hours and hours trying to teach Gabe the whole tune. It was a ritual we shared every night before bed. Gabe had listened with such interest that I just knew he was about to get it. But Gabe just liked the first line of the chorus, and that's where he stopped.

Tweeeet, tweet, tweet. Tweeeet, tweet, tweet.

He put his whole heart into it, and those three notes, I discovered soon, became Gabe's own personally assigned name for me. It was only fair, I guess, since I had given him a human name. But every morning, as soon as my feet touched the floor beside my bed, I heard my bird name—Tweeeet, tweet, tweet.

I tried to rub him one last time and offered my finger through the wires near where he was perched. But Gabe was miffed for being put back in his cage and turned his back to me. I drew back, found paper and a pen in the clutter beside the phone, sat down at the dining table, and wrote Rita careful instructions on Gabe's likes and dislikes. When I finished, I realized this was a suicide note of sorts and wondered if I should write anything else. Like "I'm sorry," or "Forgive me."

I could see no point. I was not depressed. I wasn't crazy. I was just going away. I signed my name at the bottom and pushed it aside.

Get it over with. Don't lose your nerve.

The movie versions I had seen favored a shot through the roof of the mouth. I wondered if that was accurate or just drama. At this point, I feared a failed suicide more than anything. Spending the rest of my life as a vegetable with just enough brain cells to know I had done this to myself would surely be worse than death.

I lifted the gun to my mouth, just like in the movies. My hand trembled so that I had to grab it with both hands. Still, my hands were shaking so violently I was afraid I might actually miss or just shoot out part of my face. I began to cry.

I hope you have a clear image of all of this. I want you to see it—how I cried and that made the gun shake even further, how I held the gun back down and took several breaths.

This time I would count to three and, without thinking about it, pick up the gun and shoot. I readied myself again and began to count.

Tweeeet, tweet, tweeet.

No doubt about it, I thought. There were millions of people who wanted to be me. But no one knew that my life had been so full of fears, disappointments, and crushing defeats. No one knew that at the core of all of these was one man.

It is ironic that facing death had helped to crystallize my hatred of you.

Gabe called for me again.

If I kill myself now, you will never know what you have done.

I thought about your face, on the other side of the table, watching as I put the gun to my mouth. Such perfect revenge was too appealing to dismiss so quickly. I began to reevaluate my situation. Although there was no escape from the brass bullet, it could be postponed. It would be a while before anyone found the body under the Caladiums.

I uncocked the hammer and examined the gun. I wanted to take the bullet out but knew I had to be certain of one thing before today's stay of execution could be granted.

I walked out to the Jaguar, opened the car door, and stuck my head inside. I took a deep breath and looked at the steering wheel—the keys were dangling out of the ignition. I leaned against the car in relief. I had not buried the keys with Al.

It was almost 5:00 a.m. There was a small shopping center about a mile away. I knew I could park the car there, jog back home, and be inside before the time the sun came up. That would give me plenty of time to clean up the blood.

This was a mission worthy of extending the life of the damned just a little longer—justice would be served. I jumped in the Jaguar, turned the engine, and began to plot to the end the series of steps I would need to take. It is difficult to admit this now, but I had always been afraid of you. No more.

When I returned, I sat down and wrote this letter. I will give it to you and let you read it.

The moment you finish, I will blow out my brains.

Live with that! Or better yet—die with it!

Sincerely yours,

Rod Chambers

The Selangor Club

Brent Jackson

July 13, 1993

Jason, out of breath now and gripping the letter with both hands, turned toward Charles and stared. Charles stared back soberly, looking between us, toward the street, and I began to be aware once again of city noises around us.

"When I put down the letter," he said, "Rod was sitting at the bar with a large pistol in his hand and slipped a bullet into its chamber."

Chapter Eleven

Charles Dickens

Five Days Earlier (July 8, 1993)

Los Angeles, California

"Did you know that you are my only living relative?" Rod said.

I felt my face, hands, and stomach all flush with blood at the same time. I think, however, I did a good job of masking my horror at the arrival of a weapon into our conversation. "And you are my only living relative."

He laughed. "Not for long," he said, and he held the gun to his head.

Instinctively, I stood up from my chair and moved forward, though slowly, my arms reaching out toward him.

"Stop," he commanded, and I did. He face became almost playful again as he sat there holding the gun to his temple. "So, you see, all of this will be yours after I'm dead."

I couldn't speak. I just stared at him.

"I know what you want to say. You want to tell me the money doesn't matter." Rod stuck out his lower lip in a mock whine as he waved the gun around in the air. "But I want you to have it—all of it—to remember me by."

He was too far away. There was no way I could reach him before he pulled the trigger.

"I've even written out a will. It names you, my father, as total beneficiary."

"Please let's talk about this."

"Can't you come up with a better line than that?" He feigned a look of disappointment. "Al would never have let me utter a line so cliché."

He was playing with me, but I could tell he was deadly serious and smarter than hell. "Okay," I said, and I tried to play the same game. "How about…there must be another way?"

He almost laughed but then stopped abruptly. "That was actually good. Very funny. You are a very funny guy."

The only thing I could do at this point was to attempt to engage him in conversation. "Thank you," I said. "You too."

He rested his elbow on the bar, the nozzle pressed against his temple. With his free hand, he gestured around the room. "Well, you can't actually inherit all this, as it is leased, but I have twenty or thirty mil in the bank you can buy a lot of rowboats with."

"I really don't want your money."

"Thank you for finally saying that." He lifted his shoulders. "It's in my script, you know." His smile vanished. He looked down at his glass and pulled his fingers through his hair. "In any case, you'll also need to explain to the police."

"Why don't you explain it to the police?"

"Because," he said in a loud, whispering voice, "I do not wish to go to jail. I do not wish to see my name become the biggest scandal in town splattered about on the media around the world. I simply do not wish the humiliation, nor do I wish to endure the loss of my freedom."

I don't know how I knew he had just lied to me. "I don't think so," I said.

"You don't think what?" His free hand slapped the table.

"I don't think that's why you want to kill yourself." The ground I was treading on was not only dangerous but also unexplored. There was a multitude of land mines here. As I look back, I realize he could have shot me straight away. But that didn't concern me then.

"Ah, of course," he said, "you are my father, after all. And we have spent all of, what…two hours together? I'm sure you know me well."

"Well, I know you're not very good at using sarcasm. It doesn't fit you."

He stuttered and looked disgusted. "Dear, dear father, if only you knew how little I care how anything I do appears to you."

"You're lying again."

His eyes turned red, and the veins pulsed in his neck. "You're as arrogant as I thought you would be!"

"If you don't care what I think, then how can I make you so angry?"

"Arrogance! Unbelievable!"

"If you don't care what I think, than why am I here?"

He exploded for the second time in front of me. "Because I want you to see it! Because I want you to take the memory with you to your grave!"

I was beginning to get a good idea of how Al got killed. "But why?"

"Because you deserve it." His hand clenched the gun so hard I was afraid it would go off.

"Why do I deserve it?"

"Because you never did a thing for me."

"I didn't know about you."

"I needed a father!"

"I didn't know."

"You were never there!" he screamed, and his whole body shook.

I fell back in the chair. Breathing heavily, he laid the gun down on the desk. "I'm sorry," I said.

"Just shut up."

"Is that how you killed Al? That explosive temper?"

He sat up and blew his nose on a napkin. "I told you. It's in the letter. I didn't mean to kill him. He made me so angry. I just wanted him to shut up."

He grimaced. "He fell over there." He pointed at a marble statue of a horse rising up on a platform with four very sharp-looking corners. "Al was the closest friend I ever had."

"Was he really a father figure?"

Rod glanced at me and then looked away. "Perhaps at first."

"So it isn't jail that you are afraid of, is it?"

"I give up. What is it?"

"It's the guilt," I said.

His glare and ensuing silence told me enough to go on.

"You don't think you can live with the knowledge that you killed your friend."

Rod lifted the gun slowly to his head again. He seemed tired. "It doesn't matter. None of it matters."

"It was an accident."

"I hit him. I knew what I was doing. I can't go to jail."

"Yes," I said quickly, "and that was wrong. But you didn't mean to kill him."

"But I did kill him." The gun began to shake in his hand. He put his finger on the trigger.

"Intent means something. Intent is important."

He ignored me. "I think I have to do it like this. I don't want to screw this up." He took the huge pistol with both hands and turned the gun toward his face.

"Please don't do this." I stood up.

He put the nozzle in his mouth.

I stepped forward slowly again, holding my arms out to him. "Please, wait."

He cocked the Magnum and began to put pressure on the trigger. He closed his eyes, struggling to hold back the tears.

"You're right!" I shouted.

He opened his eyes and looked at me.

"I would take the memory to my grave. I would have to live with the same pain and guilt that you say you can't endure."

He took the pistol out of his mouth and laid it on the table. He coughed. "I really am crazy. This is stupid. And I wouldn't do this to my worst enemy," he said. "You should leave."

"Leave?"

"Just get out of here, or I'll blow myself up all over you."

"Just listen for a minute, and then I'll go."

He let his exhaustion out in a long breath. "You've got one minute, and then I've got to go."

I figured he was right. I had one minute. Being with Rod like this was surreal, like a dream. I had lost my sense of reality and fought for a foothold.

But another part of me realized at the same moment that I had a valuable resource I could draw from. I had some negotiating skills that might get both Rod and me through the most important moment of our lives.

I skimmed through the most important techniques in my mind. The first was relationship. But there was no time to establish that. I skimmed through others—rationale, quick response, give them something else, increase their desire, sacrifice now for the payoff later. I had no time to develop any of these. Last resource when the deal is falling apart—get more time and promise them something extraordinary.

Rod was watching my face. "You've wasted thirty of my last seconds," he said bitterly.

"I can save you."

"I think I've made it clear that I don't wish to be saved."

"No. I mean really save you. I know you didn't mean to kill your friend. People kill people every day they didn't mean to kill. That's involuntary manslaughter. Sometimes it's just called an accident. He was your friend, you loved him, and you don't think you can live with yourself. You're repentant, and you're suffering."

"Is this the best you can—"

"Repentance is a good thing." I was talking fast now, emphasizing points with my hands. I had to get him to focus away from his current mission. "Many people kill, both accidentally and on purpose, and never feel any remorse whatsoever. The fact that you do gives me the only clue I need to the real depth of your character, your integrity, even your honesty."

"The depth of my character?" He repeated it slowly, like it was a foreign phrase he was trying to understand.

"You think you cannot live because you do not deserve life, that you deserve death. But I see you full of life. Plenty of life to give and to share."

I took a breath.

He was scrutinizing me. Searching my face for a lie.

The smallest exaggeration in negotiations with the Asians could be detected in a moment. Instinctively, I knew that Rod would know as well. I stood up and walked as close to him as I could before he flinched and clasped the gun. I stopped and waited until he relaxed. "True words," I said, never meaning anything more in my life.

Hope was clearly in his eyes. He closed them momentarily; when he opened them, I saw confusion, and I knew I had a chance.

He shook his head slowly. "It doesn't matter."

"It matters a lot."

"I have buried a body. I have attempted to cover up evidence."

"Attempted?"

"Yes, of course. Even if I had been smart enough to take the body somewhere else, traces of his blood are all over the house. I am the suspect, and it is only a matter of time before they serve a search warrant."

"How much time?"

"Who knows? They have to have reasonable suspicion. A month, maybe two tops."

"You seem to know a lot about murder investigations."

"*Murder on 122nd Street*."

"What?"

"That was the name of the movie where I was an eighteen-year-old detective who naturally outsmarted the whole Chicago Police Department in solving the case."

"I missed that one."

"In addition, the lease is up on my house in two months. The original owners are moving back in. Eventually they're going to find the body. I can't live with that hanging over my head."

His dilemma was apparent, but it was significant that he was now talking to me about the problem. I had to choose the next step carefully. I toyed with the idea of talking to him about confessing, throwing himself on the mercy of the court. But I knew that he would still spend some years in prison. The Rod that was sitting in front of me now could never do that.

"You've had me checked out for some time, haven't you?"

"Mom helped me. We started about six years ago. It started as curiosity—"

"Then you know what I'm good at."

He turned his head sideways.

"Come on," I prompted. "I make deals."

"Yes," he said, "I was told about some of your deals."

"I hope you were impressed."

"All right. I'll give you that—"

"When I was in Korea," I interrupted, "I was told that everything is impossible, and everything is possible."

"So?"

"It's true."

"What's true?" The gun was on the bar, the tips of his fingers draped casually over it.

I breathed slowly. "I can make the impossible happen," I said. "I can save you from a suicide, the death penalty, and further embarrassment. If you will agree to live, I can even save you from going to jail."

He began, in slow rhythm, to tap one finger against the barrel of the gun. "You'll pardon my extreme skepticism."

"You don't have to believe me. Believe my past record."

"How would you do that?"

He was looking me directly in the eye. I couldn't lie to him. "When a client comes to me, he brings me a problem—"

"You don't know how, do you?" The rhythm of the finger tapping increased.

"I find the solution. I always find the solution. I promise you. I can make this happen."

"You say you will keep me from going to jail?"

"From that, from humiliation, from everything."

"Except, as you pointed out, the pain and the knowledge that I have killed my best friend."

I stepped forward again until I was four feet from him. I glanced toward the gun to see if his fingers had tensed. They hadn't. "Then give ten million to an orphanage. Be a comfort to Al's family—someone they can depend on. Become an advocate for the environment. There are a hundred ways you can use your guilt constructively. Use your pain for living, not dying!"

Rod slid off the barstool, laid his gun there, and stepped back away. He looked back at me and walked back to the bar. He walked away once more, and when he returned, he opened up the refrigerator, took out ice, and poured himself a drink. His hand was shaking again. When he turned back to me, he was breathing heavily. "It's impossible."

"Give me a chance."

"You're stalling for time. You plan to talk me into going to jail."

"No! You have to trust me."

"You're lying. You're not God."

"I promise it. I swear it. Give me three months."

"No. You can't!"

"Then give me eight weeks!"

"I'll give you six!"

"Done!"

His mouth gaped open. "I can't believe I just agreed to this ridiculous…"

I smiled; it had been a classic closure.

He stared. "Tell me that's not a grin on your face."

"Sorry," I said, not able to stop.

In the next moment, Rod relaxed visibly, nodded his head, and tipped his glass to me. "You're very persuasive."

"Thank you."

"Or manipulative."

I sighed. "Manipulation is when you get what you want by lying about it." I stared directly at him, straight into his eyes. "I'm not lying."

He stared back for a long moment and then, in one gulp, drank the remainder of his drink. "We have six weeks to see."

"And now I would like to ask one thing of you."

He looked at me doubtfully.

"I would like to ask that you stop trying to deliberately hurt me."

I could tell that those words stung him. He looked at me like a puppy that'd just been told he couldn't go with you in the car. He returned to his glass and shrugged. "Fair enough."

"I also have a question I'd like you to answer."

Rod shook his glass lightly, but I could tell he was listening.

"Why didn't we have this whole scene in Singapore?"

Rod lowered his head and looked up at me, squinting. It was a you-sure-must-be-dumb squint. "Of course," I said. "Getting a gun into Singapore…"

Rod went back to his drink.

I looked at my watch. "Since that's settled, I guess I'd better go to my hotel." I could see at least three phones in this massive room. "Do you have the taxi number?"

Rod paused. "Well…I've got lots of rooms you can crash in," he said, surprising me for yet another time.

I looked at him.

"You're not going to argue with me, are you?" He said this more as a comment than a question.

"No," I said. "I'm exhausted."

He took me to an extremely large bedroom that made me wince.

"Hate to be picky," I asked. "I'm not really a red velvet wallpaper sort of guy."

He shrugged and led me to a room that was surprisingly out of character to the rest of the house—paneled walls, bookshelves covered with collections of *National Geographic*; only the extra-large chandelier gave away the notion that the room was still waiting transformation to become one with the rest of the house. "This is fine," I said.

Rod tossed me some shorts and a T-shirt that fit perfectly. I did a few things in the bathroom and went down to say good night. Rod had passed out on the den sofa. He was lying on his back, breathing heavily, with one arm folded over his chest. His right leg hung limply over the edge of the sofa.

I stared at him for a long while. He looked uncomfortable, and so I carefully lifted his right leg back up on the sofa, being aware, as I did so, that this was the first time I had touched my son. He was out cold and never even noticed the movement. I hesitated and then very gently pulled on the end of one of the shoestrings. After it came unraveled, I slowly moved the shoe back off the heel of his foot. I knew clearly what I was doing. Fulfilling some kind of fatherly need that I had but doing it in a moment when Rod could not protest. I had an odd feeling of guilt that I dismissed. I slipped off the right shoe and then the left one.

There was a hole in his left sock and a well-manicured toe stuck out of it.

I laid his feet on the sofa, went two rooms over, closed the door, and cried as quietly as I could for five or ten minutes. I then went searching for a blanket. When I returned, Rod's eyes were open. I continued as though I hadn't been discovered, though it now felt awkward. Covering him almost ceremoniously with the blanket, I had to explain myself. "You looked cold."

He watched the action without interruption. When I sat back, he said, "I was just thinking"—he folded his arms behind his head—"you gave up thirty million."

"Eighteen point five million after taxes." I shrugged. "Not that I've thought anything more about it, of course."

He watched me soberly for a moment. "Funny guy, very funny," he said finally.

"Thanks." I moved a vase and sat on the marble coffee table beside him.

"Okay. Eighteen point five million, then," he said. "I still don't know why."

I met his stare. "Maybe because I'm feeling some kind of fatherly thing?"

His expression didn't change. "That's not good enough," he said evenly.

"You're right," I said. "It's the truth. But it's not enough of the truth."

So I told him how the plane carrying my wife and daughter had crash-landed on the airport runway in Seattle, Washington, and that I had been the only one who had survived. I told him how I wasn't able to save my wife or my little girl.

He was silent for a bit when I was done. "What was your little girl's name?"

"Petra."

He thought about that for a minute. "And so you think that if you save me, it will ease the pain you had for not being able to save your daughter." He didn't speak cynically. Perhaps he liked the clarity.

"Maybe." It was a fair question, and I thought about it for a moment. "Nothing ever eases pain like that," I finally said. "You get up in the morning, you think of the pain. You go to work. You meet your friends and laugh. You sit down later alone and enjoy warm apple cider in front of a fire. You play music. You get ready for bed. You lie down. You think of the pain. You go to sleep. It never goes away. But it stops navigating your life and eventually just becomes part of it. That's the way it's been for me. That's the way it can be for you."

He stared at me so long I eventually became uncomfortable. "So is this something of what it would have been like to have a father?"

"What?"

"Circumspect advice, wise admonitions, being tucked into bed, and having one's shoes taken off."

I felt the heat come to my face and turned my head away. "I guess that's part of it."

A pause. "So what else did I miss?"

I thought for a moment. "I guess you missed a lot of tickling and wrestling. Long, good-night talks. Bedtime prayers and stories, and as you said, advice, more advice than you would ever know what to do with or want."

More silence. "You're not going to try to tickle me, are you?"

"I wouldn't dream of it."

He laughed. It was his first real laugh since we had met. Then it ceased as abruptly as it had began. "I want you to know," he said, "that I believe none of what you have told me tonight, except for one thing."

I waited.

"I believe that you believe."

"Thanks for that."

He shook his head. "It's just that I don't believe in belief."

"Rod…"

"So then how about a bedtime story?"

Once again, he had surprised me. I wondered if he was joking, but his eyes told me otherwise. And I got sad all over again because I knew that he really didn't believe, that he expected to end his life in one and half months. I understood. “All right,” I said, as though we were about to do some ordinary thing. I pushed the coffee table around and pulled a chair up beside him. “What kind of story?”

“One that you made up.”

And so I told him a story—a silly little kid’s story I had made up for Petra. How Squishy the raccoon and his slowpoke friend, Tim the tortoise, had fallen into fairy-tale land. In this one, Rapunzel had let down her long hair, but her prince was in jail waiting to be cooked by Hansel and Gretel’s wicked witch of the gingerbread house. Squishy and Tim had to save the prince and get him back to Rapunzel before her next scheduled beauty appointment where they were going to cut off her hair.

Petra had always interrupted my stories with hundreds of questions, mixed with advice and directions now and then. Rod listened raptly until close to the predictable end. As Squishy gnawed away at Rapunzel’s ropes, Rod’s eyes began to shut. By the time the prince caught Rapunzel in his arms, Rod was snoring lightly.

Chapter Twelve

The Selangor Club

July 13, 1993

Brent Jackson

Charles became silent as the remnants of his story transmuted into vivid thoughts. Jason and I sat, watching him tap his fingers absentmindedly. He was looking deep into the table. Charles looked up and slowly focused his eyes on Jason.

Jason cleared his throat. "So, uh…how are you going to do it?"

"It?" Charles asked.

"You know…save him."

I raised my finger to beckon at the waitress and pointed to our glasses. She scurried off. "And how are we part of this plan?" I asked.

"For reasons that will become clear later, I cannot tell you."

"Will it be dangerous?" Jason looked as though he would be disappointed if Charles said no.

"In a way, yes," Charles said quietly.

Jason thought about that for a moment and then nodded his head. "Cool," he said.

Charles was about to say something but looked at me instead. "Sorry about the incident earlier, Brent," he said. "Didn't mean to appear harsh."

I was silent for a moment. "It's okay. You're right."

"How am I right?"

"I've been kidding myself," I said. "The day of empowerment is important in any man's life. But for me it was only a Band-Aid. The truth is," I hesitated, "I'm not a very good father."

The bright outdoor lights of the Royal Selangor Club snapped on suddenly and filled the previously dim lawn with the kind of splendid emerald green that only materializes in artificial light. The sun was almost completely gone now, and the cars had filled the streets surrounding the club to a standstill with homeward-bound traffic. Bicyclists dressed in three-piece suits rang their bells and weaved in and out of cars that measured progress in inches.

The story I knew I had to tell next filled me with a sense of dread.

Five Days Earlier (July 8, 1993)

Oklahoma City

Two days before I left for this trip to Taiwan and Malaysia, my appointments stacked one on top of the other, the CEO of the company had decided he wanted me to squeeze in a half hour with him, and I had to entertain a visiting client from Bulgaria who had been peppering me with questions since he arrived.

"This my first time out of Bulgaria." Dr. Manolov, a pale middle-aged man with a bushy mustache, sat at my conference table with his arms folded.

"I believe you mentioned that." I was at my desk pulling a stack of faxes out of my inbox. Three faxes from China, two from Taiwan, four from Korea.

"I grew up in behind Iron Curtain. Now am seeing what really freedom is." Dr Manolov's grasp of English grammar lagged behind his unusual high comprehension of the language.

"Uh huh," I said. My client in Taiwan was asking me again for the contract that I was to have prepared. I had already e-mailed the message that the contract was at the attorney's office and it usually took about three weeks for approval. I e-mailed yet another note asking for his patience when it occurred to me that he might not have gotten my first one; e-mail in Taiwan was not as advanced as in America. I decided to redo it as a memo and fax him.

"I noticed while we were driving in that there were no people walking on street," Dr. Manolov said. "Where are the people?

"They are in their houses, in their offices," I said as I continued to write. I had been entertaining Dr. Manolov and his questions nonstop for three days.

"But they don't work at home, do they?"

I looked up, puzzled by the question. "Not usually," I said hesitantly.

"So how do they get from home to work?" He took a breath and waited for my answer.

"They take their cars," I said.

He looked amazed. "Their cars?"

I put my pen down. "Most families in Oklahoma have cars. Public transportation exists but is not as well established as in more populated cities. It's something we hope to improve someday."

This appeared to be an amazing revelation for him. He nodded to himself, took a small notepad out of his back pocket, and began to write something down.

I picked up my pen. "I'll just finish writing these faxes, and then we can talk more," I said.

Dr. Manolov was the owner of a manufacturing company in Bulgaria that produced black plastic garbage bags. As monopolies are not illegal there, he made the bags for every home, hotel, factory, and business from border to border. But until I came into his life, he had never considered exporting them. In fact, although black plastic garbage bags were not actually a monopoly in America either, it was well known that different branches of the same family living in New York owned all the major companies.

Not exactly a monopoly, but their prices were remarkably close and had been so for the last thirty years.

A large retail company had come to me with this problem: The prices for the bags had been going steadily up and their profit margin steadily down. What could I do?

I could do a lot. Thanks to a tip by a friend of mine in the US Consulate, I was on Dr. Manolov's doorstep in less than a week. His prices were one-tenth the prices of the New York firm. Even with the 100-percent mark up I recommended to Dr. Manolov and the 10-percent shipping costs to America, we could offer the prices to the retailer at one-third of their current cost. They could keep the price of the garbage bags stable to the consumer and, after my fee, still make twice the profit for the retailer.

There was one additional challenge, however. Dr. Manolov's existing factory didn't have the capacity to overflow into the American market. He would have to build two more factories and hire three times as many workers. Dr. Manolov couldn't possibly get that type of loan or find such a capital investor in Bulgaria.

I recalculated and asked the retailer to take less profit so that we could bring in a third party. The retailer agreed so long as the prices remained stable and they exceeded their original profit. That is where my Taiwanese friend, Mr. Chang, would come in. I would offer him an opportunity to go into partnership with Dr. Manolov. If Mr. Chang would put up the needed investment capital, Dr. Manolov would manage and conduct the affairs. Dr. Manolov had flown in to help me prepare the presentation for Mr. Chang.

"How many Bulgarians live in Oklahoma City?" Dr. Manolov asked.

"I'm not really sure," I said, knowing full well that that answer would never satisfy Dr. Manolov.

"Approximately?"

"I really have no idea."

"Guess."

"One hundred fifty-three."

He pondered that for a while. "That's more than I am now thinking." He pulled his notebook out of his pocket and wrote something down. "So cars are how many in this Oklahoma City?"

I had just started on another fax. "I'm not really sure."

"Approximately," he said.

"I just would have no idea," I said, scribbling rapidly on my paper, but I knew he would never accept that answer.

"How can we learn the answer?"

"Half a million," I responded, not looking up.

He paused and digested this information. The phone rang, and I answered it. It was the CEO wanting to know when I could meet him. "Give me fifteen minutes, Mike," I said, and I hung up.

"You tell me earlier there are a million people in Oklahoma City?"

"One million people in the greater Oklahoma City area, half a million in Oklahoma City proper, not counting its suburbs," I said mechanically.

"Did you think my question means the greater area or this Oklahoma City proper?"

I put down my pen and looked at him. "I'm not sure which one I thought you meant." My stare dared him to ask another question. He was not a gifted reader of American stares, however.

"So which question did you answer?" He was looking at me with the same unfazed intensity.

I sighed. "I think I was referring to Oklahoma City proper."

"This is incredible!" he exclaimed loudly. "Ever man, woman, and child has car?"

"Actually, I think I meant the greater Oklahoma City area," I said soothingly.

"Half then," he said and slapped himself on the face. "Half the people has car?"

"Perhaps my guess was a bit high," I said, smiling.

He stared at me intently while pondering that, and I wondered if his latest puzzle was the transportation system in an American city or if it was me, who gave him inexact answers.

My intercom rang, and I pushed the button on the phone. Lilly's deep bass voice, acquired from heavy smoking, boomed out over the speaker. "Brent, your ten-thirty appointment is here." She said the words slowly, almost cautiously, and I guessed there was some more that could not be said.

"I don't remember a ten-thirty appointment," I said.

"I put it on your calendar last month." Again, her voice was even and mysterious. Clearly the person I was to meet was standing next to her.

My electronic calendar rested a few inches from my fingers. I picked it up, slipped it out of its plastic case, pressed the on button and then today's date. It steadily flashed my ten-thirty appointment.

There was no name beside it.

"Yes, Lilly, it's here," I spoke at the phone. "But I still have faxes to answer, and I have a very important guest," I said the last part loudly, "and the CEO wants to meet me for thirty minutes this morning."

She knew I was asking her if this could be postponed. I hadn't made the appointment; she had. I was almost accusatory. "I think you had better take this one," she said in an un-Lilly-like soft voice.

"Give me one minute." I sighed. Lilly always knew best. I turned to Dr. Manolov. "Sorry to trouble you—"

He interrupted me. "Please, please, you do business. I wait in lounge."

"You might ask Lilly to give your some statistics on single mothers in America," I said. "It's a favorite topic of hers." He nodded enthusiastically and left my office, shutting the door behind him.

I looked at the next fax. It was a letter from a gentleman who said I had met him in China. He was building a huge golf club near Beijing and had an idea for a joint collaboration. I scanned the letter to find the signature. Mr. Wang... I could not remember the name or the situation where I had met him. I pulled open my desk drawer where my business cards were kept. There were several stacks with rubber bands around them. I pulled out the stack marked China.

I heard a firm tapping at the door, which I recognized as Lilly's. "Come in," I said, now leafing through the business cards.

"Please go in, sir, and have a seat." Lilly's voice was again so soft that I looked up.

The eleven-year-old boy standing in the doorway was dressed in khaki slacks and a white shirt with a blue necktie tied in a twisted granny knot. His hands were folded in front of him, and his shoulders slumped. He did not make eye contact. In his hand, he held a folded piece of white paper. He waited for me to say something.

"Daniel," I said to my son. "What are you doing here?"

He lifted his head and looked at me. "I have an appointment with you." He looked back down again.

"Is everything all right?" I said, somewhat alarmed.

He remained fixed on the floor. "If you are referring to an accident or something like that, everything is fine with Mother, and everything is fine with school."

For the latter, I assumed as much. Daniel was a straight-A student who had skipped the second grade.

His head tilted back again. "May I sit down?"

"Uh, sure." I gestured to the seat in front of my desk. He moved forward and fell into it. He held the white paper tightly. His hands were shaking.

He did not speak, and while I waited for him to say something, I remembered where I had met Mr. Wang. I had been a dinner guest of China's Ministry of Commerce. We were at the famous

Peking Duck restaurant located in Beijing. Mr. Wang had been a dinner guest also. I began to flip casually through the cards again. "Is there something I can do for you?"

"What if," Daniel said, "what if I had just come to see you?"

"That's nice, Daniel." I had found a Wang, but I was sure it wasn't the right one. I kept looking. "But you know how busy I am at the office. Can this wait until I see you at home?"

"And when would that be?" Daniel spoke in such a trembling voice that I looked up. "You've been home one evening in the last two weeks, and then you said you were very, very tired." He stretched out the words *very, very*.

His head bent back down, and he fumbled with the paper.

"Daniel," I said, "you're obviously upset about something." I had just remembered that Mr. Wang was one of the few multimillion-dollar Taiwanese permitted to do business in China. "Give me five minutes to find something before I forget it, and then we'll talk, okay?"

"Is this how you treat all your clients? You work during their appointments? This is my time!" He said it so loudly that it sparked my own anger circuitry. Heat rose to my temples.

I opened the drawer as calmly as possible and dropped the business cards into it. I scraped pieces of paper and the rubber bands into the drawer, closed it, and folded my arms over my now clean desk. I took a deep breath. "I give my clients my time, but I do expect respect from my son."

He glared at me. "And why would that be?"

This tone, these words—this was not the Daniel I knew. Something was up. I raised my voice only slightly. "Because I am your father."

He considered this for a moment, and I saw him relax. "That's good." He took the white paper, now very wrinkled, and spread it out on the table in front of him. "Because that is what I am here for."

"What is what you are here for?"

"To discuss your position as my father."

I wasn't sure what he meant, but I was intrigued by his advanced sentence formation. As an international person, I have learned to be very aware of a person's language ability. I am cautious not to correlate their intellectual capacity to their level of English advancement. However, even though Daniel was speaking his native language, I found that his vocabulary level was clearly higher than what I would expect from an eleven-year-old. I felt my anger subside. Daniel might make a good businessman someday.

"I know you are upset because I have not been around lately," I said as calmly as possible. "You're clearly a bright boy, and you have felt that I have neglected you. I'm sorry. I'll try to be better."

Daniel's eyebrows folded into the corners of his eyes. "I've heard you talk like this before. This is how you were when Mr. Reardon was complaining about how people treated him here. Remember, he had dinner at our house."

"I remember." Mr. Reardon was one of our top managers.

"That's how you talked to him. Now you're talking to me like that. You're paternizing me."

His blunt expression should have sent me into a new round of anger. But I continued to be caught up in the sophisticated patterns of his sentences. Even his mispronounced attempt at "patronize" had been deployed successfully. I wondered if his school was challenging enough to him. Perhaps I needed to place him in a more advanced institution.

He sighed heavily. "You are not listening to me, are you?"

My eyes shot to his. "I was thinking about you, Daniel." But he was right. I needed to give him the same attention I would give to anyone who had contracted for thirty minutes of my time. "You have my full attention."

"Good," he said, and I noticed he had stopped shaking. He glanced down at his paper.

"When I do see you at home, you usually have a client. I am told to sit quietly, but I have tried to pay attention. I know that there is first a need and then what you call 'terms,' and then you sign something."

"A contract," I interrupted.

"Or an agreement," he said.

"Or an agreement."

"I made this appointment to explain my problem and my need."

"Please go ahead."

He leaned back. "I am being cheated out of my childhood."

"Cheated out of your childhood?" I repeated slowly.

"See, I had to bring a copy of my birth certificate to school recently. It was the first time I had seen it…"

"Yes."

"There's a line that says, 'father.' Do you know whose name is listed?"

"I would hope mine."

"That's right. Your name is there. But, in fact, you aren't."

"What are you—"

"Please let me finish," he said, waiting.

I leaned back in my chair. He looked at me calmly and seriously; there was no anger in his voice. "All right," I said, "continue."

"I see the other kids at school. Half of them have divorced parents. But even they have fathers who will see them at least twice a month. I don't even have that."

I sat up straight. "Daniel, you know how busy my job is. You know I provide for you and your mother. Is there anything you want that I don't buy for you? I'm doing everything I can. This job takes a lot of my time."

Daniel listened but glanced at his paper again. "Yes, I have heard that before. You have said it to Mother. It may be all right for her…but it is not all right for me!"

I handle these situations well. I have had many employees snap and flare up in front of my eyes. Through experience, I have learned the proper thing to do. I sit back calmly and let them vent. Once the anger has passed, I give my point of view. I get big points from my staff on how effectively I handle people. Daniel was now red-faced and fighting to keep back the tears. I sat back, crossed my legs, and put on my quietest, most soothing voice. "Please go on."

He wiped his eyes and took at deep breath. "I don't know what you want from me, probably nothing, but I have prepared a list of what I want from you."

"I would like to hear it."

He looked at me, crossed his legs, and sat back in his seat. He seemed frail, gaunt—almost pitiful. He looked at his paper and began to read.

"This is an agreement between Brent Jackson and Daniel Jackson. That both parties do establish the conditions and expectations of both parties as they pursue the relationship of father and son." He stopped and then looked up shyly at me. "I copied most of the wording from one of your agreements on the computer at home." He paused. "Hope you don't mind."

"Very clever," I said. "Please go on."

He continued reading. "Section one. Terms and conditions. That Daniel Jackson, here forth referred as 'son,' does expect from Brent Jackson, here forth referred as 'father,' the following minimum requirements.

"One: That father will spend one Saturday afternoon every other week with son and that there will not be any clients with them.

"Two: That father will attend son's Cub Scout meetings no less than six times per year and will help son achieve at least one Cub Scout merit badge per year.

"Three: That father will take the son on one weekend camping trip per year. That it will be Friday night and Saturday night."

Daniel stopped. "I forgot to write it here, but Mother could go on this one with us."

"I didn't think your mother liked camping."

"I don't think she does, but we could invite her."

I looked at the clock. So much to do before noon. I felt sure I knew what the CEO wanted to see me about, and I liked it. I felt queasiness in my stomach. "Please continue," I urged him.

"Four," he read, "Father will have at least one parent/teacher meeting a year."

He put the paper down.

"Anything else?"

"That's all." He slumped in his chair.

"And out of curiosity, what do I get?"

His head bent down, and he wiped his eyes. He sniffled a couple of times and then looked up. "I don't think I…"

It was a stupid thing for me to say. "I'm sorry. I didn't mean that."

I watched him carefully, trying to decide what to say to him. He was right, but there was nothing I could do about it. We are very distant, and it is in this distance that I am the most comfortable, the most assured of my capabilities, the most focused. I share with my son more than he knows. All that I want for him is more than I can give, and what little I give will be more than I had. He wants what is not there. *This is life*, I thought, *and his is better than most. It has to be enough for him.*

"Son," I began, "I will try to do better. But my traveling prohibits me from making specific appointments and plans at home."

"You make specific plans with your clients."

"They pay the bills, Daniel. You're old enough to understand that one part."

The phone rang. I picked it up.

Daniel continued talking. "Then you don't accept this agreement?"

I raised my hand; it was the CEO.

"I'll be there in two minutes," I said, and I hung up. I began stacking my papers and pulled out my urgent-action items. "Would you like to hear what he wants to talk to me about?"

Daniel was looking at the paper in his hand, but he nodded.

"Well, our work in Southeast Asia has gotten so big that our company is creating a new division just to handle the business there."

"Uh huh." Daniel knew his geography. I didn't have to explain "Southeast Asia."

I put little yellow notes on the papers that I needed to handle before I went home. "I think the CEO is going to ask me to take the presidency of the new division."

Daniel looked down at his paper.

"The president, Daniel." His lack of interest annoyed me. "That's more responsibility—a raise in salary."

Daniel stood up and reached across my desk, taking one of my sticky yellow notes. He stuck it to the top portion of his paper and slowly slid it on my desk until it covered my other papers. He stood in front of me, his hands limp to his side.

I ignored the gesture and stood up. "I've really got to go. I'll think about what we can do, and we'll talk about it later." I slipped on my suit jacket and straightened my tie.

Daniel's eyes followed me around the room. "Let's talk about the agreement, or let's talk about the divorce." There was new bitterness in his voice.

"What are you talking about now?"

"If you won't accept being my father, then I can't be your son."

This very dramatic game had gone far enough. "Stop it, Daniel. Stop being so childish."

"It's proper for me to be childish." Daniel's voice was calm, reflective. "I am a child who wants his childhood. If you can't be my father, then I will have to find someone who can."

"And how do you plan to do that?" I grabbed my yellow pad and my calendar.

"Since all you offer is money and things," he said coldly, "perhaps you can pay someone." He walked to the door and then stopped. "You have many employees. Pay one of them to be my father." He closed the door quietly as he left.

THE SELANGOR CLUB

JULY 13, 1993

The sun had set in busy Kuala Lumpur. A lone janitor, dressed completely in white, pushed a broom slowly across the polished white boards of the veranda. He whistled a sleepy, end-of-the-day tune.

Jason and Charles waited as though there was more to tell. There wasn't.

"So when did you talk next?" Jason asked.

I shrugged my shoulders. "Remember Dr. Manolov? He took up my time for the next two days. I told him I'd talk when I came back from this trip."

Our table filled with silence. They both stared at me. Charles should have understood, I thought. He's as busy as I am.

"Don't look at me like that," I said. "I didn't have time. I'm doing the best I can. I'll talk to him when I get back."

Charles drummed his fingers on the table.

"Daniel is a very precocious boy," I explained. "He's gifted, and the gifted have special problems. But he's strong. He'll work them out."

Jason turned toward me and this time had a soft look in his eyes. "Uncle Brent," he said, "I think your story has helped me see something a little more clearly."

I looked at him and waited.

Jason turned his head away from the table and stared thoughtfully. "Perhaps my father is still teaching me. And now, he has something to teach you." Jason smiled and looked ahead, into the streets of Kuala Lumpur. After a moment, he picked up his tea, sipped it, and we watched part of the liquid dribble down his chin. Jason grabbed a napkin and dabbed frantically. "There must be a hole in my chin," he said. "I always do that."

Charles looked at me and nodded. Jason's expression, his gestures, his smile—it was Richard.

Chapter Thirteen

Jason Young-Soo O'Leary

Six Months Earlier (Jan 5, 1993)

Boston, Massachusetts

I woke up at 3:00 a.m., last July, sat up in bed, and was filled with the cold certainty that my father had just died.

I sat up, put my feet on the carpeted floor, and listened. There was a middle-of-the-night stillness—no traffic, no birds—the air conditioner clicked on, and the familiar sound of the fan filled the room. The blue silk pajamas that my father had bought me in Hong Kong were very light, and I crossed my hands over my shoulders and shivered.

I walked across the room, opened my closet, and took out a light jacket. I slipped it on as I stepped into the hall that leads to my father's room. I took two steps forward again and then stopped. There was light coming through the skylight above me, and I looked up to see a single but very bright star in the center. The house my father had chosen for us was turn of the century; the floors in the hallway were wooden and cold to my bare feet. I took another three steps and reached the door.

For a long time I could not go in. Though I had felt his death, I would not be sure until I entered the room. As long as I stood there, on this side of the door, he could be alive to me. Some say that the truth will set you free. But I feared that on the other side of the door I would find truth there that would bind me forever.

The air conditioner shut off, and I was, once again, engulfed in the eerie stillness of the house. I took another step and stood in the doorway. His bed was in the center of the room, where it had been turned two weeks before so that he could see the sunrise each morning. I stepped farther into the room and stopped again a few feet from his bed. Even though there was enough moonlight to make out objects in the room, I could not see his face clearly.

He had been in this house for three weeks, mainly I think, because I refused to leave him while he was in the hospital. He worried about me and said we would both be better at home. He knew I wanted to be with him when he died, and he felt the same way. I cursed myself. I had failed him.

I stepped forward again slowly and began to hear a muffled noise, like the low warning growl of a cat. I stepped quickly to the bed. That noise came deep from within my father's throat. The doctors had told it might happen—his death rattle.

I touched his chest. "Dad!" I said and sat down beside him. I grabbed his hand and held it. "Dad!"

There was no movement, but after a long moment, I heard him take another long, gasping breath. I jumped up and found the small night lamp that stood on his antique Korean chest. I snapped it on and returned to his bed and leaned over him.

His eyes were open, and he was looking at me.

"Dad." My face moved close to his. "Can I get you anything?"

His eyes never left mine, but it was clear he couldn't talk, so strained was his chest with the burden of breathing.

His eyes showed fear, and this disturbed me even more than his impending death. I had never seen my father afraid before. We had discussed his death, with the casualness of a planned trip abroad. I knew that he was not afraid to die, that he had had a deep faith in God, that his only sorrow to leave was his concern for me. What was the source of this fear?

I clutched his hand with both of my own. I felt helpless and stupid. "Is there anything…anything you want, Dad?" His mouth was open and laboriously involved in inhaling. But he looked at me, managed an almost imperceptible nod, and then closed his eyes.

"Then there is something?" I asked. "Should I call the doctor?"

Continued heavy breathing, but he shook his head. He opened his eyes and this time looked down at the foot of his bed, out the window.

I looked at the window and looked back at him. He was again looking at me.

"You want something out there?"

He nodded.

"I don't know, Dad." The frustration must have shown in my voice because his eyes softened.

I looked again out the window, at the quarter moon, at the dark silhouettes of the trees.

Then I remembered something he had said to me long ago. I took a deep breath and waited until I could speak without emotion. "You want to live until morning?"

He nodded.

"Okay," I squeezed his hand. "I promise."

He nodded, gave me a smile of relief, and then exhaled slowly.

"Are you in any pain?"

He was thinking about how to answer me. He took as deep a breath as he could, and I could see that he was going to try to say something. I leaned over him and placed my ear just above his lips.

"*Chokumman*," he whispered, the Korean phrase for "only a little."

Since no one in our immediate group in Boston spoke Korean, those phrases had become our own special language. Dad often spoke Korean to me, although lately we mostly used it when we were teasing each another.

"Can I give you some of your pain medication?" I asked, wondering how it would be possible to get him to drink something. He thought for a moment and mouthed the word *no*. It was like him to want to stay as alert as possible.

I considered getting a cold rag for his forehead, but I touched his face and found it to be cool. I sat down at his side again, facing him.

"Would you like me to talk for a while?" I asked. Dad's eyes, calm again and full of interest, turned toward me. The fear in them was gone. "There are some things left I still haven't told you." He smiled.

"Do you remember when you asked to be my father?" Dad's gaze remained fixed on my eyes. He remembered. It was the most important moment in our lives. "I'll bet I never told you how surprised I was," I said, "after you saved me from the ice storm.... I thought you had brought me to your room to be your servant. I thought I was there to take care of you, in exchange for my meals, just the same way I had worked for my master.

"I did not mind. I was again in a warm place. You gave me so much food that I was worried you would spend all your money, and then we would have nothing.

"I knew immediately that you were a kind man, but I honestly thought that sometimes you drank your tea with chopsticks. You know what I mean," I said, whirling my finger around my ear.

Dad blinked twice and seemed to almost smile; then he winced slightly as he fought to push the air out of his chest.

"Like the time you decided I should go to school while we were still in Korea. You went down and visited the schoolmaster, paid the fees, and bought me a school uniform. And despite my many protests, you sent me off to school.

"Of course because I had been a beggar, the students would never accept me as one of them. I came home with many bruises. You gave up."

He looked at me sadly, with concern.

"Don't be sorry," I said quickly. "It was an experience. I just didn't understand why you didn't understand. I had accepted my place in society, and I didn't understand why you couldn't.

"Then on November twenty-seventh, at six o'clock in the evening, you told me to sit down in front of you. I remember your hands were shaking, and there was sweat on your forehead. You began to talk about your classes at school, about a student who was learning English very quickly, and then in the next sentence you asked me how I would like to be your son.

"I really thought for sure that you had gone fishing in the trees, Dad. What you asked was impossible. I had already been born, and I already had had a father who was probably dead somewhere. To me, it was as impossible as saying to a pine tree, 'Now you're an oak!'

"Then you introduced a new word to me. Do you remember that word?"

He nodded several times.

"I had never heard the word *adopt*, even in the Korean language. You explained that we could go to a judge, and he could legally make us father and son and that you would swear to the judge to take care of me and love me like your own son.

"But, Dad." I shifted position and placed my feet on the bed beside him, crooked my elbow, and rested my face in my left hand. "The Korean word you used for *love* was 'romantic' love. Like how a woman tells a man she 'loves' him. It sounded so funny, and that's why I laughed.

"I remember how mad you looked after I laughed. I tried to explain, but you picked up a book and read the same page for about an hour.

"But you didn't give up. Every evening you talked to me about it, and little by little I began to understand some of it. Of course I still didn't understand the real meaning of adoption, but I understood that it was the most permanent relationship that I had ever had. I understood that you would take care of me until

I was grown and that I would go live with you in the 'beautiful country' across the ocean."

Dad winced suddenly, as if in pain, and I realized that he hadn't taken a breath in several seconds. "Breathe, Dad," I pleaded, and I waited, but I saw him look into the darkness of the window. His eyes saddened; hope began to fade from them.

I leaned over his face and slowed my breath down to match his. I took a slow, deep breath and then exhaled slightly. He relaxed, and the second time, his breath matched mine, and we continued this way until he was breathing more comfortably. He looked at me and nodded; he wanted me to go on.

A wave of distress engulfed me. So that he would not see my face clearly, I sat beside him with my back to his headboard. *The sorrow can come later*, I thought as I fought back tears. He had always been strong for me. It was my turn. I measured the tone of my voice carefully and spoke to him with the same tone as if we were sitting beside a lake with two poles in the water. I knew he would want it that way.

"Many things happened. We went to the judge. We received adoption. I remember how the US Consulate had fought the adoption. They had said I was too old. They also didn't like a single father adopting. But you solved each obstacle step by step. I went through the process, and I began to call you 'Dad,' but I didn't let you really adopt me for a long time."

Dad looked out the window, at the moon. But I knew he was listening. I had never told him this.

"Even after I came to America, it took me a long time to understand. Koreans say that soybeans come from soybeans. But I was a soybean, and you were a carrot. How could we be father and son? I accepted it as best as possible but decided that everyone else's understanding of a father had to be different than my own."

I looked down at him and grinned. "You want to hear it?" I knew he would be grateful for the teasing.

"There were a few things," I began. "You remember that day I had a cold and you had an important business meeting that you said was critical to our future?

"You took me with you and sat me in the corner all bundled up. It was a funny meeting. As usual, you were the only white guy at a table full of Chinese. You all had on suits, and the room was warm. Finally you asked the man I assumed was the 'big boss' if you could take off your jacket. He nodded, and of course they all had to take off their jackets too. But the big boss whispered to another man, and he got up and turned the temperature down.

"About ten minutes later the room was freezing. You were looking uncomfortable, and also, I think, you were worried about me. So without a word, you slowly slipped your jacket back on.

"The big boss paused, nodded at everyone, and they dutifully slipped their jackets on. The big boss whispered to the same guy, who then turned the temperature back up.

"Your jackets went on and off several times during that meeting. It was very funny. But while you were there discussing some kind of merger with a Malaysian corporation, I began to think about you.

"I had been sick. You put a cloth on my head and took my temperature. You gave me aspirin and fretted over me. During the meeting, you kept a lifeguard's eye on me. What was this in you that I had never had from another person? I asked myself.

"It was attention. You gave me lots of attention. As no one else ever gave me this, I decided that this must be something a father does—he gives lots of attention."

Dad was watching me carefully, although his breathing had become laborious again. I watched the slow rising and falling of his chest carefully while I spoke.

"You really did many things that I never understood. There was another very unusual thing that you did over and over. I could never quite predict when you would do this thing, and at first it frightened me.

"Almost every day, with no warning whatsoever, you would grab me and shake me about. I didn't know why you did this. Sometimes you grabbed me by my shoulders and picked me up, my legs dangling loosely in the air. Sometimes you grabbed me and squeezed me. I could not move, found breathing uncomfortable, and felt strange to be so close to you. I tried to be obedient and waited until you stopped.

"The only time I began to predict it was in the evening, when you would come to my room and throw your shoulders on mine with your arms intertwined about my neck. It was a strange ritual, and although I now understand hugs, it was something I had never seen in my country. Of course now in Korea, I think, it is different.

"But I began to see purpose in this custom. It was you drawing me closer. It was a reminder, totally out of the context of whatever we were doing, that I was a part of you. Later, I learned the English word *affection*, and it became clear. Fathers are affectionate. They draw their sons in to them."

Dad began to choke and gasp. I leaned over his head and bit my lip. I looked toward the foot of the bed at the window. The sky had turned a navy blue. Just a little longer. "Come on, Dad," I said. "Let me finish my story."

He took a long, slow breath, blinked twice, and smiled.

"It was my best friend, Ronnie, in the sixth grade, who helped me to understand the third characteristic of a father. He astounded me one day by saying that I was so much like you that we were like 'peas in a pod.'

"I asked what on earth he meant. I said, 'I am Korean. He is a tall, redheaded, white, hairy person.' But he persisted. He said that I walked like you, with one foot turned slightly outward. He said I ate like you, always wiping my silverware before every meal. He said I even laughed like you, with loud guffaws that are, by the way, very unbecoming of Korean people.

"I thought about this a lot and realized that you were a kind of teacher for me—but not just what you said to me. You were a successful businessman. You were kind to everyone. Everyone liked you, and I wanted to be like you in every way.

"Once we were at a department store buying both of us some shirts. The lady at the cashier gave you too much money back. I saw it immediately, and I thought, *Lucky Daddy.* But you surprised me again. You pointed out her mistake and gave the money back.

"I'll bet you don't know how many times that has happened to me since. But I've always given the money back. I give the money back because I saw you give the money back.

"I don't think you did this on purpose. But I later learned to call this important part of a father as 'training.' You were training me, by demonstration, how to be a good man."

I moved around to his side. The sky was becoming bluer. Dad began closing his eyes for longer moments. But when they opened, he was always looking straight at me, showing me that he was listening.

"Do you remember when I cut my foot and it got infected? You don't like penicillin, so you changed my bandages several times a day, and the doctor said that to heal, I had to soak it in hot, hot water three times a day.

"You filled the bathroom sink with hot water, just like the doctor said. I started to put my foot in, but it was so painful—hotter than the bathhouse in Korea. And I pulled my foot out and began to cry. You had just come home from work and were still in a dark suit. You sat on the toilet, slipped off your shoes and socks, and pulled the pant leg off your right foot up over your calf. The next thing I knew, you had pushed your foot into the hot water and then said, 'Now you try.'

"I slipped my foot in the water beside you and was amazed to discover that it didn't hurt so much. I could not understand why you were doing this or why, every day for the next ten days, you plunged your bare foot into the hot water beside mine, even after I protested that I could handle it."

My father was breathing shallowly but watching.

"Dad, up until that moment, I had accepted that you wanted me to be your son. I had accepted that I called you 'Dad,' and my last name was the same as yours. I accepted your love, your attention, and the fact that we both walked with our right foot turned outward. But I had never accepted the fact that I had the right to be your son. I had always considered myself a glorified visitor—an orphan boy, living for a while on the good luck side of the rice-paper door.

"I cannot explain it. But when you did this, when you accepted this pain for the sole purpose of relieving mine, it gave me value. Somehow it made me worthy. I felt it for the first time. The next time I called you 'Dad,' I knew what it meant."

The hoarse sound of a heavy truck could be heard stopping in front of our house. The gate latch clicked, and the sound of a man in heavy boots was heard walking on our sidewalk, onto our lawn, and to the storage shed behind the kitchen, where our large plastic trash receptors were kept. Soon the garbage truck's engine thundered to life and moved hastily to the next house. The air was filled with the sounds of hundreds of talkative birds, woken from their sleep. The orange and red colors that began to creep through the window were so burnt and deep that the room took the colors, for a few moments, of an ancient Korean painting.

We sat quietly for a few minutes while Dad watched the sunrise.

"Thanks, Dad, for letting me tell you what you mean to me."

His breathing grew shallower.

"I have told all the ways you were important to me. I will miss you, Dad. But we have no regrets, nothing left unsaid between us."

He stared at me, smiled, and nodded. Then he closed his eyes.

I leaned over him and put my arms around him. "I'm here, Dad. Everything's okay."

Thirty seconds and then another breath.

"I'm here, Dad."

A minute and then another breath.

"Thanks for my life, Dad." In spite of my pain, it felt so good to say that.

His last breath was smooth and silent. I fluffed up the pillow beside him and put my head on it. I knew I was no longer there for him. I was there for me. I wanted to remember it all. I wanted to stretch out this last moment.

I lay there until the sun was in the midmorning sky.

THE SELANGOR CLUB

JULY 13, 1993

BRENT JACKSON

I was not able to speak. Charles was frowning. "I'm confused." He looked at me and then at Jason. "You have told us a beautiful story about the perfect father, and you ended it by thanking him for your life."

Jason, still in his thoughts, did not look up. I responded for him. "What is the confusion, Uncle Charles?"

"What life are you thanking him for?" Charles's tone had become strangely hostile.

Jason's eyes looked up from the table but still not at Charles. Although I did not know why, I found myself rising to his defense. "I suppose for saving him from the life of a beggar in the streets." I looked to Jason for confirmation.

Charles raised his voice and aimed it directly at Jason. "Is that right, Jason? From the streets of Korea? Did he save you from the streets of Korea so that you can become a drunkard? Did his training include taking innocent women and stripping them of their dignity?"

Jason slammed his open palm on the table and glared at Charles. "You don't understand!"

Charles slammed his hand on the table beside Jason's. "Shame on you! Shame on you!" he shouted. "Your father's sacrifices, his love for you, have been turned into dirty rags."

"How dare you judge me!" Jason snapped.

"You are without excuse for your behavior." Charles turned and pointed his finger at me. "At least Brent can account for his disgraceful treatment of his son by saying that he never had a father, but you have had everything in a father."

Suddenly I was the target of Charles's attacks. "What disgraceful treatment? I provide for my son."

"Please." Charles rolled his eyes dramatically.

"Charles," I shouted, "you're out of line!"

Charles shut up, and we all stared for ten minutes at Somerset Maugham's table. The silence became unendurable, and I was about to speak when Jason broke the silence

"So, Uncle Charles," he said, "why did you cry?"

Charles didn't move.

"At Rod's home. You said you cried. Why?"

Charles shrugged his shoulders. "I don't know. I suppose I was mourning his lost childhood. The baby whose diaper I had never changed, the little boy I never held and who had never peed in my face..."

"What?" Jason said.

"You know, little baby boys, while you're changing their diapers, they sometimes pee in your face…"

Jason and I looked at each other and then simultaneously burst into loud laughter.

Charles's mouth fell open, and his face reddened. "I don't get the joke."

Jason wiped the tears from his eyes. "That's one I hadn't thought of. Definition number five...fathers get their faces peed on."

Charles protested our glee. "Well…"

"Yet that memory you never had is one I'll never be able to forget," I said, and Jason slapped me on the shoulder and laughed louder. A waiter turned around and looked at us.

"You've completely turned this around," Charles said and then, after watching us for a while, shook his head. "You guys are never going to let this go, are you? I opened up just a little with you and—"

We howled.

"I give up," he said. And then he too began to laugh.

Once again, we had made it to 4:00 a.m. Shu Ling had not returned, but another lone waiter stood in the doorway and watched us. As our laughter slowly died down, I became aware of a silence that seldom visited tropical climates.

Charles tapped his fingers slowly. Jason stared out onto the empty lawn. We knew it was time to depart but hated it. I sensed that all of us, including Jason, had found comfort at Somerset Maugham's table.

"Charles?" I said, interrupting our thoughts.

"Yes," Charles responded, so quietly I could barely hear him.

"Whatever happens with you and your son, it seems that his finding you was a good thing."

"Yes," he said in the same tone.

"Jason, excuse me, but if you still had a family, would it still be a good thing?"

Jason turned his chair around to listen, and Charles sat up. "It would be more complicated, but I would want to know."

"And I also want to know," I said, surprising myself.

They both looked at me and waited.

"I want to know who my father is. I want to meet him." I couldn't believe I was saying this.

Jason scratched the back of his neck. "Excuse me, but…uh… aren't you forty?"

"I'm thirty-eight, thank you."

Jason looked at my hair. "So how old is your dad?"

"Mom said my dad was twenty when she told him she was pregnant, and then he disappeared. She has refused to talk about him."

"And you think he'll want to see you now?" Jason asked.

I was surprised to feel a little sting in Jason's words—not surprised that he said it but surprised to feel it. I suppose it must have shown because Jason almost immediately said, "Sorry, Uncle Brent. Just thinking out loud."

"Rod had known about you for a long time," I said to Charles. "Why didn't he come forward sooner?"

Charles shrugged. "He said he was afraid."

"I can understand that. But I think we can be most afraid of what we don't know," I said. "Can a man without a father be a father?"

Jason interrupted. "You think that that is the dark emptiness in you? That that black hole that occasionally releases flying alligators and things that bite you on the back was put there by your father?"

"You can't put holes anywhere," I corrected. "Holes exist because something has been taken away. And if it is empty, nothing comes out of it. But a big, vacant hole is also an invitation for all kinds of things to try to live in."

"Your demons?" Jason asked.

"Perhaps."

Charles had been listening quietly but now spoke up. "And how will this affect your son?"

I thought for a moment. "I'm not sure. But is it possible that I can't give my son what he needs until this hole has been filled with at least something from my father."

"What does your son need?"

"I don't know. I feel so childish. Does all this seem ridiculous to you?"

"No," Charles said quietly. "I don't think so." But then he added quickly, "Nor am I sure that he can fill it up as well. This is the same question I am asking myself."

"Jason, you were right. Richard has something to teach me. I think I should try. For the sake of Daniel."

Both my arms were crossed in front of me on the table. Charles reached over and placed his hand on my forearm. "Your father may be dead," he said. "I'm sure you've thought of that, but I agree, for the sake of your son, the first thing you should do is try to find your father."

"First?" I said. "What is second?"

Charles looked disappointed. "Isn't it evident?"

"Not to me."

"Well, think about it. In the meantime, you find your father if you can."

Charles then told us some of his plan to save Rod. He told it to us in bits and pieces without ever connecting them together so that we could see the whole picture. When he finished, we were as baffled as when he had begun. Yet we had a foggy notion of what we were to do and that we were to wait for further direction. We submitted completely.

It was time to say good-bye. We were on important missions now. I would find my father; we would try to save Charles's son. Jason had sat down at this table as Richard's son. He stood up as one of us, a member of the circle of Somerset Maugham's table.

Chapter Fourteen

Brent Jackson

(Four Days Later) July 17, 1993

Oklahoma City, Oklahoma

It was good to be home. I was back in my own town, in my own bed, and looking toward the silhouette of Nicole's glowing shoulders against the star-filled window. I quietly got out of bed, walked to the window, and looked out at the star-filled night. *There is nothing like suburbia*, I thought, *to present the best view of stars.* Most of the large cities I traveled to produced too much smog and too many nightlights to be able to behold the kind of splendor taken for granted in my own neighborhood. I turned back toward my wife, lying on her left side, facing me and sleeping soundly.

I could see Nicole's face, there in our bedroom, with the stars themselves casting enough light to give her face a faint glow. She never put her hair up at night, and so it was folded in layers over the pillow; shadows vividly accented the Cherokee Indian in her cheekbones. She wore no makeup, and with her translucent skin and naturally deep-colored lips, she could have passed for a teenager.

One soft, narrow foot had escaped from the cotton sheet that hung limply over the rest of her leg. The sheet clung tightly to her hips, spread up under her arm, and draped itself over the front of her right breast. Her left breast was covered by her arm, which was crooked toward her, with her hand tucked under her chin, like a sleeping child.

I sat down on the carpet in front of her and crossed my legs. I was close enough to her that I had to look right and left to catch all the details of her body. She turned slightly and, like a swan rising in the sky, brought a delicate hand slowly over her head and placed it on her forehead. I took a breath and froze, lest any sound, any breath, might wake her.

I sat there quietly until I began to feel it deep within the pit of my stomach. *Nicole is not unattainable*, I thought. This was my wife. So why did I only feel despair and longing, as though there was a part of her, a part of me, that we could never share?

I felt the dampness on my back, and drops of sweat began to creep down my forehead. I stood up, threw my robe around me, and hurried downstairs to the den where it was quiet and I could let the shaking consume me in solitude. I pushed back my reclining leather chair and stared up, watching patterns flow in front of me, forming little eddies on the ceiling.

I fell asleep for a moment and woke to the sound of glasses clinking. Nicole had placed orange juice on the lamp stand beside me.

"Is it over?" She leaned over me and kissed me briefly on the lips. Her burgundy satin nightgown hung loosely away from her breasts until she stood up, whereby it clung to her skin, almost as though it were wet.

It was still dark, but a few robins outside our window were witnessing to the promise of morning.

I nodded.

"Bad one?" She sat on the sofa in front of me, arms crossed over the exposed top part of her chest, as though she were cold.

"Not too bad."

"You should have woken me."

"Thanks." I shrugged. "Nothing anyone can do."

"I like to be with you when it happens."

"Thanks. I'm better now."

She watched me for a moment and then sipped her orange juice. "I guess I look awful. I haven't even put my makeup on."

"You look beautiful without your makeup," I said. "You look like a young girl."

She shook her head and looked away. "But I'm not a young girl. And the older I get, the longer I have to stay in the makeup room."

"Don't be silly. You're beautiful." I changed subject. "What time is it?"

"We're losing you," she said without a trace of emotion in her voice.

I stared at her for a long moment. "You're losing me?" I repeated.

"Yes," she said. Her voice had no warmth or coldness in it. It was detached, spoken like a witness does in a jury trial, relating facts. "We have been for a long time."

"We?" I said. "I know I have had some problems with Daniel. But you and I…?"

She turned her head suddenly, her eyebrows knitted. "It makes me even sadder that you can't see the connection."

I pushed down on the footrest of the lounge chair and sat straight up. "What are you talking about? I can't have problems with Daniel without having problems with you? What kind of logic is that?"

"It's the kind of problems you're having. We're supposed to be a family." Her voice now held the quality of restrained anger, a tone I definitely preferred over the detached one but one that chilled me as well. "We are not you and I and I and Daniel. We are us. You can't just emotionally dump Daniel without dumping me as well."

"I'm not emotionally dumping…" And then I paused, remembering our conversation in Malaysia.

"That's what frightens me. Do you really not see the problem? Our eleven-year-old boy made an appointment with his own father so he could have thirty minutes to beg for his time."

"And I'll give him more time—"

"When? He was begging for his father. He was begging for you."

A new thought occurred to me. "Did you put him up to that?"

"I didn't even know about it until he told me a few days ago. It was the most extraordinary act of courage I have ever seen him perform." She stood up and walked to the window. "He's a marvelous boy, Brent," she said without turning around. "You're missing so much."

The phone rang. I walked to the table next to the sofa and answered it. When Nicole heard that it was Charles, she went into the kitchen.

"Where are you?" I asked.

"Here in Oklahoma City," he said. "But I don't have much time. I'm catching the next plane out."

"Uh, Charles." I lowered my voice. "This is not the best—"

"I need to know if you will still help me?" he asked.

"I said I would." I watched Nicole walk into the other part of the house in order to give me some privacy.

"Will you help me blindly?"

"Good Lord, Charles. How blind? I mean what are the risks here? Could I go to jail?"

The pause on the phone was so long that I finally said, "Charles? Are you there?"

"It is possible. I have to tell you that," Charles said.

"Jail, Charles? Jail? I'm sitting here with a major family crisis. Crisis! My going to jail is not going to improve things."

"It's highly unlikely that you will get caught."

"Caught? Caught! As in by the police? " I sank down on the floor and rested against the sofa. "I should tell you right now," I whispered, "Nicole doesn't like me to do things that upset the police."

"It's not as bad as all that." Charles seemed annoyed. "It won't take long."

"Am I driving the getaway car?"

"Very funny. Nothing like that. We're saving my son's life. I could possibly save him myself, but the chance of success would be greatly diminished. I'd like your help, I need your help, but I won't beg anymore. It's your decision, and I would understand."

"You would not."

Charles laughed softly. "I would too understand. Maybe Jason and I can do this ourselves."

"Okay. Okay. I'll do it. I think you're right. Doing it blindly is better. The more I know, the more I don't want to know."

"That's what I've been saying all along. Thank you. Now here is your first instruction. Write down this date—August sixteenth. I need you to be in LA. Are you writing it down?"

"Just a minute." I pulled open several drawers until I found a pen. "I assume this means that you have worked out all the details. You've solved the problem."

"You need to be at 1106 Mulgrove in Beverly Hills at seven thirty."

I wrote furiously. "Is that Rod's house?"

"Yes. You need to take a taxi and pay him extra so he doesn't use the meter or call it in."

"Well, at least I won't be doing anything that might appear suspicious."

Charles ignored my sarcasm. "Tell the driver you're paparazzi or something. You'll think of something."

I pondered that for a moment. "You didn't answer my question. Have you worked out—"

"I'm still working on it. I'm sure I'll have it." A pause. "Have you found out who your father is yet?"

I stuttered. "It hasn't been that long since I saw you. I'm still not sure if finding my father is such a good idea."

"Stop analyzing it. Just do it. And let me know how it goes."

"I'll think about it."

"Do it. You've got less than five weeks."

"You want me to…? In five weeks? You're out of your—"

"Aim for four, "he commanded. "So you'll be in LA?"

I groaned involuntarily. "Yeah, sure. I'll be there. What do I bring?"

"Nothing. Wear comfortable clothes."

"Okay. Anything else I need to do?"

"There may be one other thing. I'm working on something…I might need your connections—your contacts."

I wondered which ones he meant. "When will you let me know?"

"Today. For sure, today."

I tried to imagine myself getting out of a taxi in front of Rod Chambers's house. "Who else will be there?"

"That's too many questions, Brent. Blindly, remember?"

"Just one more question, just a general one. I shouldn't ask this, but I've got to. Please."

Charles sighed. "Go ahead."

"If I knew what your plan was, would I do it?"

"Oh, no. You would never do it," Charles said and hung up.

I sat on the floor and considered my feelings for a moment. What Charles was asking me to do was scary, even for a high-adventure-lifestyle guy like me. I wanted to help Charles, but I was, after all, the breadwinner of my family. Nicole hadn't worked as an advertising agent for years. We both had thought it would be good for Daniel if she stayed home, especially since I was traveling so much.

Nicole came back from the kitchen and handed me a saucer with two pieces of wheat toast on it. I wondered what I would say if she asked me what Charles's conversation was about, but she wanted to get right back into our subject.

"I know you still have wounds from an odd childhood."

"No more than millions of other kids that grow up without fathers."

"That doesn't really help you, does it?" She looked at me with big, brown, sad eyes, and I felt very small. "I can't imagine what it would have been like to have grown up without a father."

I thought of Nicole and her dad. He was as equally a part of Nicole's life as her mother had been. He had given her a credit card when she was sixteen. "Call me at any time of day or night," he used to say. "I'll be there." And she had had plenty of good reasons to call him.

Her astonishing beauty had attracted plenty of suitors, some of whom were not of the best character. Her dad had protected her like a guard dog, but their relationship was so close that she never considered it an intrusion. The first time I met him, he watched me as though I might try to hide a time bomb somewhere in their home. I was equally distrustful of him. He doted on Nicole, and she followed his wishes so respectfully that I became jealous.

Nicole was the third of four daughters. Her mother told me that when she was pregnant with the fourth child, she had asked Nicole which she wanted, a little brother or a little sister.

"Oh, it's got to be a little sister," Nicole, seven years old, had said.

Her mom was surprised by her adamancy. "Why is that?"

"For Daddy's sake," Nicole said.

They had been in the kitchen, and Nicole's mom was stirring a cake mix. She stopped and put it down. "Why for your daddy?"

"Because my daddy loves little girls," Nicole had said, shaking her head like her father had an incurable condition.

It had taken her father and me some time to make peace, but at some point, he had the realization that I was making his daughter happy. After we passed that, he released her into my arms with his blessing. Even today when they call, Nicole talks to her mother and then to her father, equally.

"I have been thinking," I said tentatively, Charles's conversation fresh on mind, "that I might like to see my father."

Her eyebrows rose. "Really? Do you know where he is?"

"I don't even know if he is alive."

"Does your mother?" Nicole changed her position and moved more in front of me.

"I've asked her a few times. She says she doesn't."

"Still…" She paused and scrunched up her mouth while she thought. "With computers and the Internet and all, if we just had a name."

I was pleased. "I thought you might think it was silly."

"It makes sense." Her eyes opened wide. "Do you think it might help you?"

"Help me?" I scratched my shoulder. "As in helping me get over my spells?"

She looked at me very evenly. There was a slight tone of sternness in her voice. "I'm tired of calling them spells. You can call them spells if you like." She looked away.

"What would you call them?"

She looked back at me. "You know how I am with Franco Zeffirelli movies."

I smiled. I had to be ready with lots of tissue when we rented *Brother Son, Sister Moon*, or *Romeo and Juliet*. "You cry like a baby."

"I don't deny it. I find them beautiful in every possible way. And I feel…"

"Sad?"

"No. That's the point," she said. "I feel good. And the crying is a kind of physical reaction to how I feel."

"Okay. And…?" I was searching for relevance.

"When you have your so-called spell, it's like…well…only when you see something beautiful."

"I'm sorry. I don't get it," I said.

"When you see something beautiful, you begin to feel something you're uncomfortable with," she said.

I was silent and thought about it for a moment. "So while most people cry over sad things, I just cry when I get really happy. Is that it?" I was teasing her, but she didn't smile.

"More than cry," she said. "Something more powerful, draining…"

"On you as well as me." I pulled her close to me and hugged her.

She placed an arm around my back. "I can live with your spells if you can. But somewhere inside there is a little boy who won't let you accept too much beauty—perhaps too much love. It's more than you can handle."

"Quite an analysis, Dr. Freud." I pressed my fingers against her bare back, rubbing them in the places I knew she loved. "You've been thinking about this a lot."

"Anyway," she said suddenly. "It does seem logical to me that to really be a father, you ought to know the father you had. There is a chain of events that needs to be broken."

"Broken?"

She took several breaths. "I don't know why your father abandoned you. Maybe his father abandoned him. But now"—she looked at me sadly—"you've abandoned Daniel."

I dropped my arms and shook my head. She was right. I had abandoned Daniel, emotionally if not physically. But as to finding my father… "I have no idea. I don't know if—"

She jumped up. "I'm going to call your mother." And before we could discuss it further, she walked briskly into the kitchen.

She lowered her voice and talked steadily to my mother for ten minutes. I couldn't hear the words, but her tone was stern, forceful. Nicole lecturing my mother—that was new.

I wanted to get up and listen, but instead I sat down and picked up one of Nicole's magazines, flipping the pages. Ten minutes of silence passed while Nicole listened on the phone. I was turning the pages so rapidly that I eventually tore one right out of the book. I could hear Nicole talking again. This time she was speaking softly, with sympathetic murmurs, an apology. I heard the click as she replaced the receiver.

I went back to my magazine.

"That was probably the best talk your mother and I have ever had," she said.

"How's that?" I asked, staring intently at an article that said, "How to Make Your Husband Say, 'Wow.'"

"Your mother's been through a lot. She has a lot of stored feelings."

I closed the magazine, leaned back, and looked at her.

"I'm having her over for dinner next week," she said.

"That's nice."

Nicole sat down and picked up my hand, turned it palm up, and placed a piece of paper in it. "Here's the name of your father."

I looked down at the paper. It was folded.

I remember the first time I had gone to Rome. I was on the top open level of a city bus, my senses overflowing with the images of a city that had stood over two thousand years. We turned a corner, and directly in front was the Coliseum. I had seen it in magazines and history books and had studied its history carefully in my guidebooks on the flight over. But here in front of me, it seemed like there should be trumpets blasting. The streets should have been lined with people applauding loudly and shouting, "This is the Coliseum! You are seeing it for the first time in your life!"

But this was real life—appreciation of which would be a quiet, solitary event, no matter who was there. The Coliseum and the people around it remained silent at my approach.

It was a feeling I would experience again and again as I traveled the world and stood in front of the three-dimensional version of a picture I had studied since childhood. These manifestations did not wait for me. There were no bands when I arrived. They were just there.

Now I was in the presence of the name of my father. It was nothing more than a name and was much less than what most sons and daughters have all their lives. The torn-off sheet of paper now lay limply on my hand and contained at least part of what was the greatest mystery and tragedy of my life.

"Would you please open it?" Nicole said impatiently.

"Right," I said, and I did so.

The name was written in blue ink. I read it out loud. "Mason Prescott."

Nicole looked at the paper, then at me, and then back at the paper again. "Mason Prescott," she repeated.

My first reaction was to say, "My name would have been Brent Prescott."

"I would be Nicole Prescott."

The room was now fully lit by the morning. I stood up and walked to the window. I continued to stare at the paper. "I can't believe Mom gave you his name."

"She gave me more than his name, Brent. She knows where he is."

"What?" I said sharply, turning around. "She's in touch with him?"

"No," Nicole replied softly. "It's true what she told you. She's never seen him since he left. She has wanted to tell you for years but didn't want you to be hurt any more than you were." She paused. "Your mom doesn't think he will see you."

I was suddenly engulfed with anger—anger at Mom for not telling me, anger at my father for the mere possibility that he might not see me. *He doesn't know who I am*, I thought. *He doesn't know how determined I can be. I will make him see me.* "Why does she think that?"

"It's because of who he is." Nicole hesitated. "Would you rather hear this from your mother?"

"It's clear that Mom doesn't talk very well with me about such things," I said, trying to hold back the bitterness from my voice. "I'd rather you tell me everything you know."

"He's very rich." Nicole leaned forward. "I don't recall ever hearing his name before. But I've heard of his company." She said the letters slowly, "GOPS—Global Oil Parts and Services.

He owns the majority of it, Brent. He's more than a billionaire." Nicole spoke softly, like a doctor would, telling a patient bad news.

I began to understand and felt a wave of sadness wash over me. On one edge of my mind was the realization that a long-lost son to a billionaire would be about as welcome as a root canal. Well, a root canal would be more welcome. This was as hard as it gets. On the other edge was the creeping awareness of something else.

"How different my life would have been," I said.

"Too different for me. You would have been a spoiled brat," Nicole said. "I would never have married someone like that."

I watched her for a long moment and then nodded. I knew her well enough to know she wasn't just trying to make me feel good—although it was working out that way. "But you wouldn't mind if I had an extra million dollars lying around."

"I just want you. Daniel and I both do," she said firmly.

I looked at her. "All I can say at this point is that I love you with all my heart."

She first nodded, but then I saw a dark thought cross her mind. She looked away and shook her head slowly. "But will you love me if I am fat and ugly?"

"That will never happen."

"I won't look young forever."

"You'll always be beautiful."

She patted my arm. "Sweet. Not true. But sweet."

"So it's an impossible situation, isn't it?"

"Not for you. You're smart. You'll figure it out," she said.

"What's going on?" We both turned to see that Daniel had walked into the room. He was standing in the doorway wearing his blue flannel pajamas. His blanket, wrapped around his shoulders, was dragging on the floor behind him. He looked thin and pale, but his eyes were sharp and aware. He had, no doubt, heard our voices and sensed a serious enough discussion to warrant his presence. "What are you talking about?" he said.

Nicole studied Daniel for a moment and then turned toward me. "This isn't just your problem. It's ours," she said. "All of ours." And just to make sure I got it, she added, "We need to be involved in the process."

I considered it for a moment before I spoke. "All right, Daniel, I'll tell you," I said, and I waited while Daniel plodded over to the sofa and sat down. I didn't know how to begin. "It's nothing much really."

Daniel watched me attentively. I don't think I had ever noticed how green his eyes were. I took a deep breath and told him how I had wanted to find my father and how, after thirty-eight years of not knowing, Nicole had extracted the information from my mother in a thirty-minute phone call. I tried to make it sound funny, but nobody laughed.

I told him what my father's name was and explained why, after all this, the whole effort could be moot because of the probability that he wouldn't even let me anywhere near him.

"What does 'moot' mean?" Daniel asked when I had finished.

"It means that it isn't relevant, that there's no point to it."

"I guess you really want to meet him, huh?"

"I don't know," I said. "But your mother makes it sound like if I don't, I have, in essence, cursed you, your future children, their children, maybe even the wives…" I laughed.

Again, no one laughed with me.

The phone rang, and I picked it up. It was Charles again. "I'm going to need one more favor from you after all."

"Sure," I said, trying not too look nervous. Daniel jumped up and ran out of the room suddenly as though he had just thought of something. Nicole got up slowly and left as well.

"Who is the richest, most powerful person you know whom you can ask a big favor of?"

It was becoming tiresome to hear such shocking questions from Charles. Yet, I thought, Charles's timing had to be coincidental, as my mind had been focused on my rich and powerful father. I hesitated but deducted that there was no way Charles could have known that. In any case, it was absurd that it would even cross my mind to ask a favor of the father I had never met and who probably wouldn't even see me. I thought for a moment. "Actually, nobody around here. The closest I can come to that description is Mr. Chang in Taiwan. I doubt that that will do."

Charles was quiet for so long I finally said, "Charles? Are you there?"

"It might still work," he said slowly. "We can make it work. It'll just be a little different. He's really rich, isn't he?"

"He flies to New York to have his suits made. His wife wanted a private retreat, so he bought her an island. He has a sixty-year-old goldfish with its own maid. He's—"

"Okay, okay. I get it," Charles interrupted. "This guy really likes you, right?"

"I think so. But he's a shrewd businessman, Charles. He doesn't give money away."

"I don't want his money," Charles said. "I want his power. I need him to make two calls for me."

Charles began to explain to me what he wanted me to ask Mr. Chang. He gave me names, times, and telephone numbers. Charles had been busy.

I wrote and listened steadily with only an occasional interruption. "You want me to ask him to ask the mayor of Los Angeles to do what?" I exclaimed once, and then I looked around to see if Nicole had heard me. I whispered into the phone, "How will I explain that?" Charles had an answer. He had answers for every logistical question, every detail. He told me to wait on the other details.

"Okay," I said finally. "I'll ask him to do as you asked. But I'm more confused than ever."

"That's good," Charles said. "Confused is good. But you won't forget?"

It would take multiple electric shocks directly to the brain for me to forget. But I just replied calmly, "Please don't worry."

"Thanks," he said.

Daniel returned the very moment I put the phone down. I had never seen him so excited. He carried with him streams of papers.

"Mom was right," he said. "He is really, really rich."

"What have you got there?" We both sat down together on the sofa.

"This company, GOPS, is more than just about oil services. It owns about a dozen oil companies and is investing in nuclear power plants in China."

"How did you get that information?"

"Internet," Daniel said simply. "There are a bunch of news articles about him. I got over 250 hits when I searched for his name. Mostly, though, they are about his company hires. He makes this announcement and that one." Daniel looked up at me. "Dad?"

I nodded.

"He's married. He's got kids." He shoved a printout of an article that contained an up-close feature about him into my hand.

I read it and then nodded. "It doesn't surprise me. I just never thought about the possibility that I would have brothers and sisters."

"Two sisters and a brother," Daniel said, and then he picked out another paper that he handed to me. "There's no picture of him. But here's where he works."

I looked down and saw a picture of a building that resembled the Acropolis, only bigger. The headline said, "Mason's Empire Away from Home." The building was located in Chicago.

Daniel watched me carefully while I read the article. "It's a pretty scary building, isn't it?" he said finally.

"Pretty darn scary," I agreed, and in my heart, I gave up.

But Daniel read my mind. "You need to meet him, Dad."

I dropped the paper on the sofa. "How?" I said, not really expecting an answer.

However, Daniel gave me one. "Well, he doesn't realize how valuable you are," he said.

"Thanks, Daniel," I said, and I lay back against the sofa.

"So you should tell him." Daniel took out a small stack of paper. He looked down at it while he squirmed in his seat.

"What else have you got there?" I asked.

"Well"—he began to blink rapidly, a habit he had developed when he was nervous—"remember when I visited your office, I told you that I had been reading about fathers?"

"I remember."

He handed me the stack. It was a collection of Internet findings he had done under the central topic, fathers.

Daniel took his eyes off my face to pull up one page, a description of a number of court cases. With his pencil, he circled one and pushed it toward me. He watched my face carefully.

I put the paper in my lap and read it. Then I reread it.

"He should know just how valuable you are," Daniel said.

I put the paper down. "You're quite right," I spoke slowly. "He doesn't know how valuable I am."

"Dad?"

"Yes?"

"What about the contract I gave you? Have you thought about it?"

"Yes. I have," I responded. "Can I work on this just a little more and then get back you?"

Daniel sighed and nodded. "Sure, Dad."

I called into the kitchen, "Nicole? Where's the address book? I need to call our attorney."

Chapter Fifteen

Six Days Later (July 23, 1993)

Brent Jackson

Chicago, Illinois

"Mr. Billings said there would be two of you."

Mr. Billings's secretary stood on other side of the gate, the inner sanctum, and looked at me tolerantly. She was petite and shapely with scattered freckles around a small, thin-lipped mouth. Her appointment book had two cards dangling from it with the word *Visitor* printed in bold red letters.

It was Tuesday, and I was at the doorstep of the GOPS building. Within the last thirty-six hours, my attorney, Robert Stein, and I had worked steadily. Robert, responding to the urgency in my voice, had spent all night drawing up the papers and then all of Monday calling various people in Mason Prescott's elaborate hierarchy of division leaders. He had threatened lawsuits and insinuated blackmail until he got as high as he could get. As high as you get and still not be Prescott was Mr. Billings, an attorney, and the apparent right-hand man of my father's oil company.

"I hope Mr. Stein will be here shortly. Mr. Billings is on a tight schedule and will have to reschedule if he is late," the redheaded secretary said, and the image of my third-grade teacher came to mind.

"Mr. Stein will not be coming. I will be seeing Mr. Billings alone."

She appeared startled. She looked at her appointment book again, as though her eyes had previously deceived her. "Oh," she said. "I'll have to check." And she moved back inside the doorway.

The GOPS building looked more like a state capitol than a modern oil company. The entryway was framed with tall Doric columns and framed at the top with crisscrossed lattices. A uniformed guard, sitting in a brown booth, assiduously looked for the red badges that identified the legitimate employees of the company. I was standing beside a short door to his right that protected those in the inner sanctum by a steel gate that looked more Gothic in appearance than Greek Colonial.

The redheaded secretary appeared once again with a mobile phone pressed to her ear. "Mr. Billings doesn't see the point in meeting you without the attorney."

"Please tell Mr. Billings that I have all the papers my attorney has prepared. I am quite capable of presenting them. I would like to do it this way for reasons that will become clear to him and that I think he will find satisfactory."

She turned her head away and spoke quietly into the phone for a few moments. After listening for a while, she turned around abruptly and scanned me from head to toe.

"Welcome to Global Oil and Products Services, Mr. Jackson." She held the door open for me, smiled, and gestured grandly for me to enter.

I almost had to stoop to get in the visitor's gate and so was not prepared when the ceiling disappeared to the total height of the building. I found myself walking across marble in an atrium where I could look up and see circular staircases surrounding all floors, of which I guessed there were more than a dozen. The natural light from a large blue dome engulfed the area.

"I'm Becky Struthers," she said, holding out her hand as though we had just met. "Please follow me."

She shook my hand briskly, and I followed her toward the back of a grand marble staircase to a large, plain wooden door. It was apparently locked, and I waited while Ms. Struthers produced a key from somewhere. She opened the door and slid back a gate. It was an elevator.

She held the gate for me as I stepped inside and watched her push the only button, which was unmarked. "Which floor are we going to?" I asked.

"The top floor," she said. "The eighteenth."

The elevator shivered, moaned, and began a slow ascent. "How old is this building?" I asked.

"Seven years." Ms. Struthers stared up where one normally looks at the blinking lights of the passing floors. I looked too and saw that there were no lights.

"Seven years?" I said, watching the floors pass by through the crisscrossed steel door. "It seems—"

"Ancient?" Ms. Struthers effused like a Vietnamese guide I had once followed around while she spoke about Chairman Ho Chi Min. "Yes, Mr. Prescott copied it exactly from a building he saw in Europe. France, I think."

A light next to the button that Ms. Struthers had pushed finally lit up and dinged. The elevator stopped, and she snapped back the hinged door as expertly, as if she had been a Sac's Fifth Avenue elevator operator.

I followed Ms. Struthers down a long hallway that had no doors. We turned to the right and were suddenly in front of a massive glass door that she pushed open and held for me. We stopped in the middle of an executive waiting room—plush, blue velvet love seat, mahogany tabletops, and a setting of coffee and light snacks. A real-life gray-hair-in-a-bun woman sat at the reception desk but did not greet us.

Ms. Struthers turned toward me and held her hand up. "Please wait here." She disappeared into the office to the right. The office in the center had two double wooden mahogany doors with the shape of a running fox carved on them.

I stepped forward to the receptionist. "Excuse me," I said. "Is that Mr. Prescott's office?"

"You'll have to get that information from Mr. Billings," she said, and she looked at me suspiciously as though I might dart for the door.

"You may come in now," Ms. Struthers called, and I entered the smaller office.

The room was massive. I was surrounded by total darkness except for the light that originated from a standing brass lamp that stood beside Mr. Billings. Even from a distance, he appeared to be a large man, but as I walked toward him, the sound of my footsteps loud on his Parquet floor, his image expanded. He was behind a conference table that came to the top of his stomach. It hid nothing, and several hundred pounds of Mr. Billings sprawled loosely under the table. He was busy with a triple-decker sandwich and appeared not to notice me.

Ms. Struthers gestured to a lean, wooden-armed chair directly in front of him. Before sitting, I looked briefly around the room. The darkness was so pervasive that I could barely see the ceiling. I caught a suggestion of large framed artwork on the walls. There was a window, but the curtains were drawn tightly and allowed no light. There was perhaps a sofa and a chair in a corner. One could have a party with a live band in this room.

"Mr. Jackson?" Ms. Struthers said without looking at me or the chair toward which she was gesturing. "Why don't you have a seat?"

I obeyed and sat in front of the caretaker of GOPS. Besides the sandwich, which occupied his total attention, he had a few papers, a manila envelope, a large glass of water, and a bowl of chocolate ice cream. Outside of those few items, the conference table, which could seat at least twenty people, was bare. There were no other chairs.

The contrast of the bright light and darkness bothered me. I wanted to see the room, and of course, I knew that was the point. Mr. Billings's long, round fingers gripped the sandwich so tightly that the cheese had begun to drip out the sides. Ms. Struthers walked briskly around the table and stood near Mr. Billings, slightly to the rear of him. During the walk around, the balance of the sandwich had disappeared into his mouth with loud, slurping noises Mr. Billings stared at his empty hands as though someone had snatched something out of them.

"Wouldn't you like your ice cream now, Mr. Billings? Mr. Jackson and I can wait," she said, graciously volunteering my time. Mr. Billings looked from his hands to the bowl of melting chocolate ice cream.

I leaned forward. "Excuse me, Mr. Billings," I said. "Why don't you have Ms. Struthers bend the lampshade a little this way? That way I can feel the full heat of the bulb on my face."

Mr. Billings paused as though considering something. He then reached for the ice cream and took a huge bite that he sucked through his lips and smacked several times jubilantly.

"If you'd like, I could come over there and get directly under the light," I said in as accommodating a voice as I could summon up.

Mr. Billings took another gaping bite and moved his eyes up to examine me for the first time. Ms. Struthers's freckles gathered all around her eyes as she glared at me.

I laughed. "Really, Mr. Billings? A spotlight? From the look of the grandeur of this building, I'm sure you must be an excellent businessman." I looked around from side to side and then lowered my voice. "But negotiating by intimidation went out in the seventies. Today you can't find a used-car salesman who can make it work."

Mr. Billings stopped chewing.

"You were way ahead, Mr. Billings," I continued in the same manner as one might discuss a football game. "This building, the whole ride up the private elevator, even making me stand in the waiting room…now that was intimidating." I pushed my chair up under his desk and folded my arms over it.

"You were way ahead," I repeated. "And if you had followed that up by meeting me graciously, offering me a refreshment, and disarming me with kindness, why…I'd be shaking in my boots by now instead of, well…" I began to laugh. "I mean, it is funny. Can't you see it? Honestly, Mr. Billings, a wooden chair? Wooden?" I laughed unreserved and then stopped abruptly. "All you've told me so far"—now I was speaking in as firm a voice as I could manage—"is that I have scared the pants off you and you're pulling out every archaic trick you can think of."

A slow redness began to color Mr. Billings's massive face. Sweat broke out profusely over his forehead. I sat back in my chair. The color continued to darken. *Have I gone too far?* I wondered. Surely he knew that in any negotiation a strong move of intimidation is met by an equally strong move of disarmament. Our pieces were now in equal positions, and it was his turn to play.

Mr. Billings's eyes flickered to his left and then back to me. He picked up his glass of water and poured it down his mouth as if it were a shot of whiskey. Mr. Billings's eyes flickered again to the left, and I decided to take a stealthy look as well.

The edges of the room were too dark to see anything well, but the corner of the room where Mr. Billings had looked contained the faint outline of a tall-backed chair. Mr. Billings's eyes flickered again, and a large drop of sweat slid down his jowl and splashed on the table.

Chills went up my legs, through my hips, and straight down my arms. I pushed my chair back away from Mr. Billings lest he see the goose bumps break out on my face. I was actually grateful for the wooden chair—any chair. I took a deep, slow breath and coughed a little to give myself an excuse for turning my head away. I couldn't let Mr. Billings realize that I now knew that someone was sitting in the chair. *Where are the trumpets?* I thought. *Where is the band?*

I took a deep breath and swallowed. I needed a drink of water, but I would not give Mr. Billings the advantage of having me ask for one. There was no question that for the first time in my life, I was sitting in the same room with my father. But this wooden chair and spotlight ploy was childish and unprofessional. I suspected that this was an old trick that Mr. Billings used and bragged about on the golf course. It may not have been my father's doing, but then he had hired Mr. Billings. He was also participating fully in Mr. Billings's Machiavellian strategy. I had not even seen my father but was learning about him by the second. I took another slow breath and coughed again. They did not know that I suspected my father was in the room. That was to my advantage. Their demonstration of old-school intimidation and trickery was also to my advantage.

I was able to find my voice and so turned back to Mr. Billings with new resolution. "Sorry," I said. "Do either of you have cats?"

Mr. Billings continued to stare, but Ms. Struthers, in the first feminine motion I had seen, touched her hand to her chest and said, "Well, I do."

"Ah," I said. "I'm allergic."

I could have, at that point, taken charge of the meeting. I could have laid down my conditions, talked through it, stood up, and left. But I resisted that temptation. I was a guest in their office, and I would not let their behavior, however rude it might be, affect mine. Anyway, it would be interesting to see where he would go next.

I waited in long silence for him to speak.

"We were expecting you and your attorney," Mr. Billings said in a voice much too high pitched for a body so large.

"I have been in full consultation with my attorney. He has drawn up the necessary papers, and I feel confident that we can handle this arrangement without him."

"Arrangement? I know of no intended arrangement. We must immediately dismiss this meeting and take it up again when you have an attorney present."

"You are an attorney, are you not, Mr. Billings?" I asked.

"Yes. Of course."

"Well, I think one attorney in a room is enough, don't you?" I smiled warmly.

Mr. Billings did not smile. He looked at me carefully. I was certain he thought me naïve at this point—like taking candy from a baby. "Very well," he said. "It's your funeral."

I showed no expression at his "funeral" comment. I waited with interest for his next comment.

"Miss Struthers?" he said sharply. She smiled and opened the brown folder that was next to him.

She handed it to me. "I believe this is for you."

It was a summons.

"We are suing you for libel and turning your name over to the district attorney for blackmail," Mr. Billings said. "You have threatened Mr. Prescott's good name and reputation with the threat of exposure and publicity. You have made false accusations about a claim to be an heir to Mr. Prescott's well-known fortune. Mr. Prescott not only denies this but has promised to punish you vigorously for defamation through every possible means of the court."

"I see," I said, taking the paper and looking at it. "Is this mine? Do you have a copy?"

Mr. Billings did not answer. "Yes, of course," Ms. Struthers answered tersely.

"Thank you," I said, opening my briefcase and slipping it into a file folder. "Anything else?" I said.

"I think that covers it. We'll see you in court." Mr. Billings turned his attention away from me back toward the empty ice cream bowl. I had been dismissed.

Good grief, Father, I thought. *Is this the best you can do?* I was actually disappointed.

"I'd like to respond," I said, and without waiting for his permission, I opened my briefcase and took out a blue file folder. The summons that had been handed me was meant to serve as a distracter to the real task at hand. Another simple chess response was required: acknowledge the distraction, focus on the desired outcome, and bring attention back to the game.

"I have two items." I pulled out a sixteen-page, stapled document with a front cover that read, *Brent Jackson vs. Mason Prescott.* I turned it around and scooted it toward Mr. Billings, who took brown-framed reading glasses out of his shirt pocket, laid them loosely over his nose, and peered at it.

"This writ, which has not yet been filed, begins on the foundation of unpaid child support." I paused. "With some expansion."

Mr. Billings began to move his head back and fourth over the document. Ms. Struthers leaned slightly forward and stared down at it as I continued. "Based upon Mr. Prescott's considerable wealth and means, my back child support would have been a considerable sum. But there are 'hardships' mentioned as well.

"I suffered from many of the normal trials that fatherless children go through, except that mine manifested itself into a psychological dilemma. You can see that attestation in Appendix B." Mr. Billings flipped a few pages from the back and began reading.

"Appendix B," I continued, "is a psychiatrist's attestation of over twenty-five years of mental treatment. Although not included in this document, I have records dating back to childhood from three different psychiatrists and psychologists who have worked with me. If you'll look at the sixth paragraph, you'll see the suspected determining cause…"

The room was very quiet while Mr. Billings read the sixth paragraph over and over. In the darkness of the corner of the room, I thought I heard a faint rustling of clothes.

"I'll read it aloud for you," I said, with the intention of making certain my father knew exactly what we were discussing.

"Mr. Brent Jackson has been under psychiatric care since his eleventh birthday. One evaluator diagnosed him with bipolar disorder. This was due to his high degree of physical activity, his creative flow of ideas, and his high sense of humor coupled with devastating depressions accompanied by delusional sessions that were frequently triggered by a single emotional stimulus."

I paused. "The next few paragraphs are even more technical. Let's skip to the third page, second paragraph of this section."

I continued, "The drug lithium was tried for a while. It had no affect on his delusions and had a strong negative effect on his creative and productive energies. It was immediately discontinued, and he was rediagnosed as having a schizoaffective disorder. Psychotherapy was determined to be the best course of treatment."

Mr. Billings interrupted me. "Yes," he said, "we can see ourselves how troubled you are, but it has no relationship whatsoever to my client, Mr. Prescott."

"Forgive me," I said, lowering my voice to a near whisper. "I know this is boring, and I know you are a busy man. Indulge me one more minute, after which it should all become sparkling clear."

Mr. Billings's lips tightened. Besides the writ, there were a few papers and a pen in front of him. He swiped the pen to one side and leaned forward, intertwining his fingers and placing both arms on the papers. "This meeting is concluded."

"Right here, Mr. Billings." I leaned over the table toward him and very gently tugged at the document that was under his right elbow. I was so close to him I could smell the onions. He looked down at the paper, lifted his elbow, and released it. I flipped the pages twice. "Right here." I pointed at the final paragraph of Appendix B. I read out loud, "The conclusion is that the cause of Mr. Jackson's illness has its origin in a recently discovered form of diagnosed child abuse…the fatherless child."

"There," I said, breathing an exaggerated sigh of relief. I would never have used such a manner in a negotiating case for my business. It would be counterproductive. I knew I was showing off for my father, but I was enjoying it. "That's why we're here."

"This is ludicrous. There are no precedents."

"I agree it would be a landmark case." The word *landmark* was carefully chosen to incite the greatest fear, and I paused for just a moment to let it soak in.

Mr. Billings took his round plump fist and pounded the table. "This is an amateurish attempt to intimidate us. You have not even established filial relationship with Mr. Prescott, and you expect us to be groveling over this imaginary case."

"You're right," I said. "Let's get that over with." I opened my briefcase and took out a small, dark-red vial. I laid it on the table and, with a flip of my finger, rolled it toward Mr. Billings who caught it.

"What's this?" he said, holding it up toward the lamp and peering through it.

"It's a sample of my blood."

He nearly dropped it. "Your blood?"

"For the DNA test."

"The DNA? My client will never agree to a DNA test. You'll need a court order, and I assure you that will cost you a great—"

"Relax, Mr. Billings," I said. "This one's a gift. You have the blood. Your client can do with it what he will." I snapped my briefcase shut. "I don't need to know, at least without a court order. But I think both of you might be curious."

"You sound..." Mr. Billings started and then snapped his mouth shut. I knew he had started to say "confident" but thought better of it. I saw the alarm in Mr. Billings's eyes for the first time. "Don't you realize," he began slowly and with little enthusiasm, "the immense resources Mr. Prescott has at his disposal to fight such a lawsuit? Even"—he hesitated—"if you were his actual son?"

"Of course I do," I said. "But don't you see how interesting this case would be?" I picked up the document and flipped several pages ahead. "There has been some remarkable research done in this area. Please take a glance, won't you?" I pointed. "It is summarized in Appendix D."

Mr. Billings would not follow my fingers. He just stared up at my eyes, trying to lock in on them.

"Well," I said. "Here are a few samples." And I began to read.

"As the family continues to be redefined, new research here shows that fathers' absences have led to numerous crippling illnesses and social dysfunctions."

I turned the page. "It goes on a bit about this. Findings indicate that the more the child is away from the father, the higher the risk for a maladjustment score.

"There's more," I said. "Findings show that children are stimulated mentally and emotionally by father's play. Findings show that children who have fathers present had a better self-concept and emotional balance."

Mr. Billings thundered at me, "No court will respect this theory!" He lowered his voice suddenly and almost looked at the darkened corner. But then he smiled. "You have forgotten a very important point. This so-called child abuse theory of yours discounts motherhood completely. You are saying that mothers count for nothing." He began to laugh. "Unless you get a jury with all men, you'll have the fury of women who think you have minimized their role in bringing up children."

"You have not read Appendix D," I said, and I raised my voice slightly as well. "That's okay." I reached over and snatched it out from under his arms, feeling the passion rise in my voice. "I'll tell you about it. First of all, the crisis of the twentieth century has not been the absence of mothers. They have stayed, as the world changed, as divorces rose in number and women took more responsibility in the workplace. They have stayed. They have accepted their responsibility. It is the fathers who have abandoned their wives, their children, and their lives."

I stood up, flipping the pages, and tore them off one by one, dropping them on the table as I articulated each point. "See Appendix D, Mr. Billings. See all the court cases, filed by women. Women, Mr. Billings! Begging the courts to find their husbands, to pay for the children they have left behind! And look at the court's responses, Mr. Billings. In the last ten years, they have responded with strong affirmation to the mothers who are on welfare, to the children who are hungry. They have responded by allowing the law to cross state lines, sending negligent fathers to jail.

"How many cases have you seen, Mr. Billings, where parents have been thrown in jail for the injury their children received when the parent left them alone? Isn't that what fathers are doing? Leaving them alone? And now, we are perhaps ready to go a step further, to declare the indigent fathers as the child molesters, the child abusers that they really are!"

I had leaned so far over the desk that both Mr. Billings and Ms. Struthers had leaned back. Mr. Billings took off his glasses and wiped his forehead. "Look at Appendix D, Mr. Billings." Women are not minimized in this court case. They are the heroes. They will not anger. They will cheer."

The only sound in the room was my breathing. Ms. Struthers was looking back and forth between the phone and Mr. Billings. I slowed my breathing down. I had let my anger show, and while normally a minus in such affairs, I felt in this case it was a wash. They had seen my passion. They were imagining its effect in front of a jury. They knew there was more on this table than the document.

"You threaten us." Mr. Billings began to settle in his chair.

I stretched out my hands. "I have no weapons. I come without arms. I didn't bring witnesses. I didn't even bring my attorney." I handed him my document. "Sorry about the pages. Here. You can have mine."

Mr. Billings replaced his glasses and began to flip to the end of the first section. He found what he was looking for and began to nod his head. "Twenty million dollars?" he said slowly with interest. "That's quite a lot of back child support."

"It's all there," I said, and I waved my hand. "My attorney explains that the son of Mr. Prescott would have quite a different lifestyle than mine. Twenty million would begin to reshape it."

"Begin?"

"Next page," I said. "A million a year, the rest of my life. I won't think the courts would find that a greedy amount for the son of a child-abusing billionaire. Of course," I said, "they may wish to add punitive damages..." My words drifted off. The dark corner of the room had been so exceedingly quiet that I wondered if he had left through some hidden door. I hoped not, I thought, with the odd realization that I had found some strange comfort in his being there.

"I will study this," Mr. Billings said, preparing again to dismiss me.

"I'm guessing, Mr. Billings, that you are now pleased to have a figure that you can work with. A figure, of any amount, gives you lawyers a starting place. Makes you feel safe, doesn't it?"

He lifted his face up slightly and again looked at me through the top of his glasses.

"What I want, you cannot give me," I said. "But you can help me get it."

"Oh?" he said, again with new concern.

"I have a second document that contains my primary objective."

"Oh?" he said again.

I pulled it out of my briefcase. I had, by this time, lost much of my energy. I was weary and emotionally drained. I wanted to stop but knew I could not break the continuum.

"A settlement?" he asked. "In the same day? I doubt your attorney would have agreed to that."

"You're right about that one. My attorney thinks I'm crazy," I said. "But we have already established that, haven't we?" I dropped two copies of the same document on the table. "This is much briefer than the other. Please go ahead and read it. I'll just wait."

Mr. Billings read slowly. When he finished the first page, he laid back in his chair and tossed the document away from him on the table. "Is this a trick?" he said simply and without accusation. "In this document, you deny any relationship whatsoever to Mason Prescott."

He continued. "You give up all rights to back child support, damages, or any consideration as his heir?"

"That's correct."

"And how much do you want for…?" he asked.

"It's on the second page."

He did not move but merely pointed at papers. It was a cue for Ms. Struthers, who came to life like a Disney animatronic. She picked up the document, turned the page, and placed it in his hand. His eyes shifted to the page and moved back and forth across the lines, down to the bottom. Then he read it again.

When he looked up at me, he looked as tired as I felt. He sighed heavily. "I agree with your lawyer."

"Perhaps," I said. "I hope not."

"For total disavowance of any claim, you desire three hours of my client's time."

"Precisely, I desire to fish with your client," I corrected him, "for a minimum of three hours."

"This is a ridiculous blackmail," he said without conviction. "He will never agree."

I shrugged. "I'm hoping that he will."

Mr. Billings moved his huge bulk forward and leaned on the table.

"And what do you hope to happen in these three hours?"

"I hope," I said, "to catch a fish."

Mr. Billings laughed, but it was not a pretty one. "You are an admitted psycho!" He picked up the first document, and for the second time in the evening, it was waved around in the air. "Appendix B! Remember? How do we know you aren't planning some kind of payback? If I were Mr. Prescott, I would be afraid of you. I'm tempted to call the guards myself for protection."

"I want to get well." I sighed heavily, talking more to myself than the members in the room. "I think knowing who my father is may help. I think so, my wife thinks so, and my son thinks so." I shook my head. "Maybe it is crazy. But it's all that I want. And I will have it."

There was a minute while all in the room ingested the fact that Mason Prescott was a grandfather.

I stood up, and Ms. Struthers leapt into action, racing around the long table to lead me back downstairs. I followed her to the door. Mr. Billings had not moved.

"So," he called after me, "you are asking me to believe that you have come here with the sole intent of bargaining for time with the man who you insist on claiming is your father?"

"I guess so." I held my briefcase handle with both hands, stopped, turned around, and looked at him.

He squinted. "And this was not your lawyer's idea?"

"Actually, no," I said, turning back toward the door. "I got the idea from my son."

Chapter Sixteen

Brent Jackson

(Seven Days Later) July 30, 1993

Chicago, Illinois

I have never been good at waiting. Though the terms of my proposal had specified that I would need a notification by 3:00 p.m. Friday for the settlement offer to remain in status, that deadline had come and gone. I had tried not to stare at the red digital numbers of the hotel clock and instead busied myself with active but mindless chores. I installed an upgrade to my Word processor, deleted old files and programs I had not used in months, and defragmented my hard disk drive. At least twice I reached for the telephone line but remembered that this hotel had only one per room, and I did not want to tie up the telephone line for the few minutes it would take to log on to my system.

At three thirty-five, the phone rang. It was Charles.

"I'm expecting a call from you-know-who, Charles," I explained.

"When are you going to meet him?"

"I don't know. I'll call you later." Charles agreed, and I hung up.

I switched off the TV, threw the bedspread lightly back, and sat at the foot of the bed until three fifty-five. I called the bell captain, walked to the window, and looked out at the steady but slow street traffic six floors below me that would, in less than an hour, be cramped with crowds of people with the single-minded purpose of getting home.

I moved across the room, opened my closet, and slipped on my suit jacket. The doorbell and the phone rang at the same moment.

I chose to answer the phone. Mr. Billings's high-pitched voice was cordial. Had I not met him, I would have imagined him much differently.

"You are asking more than you realize. Mr. Prescott is a busy man. Three hours might be arranged, but that is a lot of time for his busy schedule, especially since you insist that it be tomorrow. Could we just have a thirty-minute meeting...a lunch perhaps?"

I sat down on the bed. He had said it could be arranged. We were in the final stages of a deal. It became at once clear to me that he had had the blood tested. Due to the lateness of his call, I surmised that he had just seen the results. My father was probably standing beside Mr. Billings.

He is testing me, I thought. *He wants more information.* I would give him only what was necessary. "I am surprised that you would quibble over that point," I said. "I could have said three days, and I think you would have agreed. I do apologize for Mr. Prescott's inconvenience, but those minimal terms are not negotiable."

Billings grunted. "It's really an odd request, this fishing. Mr. Prescott is, shall we say..."

The doorbell rang again. I held my hand over the phone and told the bell captain to wait. I could not imagine what it was that was causing Billings to stutter and search for words. He said "well" a couple of times more and I said, "Yes," each time encouragingly.

"Well," he said again, "this fishing is clearly a thing that a father and a son would do together. No doubt why you've asked for it," he said quickly. "But, Mr. Jackson, actually..."

Billings's tone was much too cordial. He was choosing his words carefully. He wanted to make some point but did not wish to offend me. The positive DNA test had him on the defensive. Billings assumed that I would pursue a costly legal battle if my demands were not met.

"Actually what?" I said.

"I don't want to offend you..."

It struck me that I was Mr. Billings's worst nightmare. I was the son of Mr. Prescott, and I was, as best he could figure, a possible lunatic. He wanted this deal to happen, and he wanted it fast. "Please speak frankly, Mr. Billings."

"Mr. Prescott—and I too—think you really want more than what you've said." Billings sighed loudly. "Yes, I will be frank, as I have to say that it sounds like you might have the idea that through this fishing, some bond might form between you, and that afterward, you would expect, hope for..." He paused again.

"More," I completed his sentence.

"Yes," he said. "You're clearly an intelligent man."

"Thank you," I said evenly. Billings continued with the disappointments. He had no perception whatever of my intentions or me. "You think I am attempting to manipulate Mr. Prescott into a situation to get into his good graces, an alternative route to his money."

"Well..." He couldn't finish the sentence. He was still trying to come to an important point without scaring away the crazy man. *Actually*, I thought, *I shouldn't be so critical.* Motivation for something other than money or power was totally outside Billings's frame of reference. By his standards, I was indeed nuts.

"Mr. Billings, are you recording this conversation?"

Long pause.

"You know you have to tell me if you are," I said.

"We try to keep a record of all of our significant conversations."

I laughed. I had no idea why. "Okay, Mr. Billings, I'm going to give you one more thing that I don't have to. You want it on record that you have given me fair notice that Mr. Prescott does not wish a relationship with a long-lost son. He does this out of a sense of, shall we say, philanthropy, perhaps even pity. You want it recorded that I have been duly warned that should I renege on my promise, you can show to the court that you acted in good faith based on a promise I had given you."

Silence.

"Not bad, Mr. Billings. Good thinking," I said, returning his earlier patronization and then feeling immediately tacky about it. I had slipped into condescension and sarcasm with Billings. It was unprofessional, and I decided to be as respectful of him as I would anyone else. "Please rest assured. I formally and officially inform your recording device that I have no further expectations. I am at this moment, as best as I can tell, of sound mind in spite of the fact that I have had many years of counseling of which I am tired and anxious to draw to a conclusion. This meeting is that conclusion and is, I hope, the much-needed closure. But whether it is or is not, Mr. Prescott's obligations to this arrangement are fulfilled once the three hours are up. It's all I want from my father and, yes, I feel that I am owed it." I took a breath.

I noticed that my hand was no longer shaking. I had become tired of the game I had begun. The plan I had created just days ago could bring me face-to-face with my father by this time tomorrow. My throat felt like sandpaper, and I looked at the pitcher of water on my dresser. It was out of reach.

"And so it has to be fishing then?" Billings asked again, to my amazement.

"Fishing is what I thought of. Maybe it doesn't have to be fishing, but fishing is what I want now. I don't know. Maybe it shouldn't be fishing. Maybe baseball. Fathers do that with their sons, don't they? We could throw the ball back and forth—or maybe nothing. Maybe we should postpone the—"

"Fishing will be fine," Billings said. "Where shall we meet?"

"I assume that does not include you, Mr. Billings. I don't mean to be rude, but—"

"Of course. You and Mr. Prescott is what I meant," Billings said in his soft voice. "Could we send a car—I mean, could Mr. Prescott send a car and pick you up tomorrow afternoon at one?"

"What's the plan?"

"Mr. Prescott has a small cabin about ninety minutes southwest of Chicago. It has a pond there where, we believe, there are fish. We will also provide the poles."

"Thank you. That sounds fine."

"Not at all. Any problems with sending an attorney and a witness or two over to sign the papers tonight?"

"Without modifications?"

"I think you've thought of everything." He paused as if considering something. "Will you be having your attorney present?"

"Probably not."

I hung up the phone and immediately dialed Charles's number.

He seemed glad to hear from me. "What did the Changs say?"

"They not only were willing to help fully, they didn't even ask any questions."

"And the mayor?"

"It's done, Charles. This Detective Ryder probably has never even spoken to the mayor."

"And now he'll get a personal call."

The thought tickled us, and we both laughed about it. A long silence followed.

"How is it going with the solicitors?" Charles asked.

"Lawyers, Charles, we call them lawyers! This is America, and you are an American."

"Lawyers then," he said, overpronouncing the *R* defiantly. His voice became serious. "Well, good luck, old boy," Charles said.

I had the urge to put down the phone and run.

Chapter Seventeen

Same Day
Jason Young-Soo O'Leary
Liberal, Kansas

Charles had been right about going to a smaller airport in the Midwest. They had almost no security and were friendly and less suspicious. Yet as I stood in front of the Skyway Airlines' office manager of the Liberal, Kansas, airport and shook his hand, I felt my stomach turn upside down. It was, after all, my first crime since I had been in the streets of Korea, and I knew that if my father were alive, he would be frowning right now.

But I was not so sure that he would not have done the same thing. He would have done almost anything for Uncle Charles or Uncle Brent. It was a noble purpose, in a way. I would break a law that was intended to keep bad guys from doing bad things to nice people. But I was not doing a bad thing—I hoped, as Charles had kept me totally in the dark as to how this would accomplish his mission.

"So you're from Computer Aid Consultants?" The six-foot-four manager smiled, folded his arms, and looked down at me. We were standing in his office located around the corner of the main terminal, beside the men's bathroom. It seemed to be an excessively large office to hold only one desk, a computer terminal, and two wooden armchairs. There were deep scratches on the dark, wooden-paneled wall behind his high-backed burgundy chair.

I made a point of looking at his nametag, as though I didn't already know it. "Yes, Mr. Pritchard, I believe you got a message from the main office."

"Well, we got this." He opened up the top drawer of a badly scarred wooden desk and pulled out a slightly wadded sheet of paper. He handed it to me. I received it as though I had never seen it before, which, of course I had, before I sent it. Getting the Skyway Airlines' letterhead had been time consuming but not difficult. I had simply written a letter of complaint, and they had sent me a letter of apology. I scanned their letterhead and printed it out on my color printer. After a few telephone calls, Mr. Robert Pritchard had been identified as the manager to whom authorization letters should be submitted. The question now was, would he verify?

"It says the company is making random virus checks of local terminals and that we're supposed to assist you." He rested his hand on the top of the blinking computer terminal on his desk. Various memos, torn notes, paper clipped to other notes, and floppy disks were scattered around the keyboard, which was bright and new. "You think we have a virus?"

"It's routine," I said. "If we discover a virus, we will attempt to fix it, and then the company will probably want to launch a full examination of all terminals."

He looked at the paper again. Would he verify?

"Any questions, Mr. Pritchard?"

"Just call me Bob," he said, and he stepped away from his desk. "I guess you can use mine."

He walked around to the front. I moved to his spot. I sat down, felt a sharp sting, and immediately stood up and examined the seat.

Bob laughed. "The plastic seat has busted open. I usually sit a little to the left."

I sat down again, a little to the left.

"I can switch with one of these wooden ones, if you prefer."

"This is fine. Thank you." I pulled the keyboard around in front of me. I tapped the "space" key a few times, and the screen lit up.

A yellowed prompt blinked in the center. "Please enter your name."

I typed in Robert Pritchard.

Another yellow prompt began to blink immediately. "Please enter your password."

"I will need your password," I said, "or I need you to enter it for me."

Mr. Pritchard was silent for a few moments. "Do you need to be in the system to do this? We're not supposed to give out our passwords to anybody."

My throat constricted like I had eaten a persimmon. I fought the urge to swallow and reveal any possible nervousness. "Sorry. Have to be in the system to check it fully. Why don't I move while you enter the password?" I suggested. "That way you don't have to bend any company policies."

"Good idea." He nodded his head in agreement.

I stood up while he sat down, punched in a few letters, and pressed return. The screen flashed open to show "Welcome to Skyway Airlines Flight Information Center."

He offered me the seat again. "How long will this take?" he asked.

"About thirty minutes, "I said, "assuming that I don't find a virus."

"Want some coffee?"

"No, thank you. I just had some."

"I'll just leave you alone, then. I've got to give the ladies their orders." He laughed.

It must have been a joke, so I smiled. "Thank you. I'll find you if I need you."

He closed the door behind him. First I had to find a flight that had flown into Los Angeles on June 23 and another flight that flew out on June 25. I found three flights, looked at the passenger capacity, and then wrote down the information for one that had flown only half full.

I scrolled down to the passenger reservation and information screen and kept pressing the numbers until I got into the destinations. I typed in "Los Angeles" and then the city of origin that Charles had told me to enter.

I continued entering information as though I was making a reservation—flight, seat number, credit card information. I hesitated as I began to enter the name precisely according to Charles's instructions. This whole thing was strange, but Charles had been very persuasive. Still, it was my finger that was on the trigger. I typed each letter very slowly and, after thinking for a moment, pushed enter.

The last thing to enter was the date. I entered June 23 and then waited for the error message that almost immediately flashed.

"You have entered a date for a flight that has already been executed. Please enter another date."

I knew there was a way to enter a name on the flight that had already taken place—they had such a mechanism to correct errors—but I had to override the default system. There were several possible codes and protocols to do this, and, frankly, I had only a vague idea which one this system used. I pulled a notepad out of my pocket that contained several common and not-so-common protocols for such a case.

"Uh, sorry to interrupt." Mr. Pritchard had come in without me seeing him. "Well…my secretary reminded me that computer security is supposed to be pretty tight. She said I need to ask for your ID."

"Of course," I said, and I opened my wallet, taking out the ID I had carefully prepared a few days earlier.

He inspected it. "Okay, this looks fine." He handed it back to me. "Sorry to interrupt. But you know everybody has to be careful these days."

"Quite all right." I stuffed the ID back in my wallet. "Anything else?"

"No," he said, "my secretary is calling Mr. Spector, you know the guy who sent us the letter—you know…we have to," he said, almost apologetically.

I turned back to the computer, swallowed, and took a slow, deep breath. "Okay, but I have another appointment soon. Mind if I continue working while you verify?"

"Oh sure, no problem," he said, and he then left.

I began rapidly pushing the protocol sequence buttons. I began to shiver although I didn't know if it was from my sheer terror or from the air conditioning vent blowing directly on my head.

I entered two pages of protocols before the warning message disappeared and a new but not-so-threatening message took its place.

"You are about to override the date. This will permanently change records on the system. Are you sure you want to do this?"

I punched the "yes" key. Then to verify I had done what I hoped I had, I pulled up the June 23 and June 25 passenger list again. The name I had input was now registered in both—coach class, seat 22C. I exited the system.

My deed done, I was tempted to run out the door, but I didn't want to leave anybody suspicious if it could be avoided. There were still ways to trace my actions on this computer. Mr. Pritchard walked out of the men's bathroom. "So what's the verdict?" he asked me.

I was still so shaken from the experience that I didn't understand his question. "Verdict?"

"Are we clean? Do we have a virus?"

I recovered as best as possible and managed a smile. "You're clean, Mr. Pritchard. Would you mind signing this?" I handed him the phony invoice that I had prepared. "It just says that I came and checked your computer."

"Sure, sure." He signed the paper swiftly.

"So I guess Mr. Spector verified for you?"

"Uh." He thought for a second. "No. Couldn't get hold of him. These corporate guys always keep us on hold. I told her not to waste any more time." He smiled and shook my hand. "You've got an honest face."

"Thank you, Bob," I said, but I couldn't look him in the eyes.

Chapter Eighteen

(Next Day) July 31, 1993

Brent Jackson

Chicago, Illinois

I didn't interpret the fact that my father had sent a limousine to pick me up as anything else but facilitation. Certainly his chauffeur would know the directions better than a taxi driver. There would be no lost time.

The car glided into the slow-moving traffic and maintained a westward direction. I felt underdressed, although I had spent a good hour the night before finally deciding on blue jeans and a red, plaid, long-sleeve shirt. It was Nicole's favorite combination on me.

I pressed the metal button on the console. A panel flipped open, revealing a small collection of CDs—Dvorak, Brahms, Bach—the great composers. The previously unresponsive driver turned his attention toward my wanderings. I ignored him and flipped through the disks as though I had permission—a few Broadway musical numbers, and the last, a collection of Gilbert and Sullivan. I considered and then immediately rejected the temptation to slip in Schubert's "Ave Maria." It fit my mood but could easily send me over the edge as well. This was probably the only time I would ever meet my father, but for a reason that I would never be able to verbalize, I wanted to make a good impression.

I wondered if Rod had flying alligators visit his room. I wondered if he prayed at night for his father, or if he prayed that his mother would find him a father and that every man she brought into the living room was a disappointment because it wasn't him. I wondered if he had realized that not one of those men could possibly have lived up to the father of his dreams.

The countryside was sparse, few trees and no sign of water anywhere. The Mercedes slowed down and turned onto a bare gravel road where a solitary, weather-beaten, wooden mailbox leaned. The driver sat up straight and looked over the hood, slowly moving to the right and left of potholes, keeping his speed low enough so that no gravel struck the sides of the car. There were no houses, and save for a few trees along the side of the road that appeared to have been planted in rows, there was no sign of civilization. Soon we were passing through a grove of trees so thick that it seemed as though we had driven into the great timber divide.

I wondered, *Did Daniel pray at night for a father?*

The road began to turn downward, and within moments we were in such a decline that the driver began to rest his foot on the brake, going even slower than before as the road curved to the right and then sharply to the left. Trees blocked the bottom of the road, but after one final turn to the right again, the driver accelerated, and we smoothly drove out onto a dirt road. The trees backed away, and we were driving through a long meadow.

I had descended into a nature wonderland that any movie director would only dream of, but this was real. Tall oak and pine trees surrounded this completely hidden valley; bright red and yellow wildflowers grew randomly in the field; a walking path zigzagged off into the woods to the right. The cabin, a two-story structure built completely out of logs, rose in front of us.

So this is the noncorporate side of Prescott, I thought—a quiet place, a Shenandoah, for contemplation, rejuvenation; a place to heal, perhaps to exorcise regrets. This was his Maugham's table.

The car stopped, and the driver opened the door for me. He pointed in the direction of the cabin. I walked ahead and turned around for further directions, but he was leaning up against the

Mercedes, lighting a cigarette. I turned around again and found the winding path up to the cabin.

The cabin was built against the wall of this small valley. I assumed that by now my father was watching me from somewhere. I felt a frown stretch across my forehead and concentrated on relaxing my face. Then it seemed too relaxed, like I might be projecting a bored or uncomfortable image. I added a slight smile—not too cheerful, just enough to show some degree of self-confidence.

I came to the base of some stairs, literally carved out of stone that led to the screened doorway above. They were steep, and I watched to make sure I would not slip. I leaned forward to get a better look at the many round-shaped objects embedded in the stones. "Fossils," I whispered with surprise. "Fossils."

"Ammonites, to be exact," a voice said from above, and I jerked my head up so fast I nearly lost my balance. "Over a hundred million years old."

He was standing on the other side of the screen door but turned and walked away. "Come on in," he said, not offering to open the door for me.

I pushed the door and entered a screened-in porch area. A ceiling fan spun slowly against vaulted beams of the ceiling. Wicker chairs were scattered around simple tables that were covered with countless tiny toy soldiers. There were random things hanging on the wall, large nails placed in the wood and on some of those Salvation Army jackets that had seen better days. There was another door to the right, which apparently led to the living area of the cabin. A sleeper-sofa was pushed against the back wall. I wondered who slept out here at night.

"I know," I said.

"You know what?" My father turned around and looked at me, starting from the top and slowly working his eyes down to my shoes.

I waited until he got to the shoes to answer. "About ammonites," I said.

He looked at me doubtfully. His face was much thinner than I expected. His combed-back hair was platinum white. *And there is a lot of it*, I thought, with some odd relief.

"Cephalopods class—many legs." I managed to get this out in one breath.

"Hmm," he said, and then he abruptly stepped forward and extended his hand. "Mason Prescott."

"Brent Jackson," I said. He shook my hand in a quick, firm gesture and then released his grip immediately and stepped back until both feet were side by side. He stood up straight and motionless, slipped his hands in the back pockets of his jeans, and stared at me.

"So you know something about fossils, do you?"

There was something about the way he spoke. I suppressed a mild impulse to click my heels together and salute. Instead, I took a gulp of air and said, "I took a zoology class in college by a professor whose interest was more in dead things than living ones. I suppose his enthusiasm was contagious. I've liked fossils ever since."

His eyes were green—like mine—but I hoped mine carried more emotion than his did. His skin was so heavily tanned that I was surprised that he did not have more wrinkles around his eyes and in the cheeks. He was appropriately casual. Besides blue jeans, he wore black hiking shoes and a tan, two-button Hugo Boss shirt. His chest was large and his stomach flat. My father worked out.

He turned to his left and lifted up one of the jackets. There were two fishing poles leaning on the wall behind it. Below them were two tackle boxes—one large and one small. He picked up the small one and handed one of the poles to me. "Well, here you are." He looked at his watch. "It's two o'clock."

Duly noted, I thought. *We shall have three hours and no more.* That was okay with me.

I followed him out the door and down the winding path. We walked silently. He did not explain where we were going nor did I ask. The path was well cleared through the thick woods, and after only fifteen minutes, I began to notice the musty smell of water before turning another jag in the road to see the a large pond directly in front of us. Trees and large rocks abounded. We sat down under an old oak tree with a branch that extended out over the water. A rope with several knots hung down limply from the tree.

"Take what you like out of here." He opened up the tackle box to reveal an assortment of spinners, spoons, and brown, plastic worms. I carefully selected a silver spinner and tied it to the end. He already had a worm on his and cast it out as far as it would go, which wasn't so far.

"Is it better to use worms here?" I asked.

"I have no idea."

"What do you catch here?"

"I have never caught anything here." He looked at me out of the corner of his eye. "I don't fish."

On that thought, I cast my line out as far as it would go. It landed somewhere near his. We sat in silence for a while, and I wondered if he felt as miserable as I did. As I cast my line over and over, I turned my head and stole glimpses of him. At a closer look, minuscule, crisscrossed lines were visible on his face, as though a tiny pencil had drawn them there.

I pointed at the rope. "I guess your kids used to play on that."

"My kids rarely came up here with me," he said. "It's probably the work of the caretaker's kid."

I pulled my line in slowly, wiggling it a little, like I had seen them do on fishing shows. Unintentionally, I sighed out loud. He jerked his line and turned toward me. His face was flushed, and he was angry.

"I don't know what you hope to be happening here. But let's get this straight right now. It ain't gonna happen."

Well, something is happening, I thought. "What do you mean?" I looked away from him toward the line I was slowly pulling toward me.

"I wish you would stop with your games. It won't get you anywhere." He spun his line like he was reeling in a garden hose. "I'm only here because fifteen damned attorneys said they would quit if I didn't."

Okay, better than not talking at all. We are definitely communicating, I mused. "Thanks," I said, and I became instantly aware that the butterflies in my stomach had flown away. "Thanks for your frank comments. We can just sit here quietly until our three hours are done if you would like."

He started to say something and then closed his mouth suddenly. He cast his line out and reeled it in so fast that a fish would have needed a jet ski to catch it.

"You've opened up a big, stinking door that we would all have been better off leaving closed," he said finally.

"Perhaps for you." I pulled my line in and cut off the spinner. "Not for me."

"What is it you want, then?"

I selected a furry-looking spoon with three tiny hooks. "The truth."

It was his turn to sigh heavily while he pulled his line up out of the water. He lifted his pole, and his worm dangled above us. "What truth?"

"I'd like to get to that, if you're up to it. I'd like to ask the questions every son wants to ask a father who left him," I said.

He laid the pole beside him and sat down on the ground. "Mind if we sit for a while?"

I sat down beside him.

He folded his arms over his knees and looked directly at me. "Why the devil didn't you just call me directly and ask to speak to me? Why did you have to get the legal whores involved?"

"I tried to. And if I had been able to reach you, would you have talked to me? Would your attorneys have let you talk to me?" I looked back at him.

He watched me for a minute and then shook his head. "No. They wouldn't have."

I tied the red, furry thing to the end of my line. "And even if you had, you certainly wouldn't have agreed to see me in this setting, would you?"

He waved his arm around. "This!" he roared. "Are you really getting something out of this? Sitting here and fishing with me?"

I shrugged. "It's what I wanted."

He squinted his eyes and looked at me as though for he first time. "And you usually get what you want?"

"I try."

A couple of ducks flew out of a thicket and landed in the water. They swam gracefully to the center and then, in one splash, did that odd thing that ducks do where they stick their heads in the water and turn upside down, tail feathers and webbed feet kicking in the air.

He chuckled, and I turned my head to see what a smile looked like on him. "Well, in that regard you are a bit of a chip off the old block."

I cast my line out again farther than I had before. "So you admit it?"

"Sure I admit it," he said. "My lawyers said that that little document of yours puts me completely out of danger."

I nodded. "Good. Perhaps you can be at ease now."

"It's not going to work."

"What's not going to work?"

"Well, we have established that we both like fossils, we both get what we want, we're both shrewd negotiators, and I admit I'm impressed by how you brought me, a billionaire CEO, to his knees—I don't mind saying that, even if it's only for three hours. But it's not going to win me over." He frowned. "You are a fox trying to con a fox. It's three now. Two hours and this long-lost reunion with your old dad is over."

I was about to protest just one more time but stopped. I hated to admit it, but he was right. Somewhere down in the place where you don't like to admit things to yourself, I had wanted more than just these three hours. I had wanted, in spite of my protestations, this to be the beginning of a relationship with my father. It had taken my father's unflinching language to jostle that out of me. But in the same thought, I realized I was at least getting the bare essential of what I needed. I had met him. I was now seeing him, listening to the sound of his voice, and learning all the things about him that might someday help me understand myself.

Stop it, I said to myself. *Just get through this, and analyze it later.* "Fine," I said. "You have made your point clearly. Now can you relax?"

"I only relax when I'm alone," he said, but he pulled his brown worm up and cast it out in the water again. The ducks, now finished with their splash dance, gave up on the fish and flew back to an area in the bushes across the river from us.

After about ten minutes of concentrated silence, he cleared his throat. "You can ask your questions," he said.

"Thank you." I did not look away from my line. "First, I would like to know why you left."

"I wasn't in love with your mother. Next question."

My throat began to burn, and I wished that we had brought soft drinks down to the river. "Second, did you know that I was born? Did you know you had a son?"

"Yes."

"And why didn't you contact me?"

"You are using the word *contact* instead of *abandon*," he said. "That's very kind of you. But it is clear we both like frankness. I abandoned you. Why don't you ask me that way?"

The butterflies came swooping back, but my voice did not give away my feelings. "Very well. Why did you abandon me?"

“That’s better.” He nodded his head in a gesture as though I had just performed well for him. “I was young, and my business was budding. I did not have time for a wife—certainly did not have time for a son.”

“You weren’t even curious?”

“Ah, yes—a little curious. But my brain has always been bigger than my heart. That’s why I’m rich.” He looked at me with a mixture of sympathy and disapproval. “It appears that is one thing you did not get from me. You know you could have just as easily gotten millions out of this—maybe even your twenty million, without ever going to court.”

“Twenty million would not have gotten me this, would it?” I felt my hand begin to shake again, and I stood up to mask it. I drew my rod back then jerked it forward, and in the same motion pressed on the reel. It seemed like several seconds before I heard the splash as it hit the water. It was my best cast so far.

“Did you ever think about me?”

“Now and then, sure. I’m not a monster. But I got married, had my own kids.”

“I see. Then, there was no desire—”

“No. None.”

It was three thirty, and I was ready to go home. But at about six million dollars an hour or so, I decided I would take them all. I had given up on fish, but I was grateful for the activity. Mr. Prescott remained sitting and placed his rod down on the ground again.

“You know something, kid?”

Considering the fact that I was thirty-seven, his remark was almost affectionate. “No, what?” I responded.

“You put too much stock in this father stuff. You’re beginning to make me feel bad.”

“Gosh, I’m sorry,” I said, and I immediately regretted the sarcasm in my voice. I was here to learn—period.

“I never had much of a father either.”

I paused and looked down at him. He was staring at a school of minnows playing in the water near us. "I mean he supported me and all," he said. "But he was never home…always at the office." His voice drifted away and then came back abruptly. "What I am saying is that it didn't hurt me, and it doesn't seem to have to hurt you."

"I see." I sat down on the ground beside him. "Thanks for the advice. I understand you have a son and a daughter?"

"Yeah," he said. "Pretty grown, don't see 'em much, unless they come around for money." His formerly crisp northern intonation had begun to convert to a woodsy accent, sort of like you might expect to find in a small country town in the Midwest.

"And this is a satisfactory relationship?"

"Don't much matter." He picked up a straw and began to chew on it. I stared with fascination. He turned around, looked at me looking at him, and sat up straight. "I mean it doesn't matter to me. It's not important. I raised them, and now they can make their own lives."

"So you did feel a responsibility to raise them."

He turned to me and spat out his straw. "I raised them because when I had them, I could. When you were born, I wasn't able, wasn't ready, didn't want to, whatever you want to call it."

"Well," I said, "I guess that concludes my questions." I laid my pole on the ground and leaned back on my elbows. The sun had reached a point just behind us where it struck the water at an angle and turned the river blue. The two ducks squabbled on the other side of the riverbank, and I wondered where the rest of the flock was.

"I'd be willing to share a tip with you, however," he said.

"A stock tip?" The wind began to pick up and created little waves in the center.

"No. A life tip."

"I'm all ears."

"Well." He sat and turned to me, and for just a moment, his eyes were kind, and I thought, *For just this moment, he looks like a father talking to his son.* "What you follow follows you," he said.

"Please go on."

"That's it." The expression vanished, and he turned up his hands. "You should be able to get it from there."

"You are telling me that I have to go after what I want."

"That's right. Like most effective principles, it sounds overly simple. But it works. You want control of a business, you pursue it until it's yours. You want a million dollars, you follow the money. It'll wind up in your lap. Fame? Nothing is out of reach." He slapped both thighs, as if emphasizing his point.

"Thanks," I said. "What you follow follows you. I'll remember that." And then. "I'm finished with my questions now. Thank you."

"You've got to go for what you want." He was breathing heavily.

"I understand."

"You ready to quit? You still have an hour."

"Can we take the rest of the time and fish for just a while more?"

"It's your hour," he said.

"Thank you," I said, and I pulled out my rod. He followed suit, and we both cast out in the water.

I looked over at his face and knew that the shape in the night would never be formless again. As he pulled his line in and knew the hard part was over, he almost looked serene, and I imagined that he might even be content. It appeared that he was enjoying these last few moments that we had together—companionship without further obligation. That's what I believed.

I tried to imagine myself small and him big, and I tried to imagine that he had just taken my rod and worked out the tangles and then he had shown me how to tie the knot on the hook. I hadn't tied it right. He cut the knot and showed me again, this time taking my small fingers with his large ones and wrapping them around and around the line until, like magic, the knot pulled in so securely that it would only yield to a sharp hunter's knife.

And in my dream there was a tug on my line, and he dropped his rod and began to call out excited directions. This was my first fish. He yelled, "Pull it in!" And then he called to me, "Breathe! Breathe!" because in my excitement, I had forgotten to. And he laughed as I pulled out the biggest fish I had ever seen, almost the size of my hand, and he grabbed me around the shoulders and yelled, "You did it!" And then he got really serious and pointed out how small it was and that it was probably just a kid like me and maybe I should send it back to its mom and someday it would get really, really big and I could catch it again. And I was sad at that, but my dad always knew best, and so after he gently held its mouth and cut the hook, he handed it to me, and I, following his example, gently lowered it into the water. After we both watched it scramble to safety, he said regretfully and in the most sorrowful tone that he wished he had brought his camera because that was my first fish.

But the time was over, and I stood in front of the car and shook his hand and looked at his cold green eyes and thought that it had, after all, been an important experience, and I had learned at least one twenty-million-dollar truth.

A far worse thing than being abandoned by your father is being raised by one without a heart.

Chapter Nineteen

Sixteen Days Later (August 16, 4:30 P.M.)

Jason Young-Soo O'Leary

Los Angeles, California

Even through the thick LA airport crowds, Detective John Ryder was not hard to recognize. His dark-gray suit was ordinary enough, but he had the critical eyes of an umpire and a forehead creased with a permanent frown. He was clutching a large, golden-embossed certificate under one arm and a large box, wrapped in bright-white paper, under the other. When he saw me, there was something else in his eyes. Disdain, perhaps, though I didn't know why I should deserve it. When he spoke, it became clear to me.

"You the Chinese boy who's supposed to be helping me?"

"Yes," I said, thinking, *Why not? Dato is acting as the Malaysian Sultan. I'll be the Chinese boy.* "I'm the sultan's…uh… honorable assistant."

"Well then," Ryder snapped. "You're the one I want to give a piece of my mind."

"Excuse me?"

"I'm only doing this because I was ordered to." Ryder's voice was loud enough that a few people turned their heads and looked for a moment. "The captain ordered me, and the mayor ordered him, and for some godforsaken reason, some rich Chinese family named Chang asked him. Why would they do that? Why me?"

"I do not know," I said. "Perhaps you helped a friend of theirs once."

"Chinese? I don't have anything to do with them." He stopped, looked away, and said, "No offense, you understand. Our paths just never cross."

"I see."

"I sure never expected to be a frigging host to some Chinese big shot from Malaysia."

"Actually," I said, "he is Malay."

"Whatever." He looked at his watch. "Just what is a frigging sultan anyway?"

I resisted the temptation to clip my sentences and singsong them into the stereotypical Chinese speech. Perhaps I could stick my teeth out a little. This man would be excellent sport—and deserved it. But that was not my job. My job was to connect the chief investigator of Al Renfield's murder with Dato. Dato would then do the rest. "A sultan," I explained, "is like a king—except that he controls a province instead of a country. Actually these provinces once were countries. Now sultans rotate, in Malaysia, to be king and—"

"What the…? I got it already," Ryder interrupted. "I didn't want a whole freaking history lesson."

"I'm sorry," I said evenly, and I fell into my role again. "I am wondering if you know how to behave with a sultan?"

"What?" Ryder looked around as if to find someone to share the joke with. The lobby of the airport was filled with briskly walking passengers, pausing only to examine the bright schedule boards on the TV monitors hanging from ceilings. He stepped forward, actually pushing his chest out, like a cartoon character on TV. "Do you know who I am?"

A large number of possibilities floated about in my head, but they were all in Korean, so I said simply, "I think you are the man who is to escort the most honorable sultan today."

"Escort? Listen here. I'm a detective. While I'm out playing nursemaid to your sultan, a bunch of criminals are getting away." Ryder made a sweeping gesture that ended with a finger pointing to his chest, but as he did so, the gift slipped from under his arm. He spun around, caught it, but not before it had snagged on his belt and broken open some sort of container. A dozen bullets fell from his body, clinking noisily on the tile floor around him.

Nearby passengers paused and pointed. Ryder remained frozen, the box pressed to his stomach. I knelt down and slowly picked them up, one by one. When I humbly handed them back to him in my cupped hand, the bad little voice from somewhere inside me escaped. "Shall I throw them at the bad guys…while you holler 'bang'"?

Ryder grabbed them out of my hand and furiously stuffed them into his pockets.

"Is it permitted to have those in the airport?" I said in a low voice.

"I have a permit," Ryder said, nearly losing the box again. "If it's any of your business."

I took a deep breath. I would not be distracted from my goal. All I had to do was get him to the restaurant with Dato.

And then Ryder added, "This is America. There are many things here I'm sure you can't possibly understand."

On the other hand, just a little sport wouldn't do any real harm.

There was a stirring of the passengers just ahead, beyond the security gates. I chose that moment to lean forward. "You have a very important job here. Do you think you can handle it?"

"I think I can manage," Ryder mumbled.

"What is under your arm?"

"It's a gift."

"A gift? For who?"

"Who do you think, Mr. Honorable Assistant?"

"Not the sultan."

"Why are you looking at me like that? Listen, kid"—Ryder pointed one thumb at his chest—"I'm the American here, you guys are—"

"But the gift is white."

Ryder scrunched up his faced. "Oh really? Hadn't noticed. Of course it's white. The mayor sent me this vase with a note to have it wrapped—"

"It's death!" I feigned hysteria, waving my arms and yelling.

"Have you lost your—"

"White in our culture means that you want the sultan to die!"

"What?"

"Get rid of it. Hurry. Before he sees it."

Ryder held it away from his body as though it might be ticking.

"I think he's coming. Hurry!" I clenched my fists dramatically and looked over my shoulder.

"What the—"

"You'll insult him. The mayor will be furious."

A small lady with a white umbrella walked by. "Here, ma'am," Ryder said offering it to her, "take this."

She gasped, held her umbrella up toward him as she backed away, and ran the other direction to a security officer.

"He tried to give me a box!" She waved her finger at Ryder, who had begun to stuff the box in the wastebasket.

"What are you doing, sir?" the security officer yelled. "Everyone, stand back."

"Relax." Ryder waved his badge in the air. "I'm a cop."

"What's going on, sir?" the security officer asked. "What's in the box?"

"I'm here to meet the sultan of Malaysia," Ryder said, and then he pointed to me, though I had become very interested in a musical theatre poster. "That Chinaman thinks it means death. I'm humoring him, okay?"

"I think you'd better come with me, sir." The security officer started to reach for Ryder.

Ryder opened his jacket, revealing his badge. "I'm having a really bad day," he said, and he then picked up the white box out of the wastebasket and shoved it into the arms of the security officer. "Take this and give it to your wife. It's a really expensive vase!"

The derogative term *Chinaman* was still spinning around in my head. I had not heard that for many years. And this from an officer of the law. I motioned for him to come. Ryder rolled his eyes but then shuttled over to my side. "He is coming. Get ready," I said.

"Ready for what?" Ryder shook his head and made no attempt to conceal the contempt on his face.

Dato had appeared. He was wearing a conservative three-piece suit, carried a small brown bag, and also held in his hand a branch of orchids, which, I guessed, he had purchased in the Malaysian airport. He saw me and began to approach us.

"It's him!" I whispered.

"What? You've gotten me all worked up. This is ridiculous." And then he added, with some disappointment in his voice, "I thought he would be wearing a crown."

I tugged at his arm. "Okay. Prostrate yourself."

"How's that?" Ryder tried to pull his arm away from my grip.

"Quickly. Down on the floor." I used my right hand to push on Ryder's back.

"This is ridiculous," Ryder protested. "I don't prostrate myself for—"

I wrapped one arm around Ryder's waist and used my calves to push slowly against his legs. Ryder was strong, but I had the advantage of total surprise—shock, I would venture to say, as I looked at the expression on his face.

Ryder stumbled and slowly sank toward the floor. He had to put out one arm to catch himself until he was finally down on his hands and knees. I wrapped myself around him like we were Greco Roman wrestlers. Ryder was handicapped by the mayor's certificate stuffed under his left arm, but he reached back with his right hand to try to pry my fingers loose. I strengthened my grip.

"You…you're fighting with me," Ryder said in disbelief as he turned his head and looked at the many legs of the people who had stopped to watch.

I pressed him harder. "The mayor will be proud of you. He would do this." I gave Ryder's knee a firm kick.

Ryder collapsed, face down on the floor.

"Spread your arms and legs out," I ordered. Ryder, confused and overcome, submitted.

Dato came running up and looked at me in astonishment. I mouthed to Dato that this guy was a "jerk." Of course Dato, the king of practical jokes, understood what I was doing and nodded. Dato patted him on the shoulder and then said, straight-faced, "Thank you for your kind welcome. You may get up now."

Ryder stood, avoiding the bewildered looks of the people around us, and brushed off. "Here, Your Majesty," Ryder said, and he offered the sultan the certificate. "You are now officially mayor of Los Angles for a day." He held it out and waited, but Dato merely stared at him.

I leaned forward and whispered urgently into his ear, "Both hands. Both hands!"

Ryder's left hand flew upward and grabbed the certificate. Dato bowed slightly and took it.

Ryder let out a long, slow breath. "Okay," he said, "the car is this way." He started toward the car. At that moment Dato, anxious to join in on the fun, jabbed me in the side and whispered a quick instruction to me.

After walking a few yards, Ryder looked back. Dato and I were standing in the same spot where he had left us. Ryder, with slumped shoulders, walked back slowly. "Is there something else I can help you with?"

I took him by the elbow and escorted him slowly away from the sultan. "You do not know the protocol for moving the sultan through crowds?"

"They didn't teach that in police academy."

"Well, it's very simple," I said. "You must walk in front of him and clear the way."

Ryder grabbed the paper. "Only clear the way. You mean I don't have to sing or dance naked for him?"

"We'd prefer it if you didn't." I took the orchid branch from Dato. "Here, you will also want to carry these."

"What are these?"

"Orchids."

"Of course they are."

"You'd better get moving." I smiled and shook Ryder's hand. "I'm going to run ahead to the restaurant—to make sure everything is ready."

Ryder looked at the orchids, looked at the sultan, and then back to the orchids again. He looked at me sadly. "Why don't you do this?"

I lowered my head. "I am not an important person. You are a great person in this city. Only someone like you can have this honor."

Ryder turned slowly around and stuck the branch in the air. He walked forward as the sultan followed behind, nodding at the interested travelers who had stopped to watch.

"Make way for the sultan." Ryder's voice was robotic. "Make way for the sultan."

Same Day, Three Hours Later (7:30 p.m.)

Brent Jackson

Los Angeles, California

There is a great difference between suspecting and knowing.

Once the taxi had dropped me off, I walked through the gates, as per Charles's instructions. An apparently empty gray van was parked under the covered driveway. I did not ring the bell but pushed open the double doors and went through the house. It was as I had imagined, a house fit for a movie star.

I knew that Rod was not present; Charles had gotten him out of the house for the evening. He was told not to ask questions and could return the following morning, when all would be clear. I imagined that must have been difficult for Rod, a man who likes answers. But I knew Charles's persuasive abilities. I had a lot of questions myself, yet here I was.

I passed through the large entry, under the skylight, and into the dining area, where I found the double glass doors. A grunt escaped me as I slid one door open and then moved around a potted tree where I looked up, really for the first time, and saw where I was.

The garden, the pool, and the palm trees all seemed completely ordinary—compared to the sight of Charles, wearing a filthy shirt, old jeans, and roughneck boots; he had turned toward my direction. He nodded in acknowledgment of my arrival, but I did not return the simple greeting. In the first moment of looking at him, he confirmed my worst fears.

He had one shovel in each of his hands.

He stood there quietly and let me survey the scene. Caladiums had been pulled up gently by their bulbs and were resting on their sides near tall red amaryllis. The roughed-up earth that had once been their home was slightly behind Charles. To his side, laid out as though ready for a picnic, were three buckets, a man-sized plastic bag, six medium-sized bags of dirt, and two pairs of rubber gloves.

Everything in the garden began to seem three times more colorful than it had just a moment before. I felt like I was standing in water, looking out of a large aquarium. Flowers seemed to be poking out of every shrub and bush; tiny, spiderlike grass stems grew everywhere under my feet.

I found myself wondering—absently, irrationally, miserably—what the buckets were for.

Charles wiped his forehead on one arm, leaving a dark stain on his forehead. Without moving forward, he stretched out his hand and extended the handle of one of the shovels to me. I walked the extra ten feet and paused in front of it. I was already feeling the humidity on my back, so, like Charles, I unbuttoned my outer shirt, tossed it flat on a delicately carved hedge, and accepted the shovel. Charles nodded twice and turned his back to me, stuck the shovel in the ground, and stood on it. I walked around to the other side of him, stuck my shovel in the ground, and lifted a clump of soil.

I did my best to not betray stress or tension. I had agreed to help, and I was there, after all now, to dig up a body that Rod Chambers had buried. I wondered for a little while if Rod knew we were here, but I doubted it. I knew that anyone could walk through those double doors—the maid, the gardener, a delivery boy. The possibility didn't seem to matter, so engaged I was in the activity at my feet. As the sky seemed to darken, a new curiosity, the possibility of rain began to arrive. Soon the quiet but surreal sounds of the quick stabs of the shovel into the soil faded murkily into the background of my focus.

After one hour, maybe more, the mound of dirt behind each of us had grown higher. Charles, glistening in his own sweat, had begun to pause, just an infinite second before each plunge of the shovel. My hesitation followed his, echoing his dread. We knew that we were near, that any careless jab of the spade could mutilate our target further—a concern that I could not begin to explain logically. As we couldn't even guess which direction the body lay, we worked in a circular manner, large enough that we should eventually find some part of it, small enough that we would not expend excess energy by digging too far outside the essential boundaries.

Save for a partial moon, rising somewhere behind me, and a few lights from the interior, we worked in total darkness. LA air is sharp and clear as it approaches autumn with the smog pushed west over the ocean. The early darkness I had observed had covered the stars to the west of us. But there appeared to be no further activity. Perhaps we would be saved from the rain, which was rare this time of year and then usually only in the form of sudden gully washers.

My eyes were sharper than I was ever aware of them being before. As the hole deepened, the shovel, heavy with soil, had to be lifted higher. We groaned and gasped loudly.

My shovel hit something new—too soft for a rock, but perhaps too hard for our target. I stopped and squinted but could see no revealing shape. Charles stopped too and watched while I scratched at it with the tip of my shovel.

"Is that it?" I said, noticing the odd feeling of hearing the sound of my voice for the first time that evening.

"I've got a flashlight." Charles dropped his shovel and reached for something out behind him.

"Maybe we'd better not…" I started, but the piercing light, like the rays from a lighthouse beacon, had already filled the rapidly expanding hole between our feet. *It looks nothing like a grave*, I thought, *with its uneven surface and rough, shoddy edges. More like the aftermath of a storm, where a tree has blown over, roots and all, and left a gaping hole that has once been its home.*

"Hold this."

Charles handed me the flashlight and dropped to his knees with his head so close to the mark he cast a shadow over it. I squatted down beside him, aiming the light as helpfully as I could. He brushed the ground with the side of his hand. Soon he had uncovered some kind of cloth, probably a blanket. Being careful not to go too deep, he brushed around it further, sometimes picking up clumps of dirt and tossing them behind him.

Charles stood up and without looking at me drew an oval in the air above the hole. "His body's probably lying this way," he said.

I now knew why I had been so comfortable, so protective of our silence. I had not wanted to hear the sounds of such words. I stood there that August evening in the city of no seasons, in

Rod Chambers's back yard; the long shadow of the fortress wall on three sides, the cascading tiled roof catching moonlight and bending it in odd, psychedelic shapes; the smell of fresh dirt and salty sweat—all of it flaming the senses that I had checked in at the door. I turned the light toward Charles, who instantly covered his eyes with his hand and then peeked through his fingers in my direction.

"Charles," I said. "What are we going to do with this body?"

7:30 P.M.

Jason Young-Soo O'Leary

"So tell me, Mr. Detective Ryder, what cases are you working on that might be of interest?" Dato asked.

Ryder wadded his linen napkin and dropped it on the table next to the empty dessert tray. It was clear that he was uncomfortable in such formal surroundings. He had stared at all the silverware that surrounded his plate and didn't bother hiding his displeasure that all the courses had not been served on one plate. I felt the only thing he really enjoyed had been the dessert, full of cream, apples, and nuts. That, however, had made him sleepy. He yawned at Dato's persistent efforts to keep a conversation going.

"Oh, several things," he said, stifling a yawn. "Always got something going on."

I stared into the bottom of his wine glass. Dato had not drunk wine but had instead sipped on small, thimble-sized coffee cups throughout the meal. "Any armed robberies?" Dato enunciated each syllable strategically, like he was recording a language tape.

"I've currently got about fifteen cases I'm working on." Ryder looked at his watch for the third time since we had sat down to eat.

Dato slowly rubbed the top of his head, an old habit, I guessed, developed back when he had hair. "I'm really quite interested. What's your most puzzling case?"

"None puzzling. They just have pieces missing," Ryder said dismissively.

I pressed further. "Seems like I remember seeing your name in the paper." I took a large gulp of wine, examined the empty glass, and poured another. "In connection with some movie star."

Ryder looked at me and rose slightly in his chair. The corners of his mouth crept upward. He hid the smile by coughing into his fist. He was clearly flattered when people saw his name in the news. "Yeah, that's right," he said casually. "I'm investigating the disappearance of Al Renfield, Rod Chambers's movie agent. That's what you saw."

He pulled his chair up and leaned forward. He looked around us as though there might be listeners. "Normally, I'm over at his house checking things out. I've been watching him every night for weeks. Personal interest of mine." He looked at us with a sad expression. "Sorry to say I'll have to cut the evening short." He winked. "Duty calls. I need to run back over there and keep—"

"Ah," said Dato. "Charming young man, this Rod Chambers."

"You must mean a different Rod Chambers," Ryder growled. "Been a pain in the butt every time I talked to him."

"Has that been your experience? He was a charming child," he said. "At least, I was always fond of him."

"Fond of him?" Ryder cocked one suspicious eye toward Dato. "You knew him?"

"For a long time. But I always felt sorry for him—typical Hollywood family circumstances, you know."

Ryder leaned forward, placing both elbows on the table. "Family? His mother died several years ago."

"Well, yes." The Malaysian frowned. "But..."

This was my cue to lean forward and touch Dato's arm. He turned toward me.

"Excuse me, Most Honorable One. But perhaps such events could be considered private?"

Dato nodded. "Of course you're right." Then he turned back to Ryder. "Well, anyway, it's none of my business. Tell me about another case."

Ryder leaned back in his chair and studied us. I couldn't tell if we had been too obvious or too subtle, but then Ryder suddenly spoke up. "Now, Sultan"—he leaned back in his chair—"if you know something, you've got to share it with me. This little social dinner has just become official."

Chapter Twenty

Same Day (10:30 P.M.)

Brent Jackson

"We're going to bury him in the desert."

Charles paused to see that I had heard him and then bent over and moved his spade to the edge of the hole, stepping on it with less force than he had done so in the past. I watched him for a moment and then circled around to his opposite to do the same.

"We'll put him in the van and drive him to the desert tonight," Charles said without looking up. "But we have to hurry. It's imperative we finish this before Rod gets back."

I pressed my foot hard on the edge of the shovel and worked to keep up with Charles. We pushed easily on the soil but tossed it behind us with all our energy. There were no stones but plenty of hardened, dark clumps of mud, layered by the rains of late. The wooden handles stung our hands so that Charles and I had to occasionally pause to squeeze our fingers into tight fists, then open them wide, temporarily relieving the stretched muscles that were more accustomed to tapping on keyboards than digging. But Charles, panting deeply, pushed forward with the intensity of a dog burrowing into a rabbit hole. Caught in his inspiration, I ignored my straining muscles, and, shovel by shovel, we began to outline the length of a man in the soil.

At last we stood back, leaned on our shovels, and examined our work. The surface of the blanket, now fully exposed, was uncannily smooth. It did not allow any features of a man's face, his chest, or his feet. However, part of it was wider than the rest, like a mummy's sarcophagus, and left little doubt of the arrangement. Charles released his shovel, and it fell to the ground. He stepped behind him and reached for something in the dark that he then tossed to me. A pair of rubber gloves landed at my feet.

Lubricated from the oily perspiration on my palms, the gloves slipped around my fingers immediately. Charles fiddled for a few seconds with the zipper of the body bag, then spread it open widely, and with both arms outstretched, we laid it near the grave. He stood next to what looked like the upper torso of the body.

"We need to reach down here and each grab a shoulder," he said. "We'll pull the body out and slide it onto this plastic bag."

He made it sound so simple, and so I, with knees quaking, obediently stood beside him. We both bent over and began to slip our fingers into the moist soil, searching for shoulders. I was very grateful for the gloves. Soon I had found something slippery.

"Plastic." Charles had felt it too. "Must have wrapped him in garbage sacks. That's good."

"That's good?"

"If we're lucky, he'll still be all in one piece."

That even more horrifying alternative had not even occurred to me.

"This will be tricky, but give it a pull anyway," Charles said, and he pulled up in one strong movement so that that the entire blanket moved. What I found to grip on was not exactly solid, but as I pulled, the blanket moved as well. "You have it?" Charles queried. I nodded, and Charles counted to three, after which we both tugged together. The entire shape moved toward us about six inches.

My stomach constricted as my mouth filled with vomit. The stench from the decaying body hit me so suddenly I didn't have time to say anything to Charles, who, like me, had dropped his share of the load and had stepped backward away from it, covering his nose with his forearm. He had begun to gag but picked up something from the ground. And then Charles, left-hemispheric brained Charles, the planner of all things, shoved a bucket into my arms.

For the next few moments, the backyard of Rod Chambers was filled with the sounds of loud choking, gagging, and the ultimate cough that comes when the stomach releases its contents. Finally, I moved as far away from the putrid soil as I could, sat on the ground, put the bucket down to my side, but held on to it, as a drunk would a toilet. Charles soon crumpled beside me.

"Charles, I don't understand," I said, realizing that the effort to speak was making me sicker again. "You can move the body. But you can't move the DNA. The way I understand it, there was blood in the house…"

Charles took a deep breath and blew out slowly. "It has all been considered. We just need to move the body."

"How, Charles? How do you account for the DNA?" I asked, feeling the warmness creep up toward my head, the sweat spring to my forehead, as though I had contracted the flu.

"Later, Brent."

"Where's Jason?" I said in pleading voice. "I thought he was supposed to help."

"He's with Dato, and he is helping," Charles said. "We'll talk later. Let's get the body moved first."

7:45 P.M.

Jason Young-Soo O'Leary

"I don't know what to tell you," Dato said. "All things in our circle of friends are sacred. We never gossip. We never tell."

I could see Detective Ryder transform before us. He became alert and focused—like he'd had a full night's sleep. I could only imagine he was congratulating himself on his good fortune. This sultan appeared out of nowhere with information about his most important case. I watched his excitement build, and then I watched him try to shield it. He was going to take this slow and easy. That was good for Charles's plan. Keep the detective away from Rod's home.

"Uh…" Ryder's voice became soft and polite. "Your Highness, if you have any information that can help us in this case, you really need to share it with us."

Dato continued staring away from the table, as though he hadn't heard Ryder. *We have to be convincing*, I thought, and I turned squarely toward him. "Sorry, Detective, this is not the purpose of the sultan's visit."

"Come on now, gentlemen," he said in a voice that I assumed was to endear him to us—trust him perhaps. "You know all information could be subpoenaed. But I don't want to embarrass anyone. Let's just keep it quiet."

I laughed. "I doubt that you could find a judge that would issue a subpoena to a royal guest of Los Angles. Or perhaps we could consult the mayor about this."

Ryder looked like he wanted to punch me in the face. Still, he continued with soft diplomacy. "I don't mean to offend," he said. "But we are talking about a murder here…a man's life. His family will never rest until they have solved the crime. Don't you want to help them out?"

Dato moved his eyes slowly to Ryder and stared at him for a long moment. "You're very persuasive, Detective. But I'm not sure what I know will be of any real help to you."

Ryder pushed aside his plate and leaned on his elbows. "Anything—anything at all. Let me decide if it's helpful or—"

"This has to be confidential," I interrupted. "The sultan is leaving tomorrow and doesn't want his name linked to a criminal investigation."

"Absolutely," Ryder said, his voice full of sincerity. "Totally confidential."

7:45 P.M.

Brent Jackson

"How are we going to move the stinking thing?" I was still clutching my bucket. "We can't get near it."

Charles grabbed my arm and pulled me to my feet. I immediately felt dizzy and leaned forward, hands on my knees.

"Take a deep breath, and come with me," Charles said.

I took five deep breaths and then ran to the body with Charles. We both grabbed the shoulders and heaved together. The body slipped completely out of the grave. We started to pull one more time, but the air slipped out of me, and my lungs screamed for more. I dropped the body and ran as far away as I could, past the watering lion, past the pond, and only then, with gasping breaths, filled my lungs with air.

Charles had followed closely and was wheezing behind me. "That was good." He gasped. "Let's try that again."

My lungs expanded and contracted rapidly, but I couldn't seem to get enough air. I began to feel dizzy and sat back on the ground, placing my hand on my knees. I didn't think my body would be able to recover quickly from another retching dose of putrid air.

"It's time I knew more, Charles," I said. "I promise I won't back out. But this doesn't seem like it can work."

Charles looked at his watch and then sat cross-legged in front of me. "What won't work?"

I waved my arm toward the house. "I've already said it. There's no way that Rod's not going to be under serious investigation. They'll find the bloodstains. They'll arrest him—body or not."

Charles locked eyes with me. "You forgot to mention that once they find the DNA, they will search the grounds for the body. They will eventually find the ground we worked—full of incriminating tissue samples."

As my breath and heartbeat slowly returned to normal, I began to feel the Los Angles night coolness on my bare arms. I longed to put on my shirt but also felt the need to have something clean to put on later. "Thank you for agreeing with me," I said. "I forgot to mention that."

Charles looked at me without expression. "So how can I keep the police from digging in the back yard?"

A sharp wind had crept from the outside to the sanctuary of Rod Chambers's fortress walls and moved behind me, further chilling my bare back. From somewhere, perhaps inside the house, three notes of the *Andy Griffith Show* song rang out. The chilling silence that followed made me acutely aware that there were no other sounds, no birds, no crickets, as though they too were demonstrating quiet respect of the dead. I looked, wide eyed, toward the house.

"It's Gabe," Charles said. "Rod's pet."

I shook my head. "The only way the police won't look here," I said, "is if they are able to find the real body."

Charles nodded but said nothing. There was more. The shivers started, first under the blade bones of my back and then extending all the way to the sides of my arms. "The only way the police won't arrest Rod," I said, "is if they have another suspect."

Charles stood up. "Please. Let's finish now."

Another suspect.

The pieces of Charles's plan seemed to fall together. I stared in disbelief at the man I thought I had known, understood—believed in. Charles was not capable of this, was he? I could not hide my disappointment and remained on the ground. "So who is it going to be?" I said. "Who are you going to frame?"

Jason Young-Soo O'Leary

8 P.M.

Dato looked inquisitively at me. We both realized that this was the moment of no return. We now fully realized the probable outcome of us following the instructions that Charles had given us. I would never have been able to participate in this had I not known, with virtual certainty, that my father would have done the same thing. He loved Charles, and though he would have tried to talk him out of this, as Dato did when he first heard the scheme, he would have eventually cooperated.

I nodded, and Dato immediately turned his attention back to Ryder. There was sadness in Dato's eyes.

"Well, perhaps there are some facts of which you are not aware," Dato began, and Ryder pulled out his detective notepad from his back pocket and began scribbling rapidly.

12:30 P.M.

Brent Jackson

I had lost what seemed like three days' worth of food in my bucket. But at least we had gotten the body bag zipped up. I never could bring myself to ask Charles where he got that! The zipper stuck as we were halfway around. Charles squeezed the sides together while I pulled it along. We struggled and squeezed and managed to yank it through, but not before, in explosive gasps, we lost our precious air. We dropped the load and ran.

"Well, there it is." Charles gestured toward our work, after we had managed to breathe pure air for a few moments.

We had not spoken since I had first realized the depth of this sickening conspiracy of which I was now a full partner. Charles—my friend—was going to frame an innocent man, and I was helping him. No wonder Charles told me I would not agree to this if I knew the details. He'd asked me to trust him, willing to tell me only that I might be breaking the law, not that I was committing an act that would damage my very soul.

Charles was sitting on the ground, resting. Even in the shadows, I could see the sharp features of his face, his focused stare. He seemed, surprisingly enough, quite calm. He looked at me in such at way that I felt a melting in my chest. There is no funeral more grievous than the quiet, solitary one we have when our friends disappoint. I mourned for the loss of the respect I had had for Charles.

"It has to stop here," I said, surprised to hear myself say this.

"What has to stop here?" Charles didn't move.

"We leave the body just the way it is. We call the police. We tell them everything. We all take our medicine." I pulled off the nasty gloves and saw how my hands were trembling.

"What are you talking—"

"I'm not going to apologize for obeying the law, and I'm not going to be dissuaded from it." I threw the gloves on the ground and stood up. Charles stood with me.

"You're scaring me, Brent." Charles tore his gloves off and threw them on the ground as well.

"You're right, Charles. I would never have agreed to frame an innocent person. And the part of you that would allow it to happen is certainly one that I never knew existed." I stepped toward the house. "This was never an option."

Charles stepped in front of me, arms down by his side, legs a stance apart, his muscles tense, and he grabbed my shoulders. "I can't let you call the police."

I prepared for battle. "You can't stop me. I don't care how much you want to help Rod. It's wrong, and you know it!"

The wind picked up. As the palm trees were the highest in the yard, they began to bend slightly. It blew briefly through the yard.

A car, with the tightly belted sound of a large and finely tuned engine, drove slowly past.

I saw Charles's body relax. "What if…what if the innocent wants to be framed?"

"Wants to be?" I stood there, shifting my weight from one foot to the other, and stared unflinching into Charles's eyes.

But Charles could not look at me, and I understood who the innocent was immediately.

"Charles. This body over there is not of your doing. You don't have to—"

"I think I do," Charles said.

"But be practical. What lesson are you teaching him?" I reached forward and grasped his shoulder. I knew that there were no words that would alter Charles's careful plans, but I felt I had to try. "Are you teaching him that life has no responsibility, that there are no consequences? That people don't have to pay for their actions?"

"Some lessons are just too tough and come too late, my friend." Charles rested his left hand on my outstretched arm. There was a thickening in his voice. "I need you to be with me on this, Brent…please."

I nodded and stepped back, staggering slightly. I turned and looked about us. We still had to fill up the hole, replant the Caladiums, and put the body in the van—then the long drive to the desert. I felt exhausted.

"We'd better get moving," Charles said as if reading my thoughts.

"Where does it come from?" I asked him.

Charles wiped his face with the back of his hand. "What?"

"That strength," I said. "I'll never have it. I just spent the last two days—"

"Trying to find it." Charles completed my sentence. "But you couldn't."

"That's right. I couldn't."

He turned toward the gravesite, and I followed. We picked up our shovels and methodically began tossing dirt back in the hole. Occasionally Charles would walk around on it, pressing it as firmly down as possible. We were emptying the extra bags of dirt into the ground when Charles said suddenly, "I remember you told me your laptop was acting up on you. What was it?"

What an odd question for Charles to ask at this particular time. I had complained about a problem I was having with my computer to Charles months ago, on a long-distance telephone call. Perhaps he was trying to keep our work light. "Yeah. It wouldn't start up right. It kept searching for a D drive and showed an error."

Charles tossed an empty bag of soil onto the ground. "What was the error?"

"Well, I didn't have a D drive. Somehow the software thought I did and wouldn't let me proceed until it found it."

"So how did you fix it?"

"I tried for hours to figure out which software was making it do that. But I gave up on that."

Charles picked up the shovel, patted down the soil, and then stood on the empty grave. "But you fixed it?"

"I fooled it," I said. "I partitioned off a space on my hard drive and named it D drive."

Charles laughed. "So then when the mysterious software looked for D drive…"

"It found what it thought was the D drive and then continued. Works fine now."

"Good solution." Charles paused and leaned on the shovel. The partial moon I had observed earlier was making its final descent and hesitated over the cement walls as the outlines of a smooth, dark shadow began to flow toward the house. It took me a moment to realize how truly quiet it was. "We guys are a peculiar species," Charles said. "We will dicker with a computer, a car, or a washing machine for hours, even days, until we get it right. Yet we are defeated by the simplest of relationships."

It began to rain—not the gully-washer typical of this time of year but a soft, gentle, cleansing rain that covered our work, our tracks, cleaned us of all our business before we finally were able to get into the van and drive off toward the desert. We turned the heater on us to dry off and drove silently until city lights had become a glowing haze in the rearview mirror. Only the blackness of the sky, pierced by our headlights, was in front of us.

"How were you able to jump up that hill?" Charles asked.

I moaned from the weariness and the random questions. "What hill, Charles?"

"The one in the story you told us. You made a supernatural jump up a hill with a one-hundred-forty-pound boy on your side. How did you do it?"

"I don't know, Charles. I don't know how I did it."

As I watched Charles staring out the window, I could not elude that distractive feeling that I was not just an observer for Charles's play. It wasn't just the sheer force of his personality that had somehow solidly connected all of this. It was something else.

Charles watched the instruments closely, careful not to speed. As we approached the desert, the black night fell like a backdrop onto the rear window.

"So I wonder..." Charles said finally, "can you do it again?"

Chapter Twenty-One

Eight Months Later (April 6, 1994)

Brent Jackson

I took Daniel with me to witness Charles's sentencing. I wanted him to see the judge, watch Charles's face, and the faces of all those in the courtroom. Then someday, when he was older and had children of his own, I would tell him what he saw and what it had meant to us all.

The courtroom was filled and the hallways were lined with battalions of reporters with their cameras. The story had been sensationalized ever since Detective Ryder had made the news-breaking announcement that Al Renfield's body had been found in the desert and that the chief suspect was not Rod Chambers, as once thought, but Rod's estranged father.

I had read every newspaper and tabloid article about the "Rod Chambers Scandal" and watched talk-show hosts banter about it until I had nearly gone blind. The Los Angeles papers were full of "close-ups" about the detective who solved the case. One interviewer asked where he got his biggest tip that helped him to solve the case, and he had quipped that a "good detective, like a newspaper reporter, has to protect his sources." But his most important source had confirmed, he allowed, that there had been feuding between Rod's agent and Rod's father, who had reentered his life since his mother's death and had tried to take over his career. The detective shook his finger in the air and said that was the clue that put the rest of the pieces together. After that, he modestly declared, he had just followed good police procedure.

There had been no real trial. Charles had plea-bargained "no contest"—the equivalent of a guilty plea—to charges of second-degree murder and obstruction of justice in a police investigation. The story became talk-show material, however, when movie star Rod Chambers himself burst into the police station and personally confessed to the murder of his own agent. Detective Ryder looked sympathetic as he addressed the cameras and spoke about the star America loved. Detective Ryder had expected such a confession, he said. His "sources" had explained that Rod had developed a misguided and unnatural attachment to his father and might try this sort of thing.

But the evidence that put Charles at the time and at the scene was overwhelming. There were even airline records putting him in LA at the time of Al's disappearance. By the time Rod remembered the DNA evidence and demanded police action to take samples around the house, Detective Ryder had grown tired of Rod's outbursts and refused to spend additional time and money for a crime that was, in Ryder's mind, solved. Additionally, when Charles eventually confessed, he had told them where the body was—an important detail that Rod Chambers, also professing to be the murderer—was left without. Detective Ryder assumed Rod was trying to stay in the spotlight, like all movie stars. He wouldn't be a party to it.

The back of the courtroom door opened, and two guards escorted Charles to the desk in front of us. Charles looked around, saw me, and, with a half smile, nodded his head. His eyes scanned the courtroom. He sat down, turned his head, and continued looking. Finally he caught my eye again. I quietly shook my head. Rod Chambers had not arrived.

Charles had remained quiet since his first arrest. After he made bail, he never spoke publicly and dodged reporters as best as he could. He also avoided me, and when we did speak, we avoided any mention about the circumstances involving the trial. He told me how he had to sell his house to pay for the attorney expenses, how he had acquired a small apartment because the judge had refused to allow him to leave the LA area, how he had developed an insatiable appetite for Korean food and had stored jars of kimchi in his refrigerator.

Two weeks prior to sentencing, Charles had called me and asked if, next time I came to LA, I would meet him at the Bulgogi House restaurant in Korea Town.

"Perhaps on your way to Asia?" he offered.

I had no plans for at least three months to go to Asia, but I could hear the strain in his voice. I took the next plane to LA and walked into the restaurant according to his directions. As I entered, Charles stood up, paid the cashier, and motioned for me to follow him outside. At the street, he turned, gave me a brilliant Charles smile, and I noticed that, although Charles was as striking as ever, he had the promise of forty on his face for the first time.

A taxi pulled up beside us, and the driver stuck his head out the window. "You John Smith?" he hollered.

"That's me." Charles opened the door for me while I scooted across the back seat.

"Let's try another restaurant," Charles said when he had shut the door. "I don't think I'm being followed anymore, but—"

"I had my heart set on Bulgogi," I said, referring to Korea's most famous barbecued meat dish.

"What makes you think I don't?" Charles gave instructions to the driver to take us to the Korean Garden restaurant located in Culver City.

Once inside the restaurant, we sat down at a table that had a grill in the center and a large ventilating chimney above us. The waiter brought us a dozen or so Korean side dishes, lit the grill, and poured the marinated meat into its center. The old, familiar smell of soy sauce, onions, garlic, and sesame seed oil inflamed our appetites so strongly that we both grabbed our chopsticks and ate silently.

About ten minutes later, I was piling rice onto my tongue to rescue it from the fiery sting of kimchi. "Rod showed up at my apartment," Charles said.

"When?" The last I had heard, Rod and Charles had not seen each other since the arrest.

Charles picked up a crisp slice of seaweed with his chopsticks, plunged it into his rice bowl, expertly wrapping it around a large mouthful of rice. "Last week. He was angry."

"Confused?" I said.

"Angry," Charles emphasized. "He shouted that he would never accept me as his father." Charles picked up the teapot and filled our cups. "I told him it didn't matter. But he said that the only thing I had done was make him feel worse, that he could never live with all the guilt."

Charles picked up his teacup and blew across the top of it holding his face inches from the cup. Without moving his head, his eyes turned toward me. I then knew why I had been called.

And so, three days later, I found myself in a cheap, out-of-the-way, low-class, very dark bar with a flashing red sign because that was absolutely the only place where Rod would agree to meet me.

There was a pause in the noisy conversations of the courtroom as the judge's door opened. On first glance, she looked like a middle-aged, respectably proper judge-type lady. But on second glance, I could see that her blond hair was pulled back in a bun. Her features were perfect and her complexion even, with a slight pallor to them that I suspected was a light powder. This judge was hiding her beauty.

The bailiff called us all to rise. Daniel rose with me as though we were one. I put my hand on his shoulder and pressed it. Charles turned around again and searched the crowd. One smartly dressed gentleman moved to our row and pointed at the empty spot next to Daniel, who put his hand over it and whispered that it was saved.

I had ordered coffee at the flashing red-signed club, and the bartender, a very wide-mustached man with impressive forearms, looked at me like I had just ordered corn flakes. He asked for the two dollars in advance. I slipped two one-dollar bills across the bar to him, where he received them, picked them up, and examined them as though they might be photocopies. He stepped away, wiped the spot in front of me, and slid the cup and saucer over. There were only two other men there, each drinking alone.

I felt a strong instinctive urge to protect my back and so moved away from the bar to an empty spot at a booth. The table had the strong smell of spilt whiskey, but the seat looked dry enough. I sat down and waited.

A man entered, wearing a dark baseball cap turned backward and heavy-framed dark glasses. He walked directly to me, sat down, and tossed the glasses on the table in front of him. "I'm Rod Chambers," he said.

We shook hands, and the bartender approached us. I asked for a refill. Rod ordered straight gin.

"Gin? Straight?" I said, and I immediately regretted it.

He ignored me while the bartender brought it over. Rod picked it up and stared at me over the rim of the glass while he took a long, slow sip. "It's amazing how many people are trying to be my father nowadays."

I ignored the comment and dropped a spoonful of sugar in my coffee. I wasn't sure where to go next. "Nice cap," I finally said. "I'd like to get one like that for my son, but the stores in my city all have their bills in the front."

There are some moments when something sounds so funny when it's inside your head and then you hurl it out and it is just awful. This was one of those moments. Rod removed his dark glasses, stared at me, and shook his head, almost imperceptibly. He looked at me like I had just told him a redneck joke.

"Sorry, Mr. Jackson. I am not disarmed by your attempts at humor, nor am I drawn in to you with your attempt at informality. I really have no idea why I came here. But it's getting late and—"

"I know why you came here."

"Terrific." He nodded toward me. "Will this next approach be psychological, or is there a Gandhi moment I need to be prepared for?"

He was challenging me three steps ahead of myself. I took a sip of coffee as the adrenaline raced through my body. "All right," I said. "Since you very much like to establish that you're not a game player, let's dispense with the games."

"Ah," he said in mock agreement. "Let's play like there are no games now."

"Okay. You're right in a manner of speaking," I said. "I was trying to get you to feel comfortable. That's a little different than manipulation—just comfortable, relaxed. But since I now see how clever you are, let's put all this aside."

"Embedded flattery undercoated with a pinch of sarcasm. I like it."

I had known this was not going to be easy, but his piercing cynicism was even sharper than Charles had prepared me for. "Let me try another approach," I said evenly. "Everything I heard about you and now witness here tonight has told me that you are exactly the selfish, spoiled, Hollywood urchin that I thought you were."

Rod clapped his hands. "Bravo." His mouth was smiling, but his nose was crinkled in distaste, like he had just eaten a lemon slice. "Very good attempt at the honest approach. I should now be hurt, rebuffed, and eager to prove you wrong."

"Good idea. Why don't you prove me wrong?" I said. "You're so sure everything I'm saying is a lie, everything Charles is doing is a lie—how would you be able to detect the truth?"

Rod started to speak but instead picked up his drink, sipped it, and shook his head slowly.

"You know so much about lies. What do you know about truth? You say you know immediately when they are lying. How do you know when they are speaking the truth?"

Rod thumped the rim of his glass twice, making it ring.

"Or perhaps you think everything anybody says is a lie?" I continued.

One of the men in the bar began to raise his voice at the other. The bartender stepped between them.

"Okay, I'm going to help you out. I'm very tired," he finally said. "You have said one thing that I cannot so easily dismiss. I don't know what is a lie and what's not."

"That's because you don't have all the answers. I could be your greatest con or your greatest friend, and you can't tell the difference."

Rod studied me for a long moment. Finally, without even turning around, he lifted his hand above his head and raised one finger.

"What are you doing?" I said.

"What does it look like I'm doing? I'm ordering another drink."

I laughed, and Rod's faced reddened.

"Nobody's paying attention to you," I said very slowly like I was talking to someone who had just started speaking English. "You have to turn around and get their attention. Nobody here knows who you are, remember?" I pointed to the hat.

"Oh…right." He blinked, turned around, and waved at the bartender.

He wiped his hands on the front of his shirt. He examined his empty glass for the third time.

"So why don't you tell me?" I said.

"Tell you what?" He looked up at me in surprise.

"Don't make me tell you why you came here. You tell me."

"Why don't you—" he raised his voice.

"Games," I interrupted him. "Games. Honesty. Didn't we agree? You laughed when I suggested them."

The bartender brought the gin and set it down in front of him. Rod dug in his pocket for a bill and placed in the bartender's outstretched hand. "All right," he said to me.

I waited.

"I came here," he spoke slowly and so softly I had to lean forward to hear him, "in the hope that you could give me one reason why I shouldn't kill myself."

He slipped his cap off and laid it on the table. We both stared at it for a moment.

"I can't do that," I said.

The judge hit the bench with her gavel and brought the courtroom to order. She asked for Charles to stand.

"Do you have anything to say before I pass sentence?" she said. The judge was alert, tensed, and looking at Charles as though he was the only one in the room.

Neither Charles nor his attorney moved for a moment. "No, Your Honor," Charles said finally.

The judge's shoulders fell. She pulled out a handkerchief and slipped off her gray-rimmed glasses, polishing them. "This case has many questions that have still not been answered to my satisfaction."

Someone coughed in the courtroom. The stirrings of the press, moving noisily about outside, leaked in just enough to give a background sound—the rumblings of a crowd.

"The prosecuting team has offered you up to this court on a platter of culpability. They have placed you at the scene, found your prints, even offered a motive. Yet you have not a hint of a record—not even a traffic ticket—and no history of violence. You plead 'no contest,' which I must accept as a guilty plea. Furthermore, you have remained mute, offering no defense—not even permitting a character witness to plead for the mercy of the court."

She paused and stared at Charles for a long moment. "It is also possible, from the forensic studies, that Mr. Renfield was killed from a fall and not a blow to the head, as was originally thought. Still, you do not offer this court the slightest encouragement to consider that theory."

What she said is true, I thought. But I also suspected that Charles feared that if he prepared any defense at all that the prosecution would go after more evidence. This might lead to the feared DNA evidence at Rod's home.

She slipped her glasses back on. "I am very uncomfortable with this case," she said, "very uncomfortable, indeed."

Rod looked at me as though I had struck him. I could see the anger rise and fall in his face. I repeated the words. "I can't do that. I can't talk you out of killing yourself."

"Well, I wanted honesty," he said, breathing hard.

"You have all the information you need to make that choice."

Rod glanced at me and looked away. "I see where this conversation is going. Thanks then—for nothing." He spat out the words bitterly, picked up his gin, poured it down his throat, and stood up.

"Wait." I stood up with him.

His face was flushed. "What do you want me to say? That I've been given a second chance, that I can take up tennis and travel to Europe while that…that…man sits in jail in my place!"

"Don't ask me about that. Ask your father."

"I do not accept him as my father." Rod threw the glass at the wall, smashing it. The bartender turned sharply. "Did he do this to make me love him?" Rod shouted. "Is this some perverted way of trying to make me accept him?"

The bartender walked around the bar toward us. I grabbed Rod's shoulders, trying to calm him, but instantly realized my mistake. He broke loose of my grasp and swung his right fist on the left side of my face. I flew back against the wall, hitting my head, and then slid down to the floor directly onto the broken shot glass; searing pain flowed from my head into the cavity of my back. I felt warm blood drip onto my forehead.

Rod stood above me, frozen, looking like he had been the one struck. "Brent. I…" He didn't finish his sentence.

"What the…!" The bartender bent down to look at me. "I'm going to call an ambulance and the police," he said.

I found that I was able to move. "No police," I said. "He'll take me to the hospital." I pointed to Rod and extended my hand.

He stepped forward, robot-like, and helped me to stand.

"You'd better pay him something for the damage," I whispered into his ear.

Rod opened his wallet and pulled out a wad of hundred-dollar bills. He stuffed them into the bartender's hand, put his arm around me, and helped me to the door.

Once in the car, Rod pushed his foot on the gas and squealed the tires as he turned around the first corner. I asked him to slow down. "It doesn't feel that serious," I said. "Probably needs a stitch."

Rod slowed down in perfect obedience. His anger was spent. We drove silently through the dark streets toward the hospital.

"I know what you're thinking," I said.

Rod held the steering wheel with both hands, a light far ahead of us changed to yellow, and he slowly applied the brake.

"You're thinking," I said, "that this is the final straw, that if there were any doubts before, there are no doubts now. You can't be trusted. Your temper can't be trusted. You are thinking you should have pulled that trigger months ago."

The light changed to green. Rod looked both ways and slowly accelerated.

"There's some tissue in there." Rod pointed at the glove compartment. "You should hold it against your head."

"It's a very long story that I don't have time to tell now," I said as I pulled the tissue out, "but your encounter with your father encouraged me to look for my own." I dabbed my face and forehead and looked at the tissue. It was soaking.

"Did you find him?" Rod stared straight ahead and accelerated.

"Yes."

Rod turned to look at me, gave me a double take, slowed the car down, and pulled over under a street lamp. "You're a mess. You're going to scare the emergency room attendants." He took the tissue from my hand. "Your spit or mine?"

"Mine, please." I stuck out my tongue.

He pressed the tissue against my tongue and then began to wipe the right side of my face.

"So how is your father?" he said.

"Very rich. Very set in his ways. I felt sorry for him."

"Will you see him again?"

"No."

He pulled the last tissue out of the box. "Hold this one here." He guided my hand to the place on my head where it was throbbing the most. I pushed it against my head as hard as I could stand it. Rod put the car into drive, and we moved forward.

"I'm glad I met my father," I said. "It's nice to know. But it was what I learned from the search for my father that was the most valuable to me."

The hospital direction signs began to appear on our right. "We're almost there," he said.

"I learned that there are many people like us," I said, "like you and me—sons and daughters raised without a father."

"Yeah, I know. And we're all a mess." Rod slowed down and turned into the emergency entrance.

"Not all, but many of us," I said. "I have psychotic episodes. You have rage."

"*Rage*..." He said the word slowly.

"I saw on the news this morning that a woman driver accidentally cut off a man in traffic. He pulled up in front of her, ran her onto the shoulder, and got out of the car. Before she could get her window up, he reached in, grabbed her dog, and threw it into the traffic."

Rod pulled the car in front of the emergency door and shut off the engine.

"Guys with rage beat their wives, break things, pick up guns, and start shooting people."

"Thanks for telling me that," Rod said. "I feel a lot better."

The tissue was soaked. I threw it out the window and pressed my bare hand against my forehead. "But I also found really good news. There is help. There are mild medications that have almost no side effects but kick into action when a man's temper begins to flare. There's counseling. There's God."

"You're bleeding badly," he said. "I'll help you inside."

I held my hand up. "No. I'll go alone. They'll recognize you."

"That's ridiculous," he said. "Let me—"

"No, let's not. Trust me on this."

He looked down at his hands. "I don't know what to say."

"Say you'll keep the promise you made with your father. He promised that he would get you off with no consequences. He has kept his part." I said this sternly and then added, "Also say you'll get the help you need. I know it sounds like a Band-Aid, but it works. It's easy, and it's available. Your father gave you your life back. It was his gift to you. You just have to take it."

Rod leaned back against the car seat and placed his hands loosely on the steering wheel. "I don't know why he did it."

"I'll bet you know the answer to that too."

"I don't know. I don't." Rod leaned his head against the top of the steering wheel. "Maybe out of the guilt of losing his daughter. Or maybe…"

"Maybe what?"

His lower lip began to quiver. "Maybe to give me another chance." His voice was hesitant, fearful.

As an attendant approached our car, I opened the door. "I'm not sure either. But I think you're on the right track." I put one foot on the curb. "I've thought about it a lot, and my theory is this. By the time he met you, you were all grown up, and 'one more chance' was the only thing left he had to offer."

"You give me no choice," the judge said. "For involuntary manslaughter, I am sentencing you to ten years, and for willfully plotting to block criminal justice, ten years—to be served consecutively." She slammed her gavel down and stood up.

Twenty years! The two guards put Charles's hands behind his back and cuffed him. He turned around and looked at me, then at the door. He was still watching it as they led him out of sight.

But the door did open, and Nicole came in. She sat on the other side of Daniel but reached over and put her arm around my shoulders. We were there a long time, until the last reporter had left and we were alone in the courtroom.

As we sat there, I turned the next corner of my life.

"Daniel?" I said, looking into his eyes.

"Yes?" he said.

I tried to match his matter-of-fact tone. "I finished reviewing your proposal, and I have some changes to make."

"What changes?" he said without expression.

"Instead of meeting every Saturday afternoon," I explained, "I'm scheduling us for Saturday and Thursday evenings as well."

There was a pause. "I have baseball practice on Thursday night."

"I know. I'll go with you."

Daniel made no comment.

"Daniel?"

"Yes?"

"Are you listening to me?"

"Yes."

"And another thing."

"Yes?"

I took a breath. "How'd you like to go to Korea with me?"

"Korea?" he said, his voice suspicious. "Why?"

“I’d like to show it to you.”

Another long pause. He looked at Nicole. “I think Mom would like to go with you,” he finally said.

I looked at Nicole and then back at Daniel. “She can go with us next time.”

“Next time?”

“This time will be for us,” I said. I knew I was giving him too much information, but I had to say more. “And, Daniel, what would you think if I didn’t take the promotion to president?”

No delay this time. “That would be great,” he said with a slight lift in his voice. “But, Dad?” He stared, his green eyes regarding me—puzzlement, interest, skepticism. “Why?”

Everyone else had left the courtroom. Nicole and I sat there on the bench soaking in the absolute silence while each of us held one of Daniel’s hands. It would be tricky. I would have to work extra hours some evenings, be ferociously protective of other nights. But my job was secure. They knew they were lucky to have me. They had always thought of me as a rising star, and when I tell them this was as good as it would get, they’d be disappointed. *But*, I thought, *they’ll get over it.*

“Why, Dad?” Daniel repeated.

“It was something my father said to me,” I said.

“Something your father said to you?” Daniel repeated.

“Yes,” I said, and I smiled.

I laid my hand on the back of Daniel’s head, smoothing out a cowlick. “I think he may have taught me something after all. Someday I’ll tell you.”

Epilogue

Seven Years Later (2000)

Kuala Lumpur

Brent Jackson

I stood alone on the veranda of the Royal Selangor Club and wondered if Somerset Maugham had actually written at his table. *Perhaps not with pen and paper*, I thought. That came afterward, the finishing stroke on the masterpiece. But he must have sat out on that veranda looking across that space of green grass—men and women playing cricket on the lawn; elderly; newlyweds; the engaged; the hopeful; radiant, slender women in long, pressed dresses; lean and dark young men building an office complex in a once vacant field to the south. The air teemed with the smells of chicken and beef satay dipped in spicy peanut butter sauce; Indian curry sprinkled with sliced coconut and coriander; tangy orange shrimp dipped in fresh roasted sesame seeds; happy discussions that juggled multiple languages; the clip-clop of horses pulling their masters up to the great doors; the ceaseless ring of the bicycles rolling back and forth across the road.

Somerset Maugham must have sat on the veranda, his arms resting limply on his specially fitted teak cane, and with no more than the mere effort of moving his eyes across the sights of the Royal Selangor Club, he began to create his stories.

I sat down at the table on this warm September evening and waited. By seven thirty, the front lawn was packed. Couples sat on the ground with their children clustered under their arms; groups of men leaned against benches and trees. They were intensely focused on the bright lights of the seventy-five-foot color television screen, created by stacking monitors like building blocks, as they watched their Malaysian team play in the World Cup finals badminton tournament. The television announcer dominated the attention of the crowd with his rapid-fire descriptions. Occasionally, the Malaysian team made a point, and the cheers from those gathered around the club, even in the great room, vibrated the windows with the excitement.

Nicole had not wanted me to be too early or too late, so at the appropriate time, I stood up, glanced briefly toward the table, and then made my way slowly into the entry, up the stairs, around the corner, and pushed open the doors. Those inside the great room were preoccupied, at least for the moment, with the business of reuniting—seeing the faces that time had separated. Some of them stood on the dance floor; others formed small circles throughout the room. Conversation was seasoned with the soft flow of piano music played by an elegant young Chinese woman in a blue satin dress.

Several tables scattered about the room were covered in a multitude of dishes. A large, round, hunter-green birthday cake with three layers occupied one of them. I moved to the western table, the one with cheese dip and Western-style potato chips. I searched through the bottles placed on ice in a large bowl, moving them about and digging deep within the ice where I found a bottle that had been hidden. I picked it up and was about to twist the cap open when a waiter rushed to my side, gingerly removed the bottle from my hand, opened it, poured it into a glass, and with both hands, returned it to me as I nodded my thanks.

I examined the wine glass, sniffed it, and held it up in the air toward the frosted glass light globes, swirling the yellow liquid around the sides.

"So how did you get the only bottle of mango juice?" a soft voice said to my side. Nicole was wearing a gold-sequined dress that could have been painted on her. It was conservative enough for Malaysian standards but still revealed the distinguishing mole just off center of her perfectly shaped breasts. I was in my standard black tuxedo.

"Dato takes good care of me," I said, and I took a long, satisfying drink.

"Well, this is your party." She smiled, clasped my arm, and leaned her head onto my shoulder. Her eyes turned to the dance floor to see how well her aunt Ginny was holding up in bright conversation with Dato.

I watched with her. "Look at that. All these people are here because of you," I said. "Most traveled halfway around the world because my wife can talk the Japanese into buying rice."

"I think that must be your way of saying that I'm persuasive." Nicole brushed something off the front of my black tuxedo jacket. "But they're here because of you. It's your forty-fifth birthday."

"But Malaysia?" I laughed. "Some people have trouble organizing a party across town. You've persuaded my family, your family, more friends than I knew I—"

"That's just it. Most of your friends are on this side of the world," she said. "For our families, it's an adventure."

I put down my glass and looked for a long moment at my wife. *How is it*, I wondered, *that the guy here, who had visitations from flying alligators, who cried like a baby at concerts, who tiptoed around bullies in high school—how is it that this guy has the most beautiful wife in the room?*

"You're beautiful," I said, and I wondered at how insufficient those words were.

She reached up and adjusted my tie. "I'm getting old."

I looked down at her and pressed my hands to her shoulders. "I'm so sorry."

"Sorry I'm getting old?"

"No...that I always tell you how beautiful you are."

"And you're sorry because..."

"Because you must think that's all that I love about you."

She turned and looked out the window. "Sometimes I wonder…"

"Nicole, we've been married twenty years. It's…" I shook my head. "I don't know how to explain this, but it's not just your eyes that I love. Well…it's the way they see things. And"—I reached forward and ran my fingers over her mouth—"it's not just your lips that I love. It's what they say."

I ran my fingers across her soft shoulders. "You have the most beautiful skin I have ever seen, but what I love most is how it feels to me." I lifted up her chin and kissed her lightly on the lips. "You grow more beautiful every day."

She studied my face intently while I spoke and then was quiet for a long moment. "That was a good one."

I fixed my eyes on hers. "I meant every word."

"You're sweet." She squeezed my arm. "I haven't seen you act possessed for a long time now."

"I'm getting better."

"I can't remember the last time. Do you?"

"It's been a while." I took a big swallow of mango juice. "They're definitely not as strong."

"So what do you do?"

"Sometimes I just cry."

"That's very good, sweetie." She raised her hand to my cheek and stroked it. "I love a man who can cry." She rested her hand there for a moment. "And I promise not to get offended if you want to tell me I'm beautiful now and then."

I took her hand and kissed her wrist.

"Uncle Brent?" a familiar voice called out, and both our heads turned to see Jason, arm in arm with a petite young blond in a long blue maternity dress.

"Isn't Daniel here yet?" he asked. Jason, in his white dinner jacket, was exactly the height as his wife.

"He said he had to iron his pants," I explained. "He should be here in a moment."

"Hello, Julie," Nicole said. Julie smiled and stepped forward, taking both of Nicole's hands.

Jason watched Julie walk away. They had been married three years.

I leaned close to Jason. "Your father would have loved her."

"He sure would have," he stated enthusiastically. And his voice became solemn. "I really enjoyed myself at your house last Christmas."

"We enjoyed having you."

"You and Uncle Charles have been great. Last March I got a birthday card signed by him and all the members of cell block three."

I laughed. "Yes, I heard."

"I've received a letter from him weekly and a call once a month. His letters were full of"—he looked up—"joy."

"I'm sure Charles would like to hear you say that," I said.

"Oh, I've told him," he said.

The doors flew open, and a young man entered the room like a thoroughbred starts from the gate. His body quivered with the energy of a stallion. His brows furrowed, and his eyes darted back and forth across the room, pausing only twice, when he appeared to spot a familiar face. Each time he smiled, raised his hand, and then continued his search. Only when his eyes rested on me did he stop.

He didn't smile but nodded his head firmly to show that he had seen me and moved steadily through the crowd in my direction. He got as far as Jason. Jason Young-Soo O'Leary grabbed him by both arms and picked him up. Not an easy feat since Daniel was about eight inches taller. "Daniel, have you grown since Christmas? We're going to have to put a kimchi pot on your head."

Well, almost, I thought. He was still quite lean, but the clumsiness of puberty had passed, leaving behind a solidly muscular man with his mother's beauty on his face—sculptured cheekbones set-off emerald eyes framed by eyelashes that any woman would envy. Out of self-defense, I had gotten him his own telephone because it rang constantly by different female classmates asking him for "special" help with their homework.

Daniel pretended to give Jason a karate chop and then stood back, fixed his eyes on Jason, looked him up and down, and pulled him close, wrapping both arms tightly around him.

"So I hear I'm getting a nephew," Daniel said over Jason's shoulder.

"Or a niece," Jason added quickly, patting Daniel on the back. "We told the doctor we want it to be a surprise."

Daniel released his grip but kept his right hand loosely on Jason's shoulder. "I've missed you," Daniel said.

"Excuse me." A young woman had walked slowly up and stood behind Daniel. She had the face of one on the brink of womanhood. She wore almost no makeup, but her complexion was sunny, her velvet brown eyes almond shaped. Her long black dress revealed a slender shape but modestly covered her shoulders.

Daniel turned swiftly around and nearly bumped into her. He backed up sharply, knocking Jason away from him.

Jason stumbled and caught himself. "Excuse me." He shoved Daniel in the back. "I seem to have been standing in the place where you wanted to be."

Daniel ignored him. He stared. He gawked. He looked from her shoulder-length auburn hair down to her pink-painted toenails revealed through the black, open-toed evening shoes. Nicole stepped forward and took Daniel by the arm as though holding him up. "Daniel, this is your cousin, Kate. Kate, this slobbering young man is my son, Daniel."

Daniel's face scrunched up. I could read his mind—*Not my cousin!* he was thinking. His face clouded with disappointment, but he extended a hand. Kate took it firmly and greeted him.

Nicole let go of his arm. "Excuse me," she said. "My aunt Ginny is alone. I'm going to go talk to her."

"So"—Daniel shifted weight from one foot to the other—"how's Uncle Roy? I haven't talked to him yet."

"He's fine." Kate pointed to a gray-haired man who had joined a few of the Malaysians by the window, where they stood looking outside, watching the game on the giant TV screen.

Daniel didn't look but nodded. "That's nice."

Kate took a deep breath. "You don't remember me, do you?"

Daniel blinked, "Well…"

"I didn't think so." Kate frowned and looked toward her father as if remembering something. "Thanksgiving, about six or seven years ago. Uncle Roy and Aunt Ginny?"

Daniel frowned again while he thought. "Well, I remember Uncle Roy and Aunt Ginny coming to the house. Mom never prepares turkey, so we had had Cajun food. Afterward, Dad had put on a karaoke CD and forced everyone to sing songs. Uncle Roy and Aunt Ginny had their three kids with them, two boys and…Bucky?" he said in disbelief.

She shook her head. "How lovely. So sweet of you to remember."

Daniel protested." I…I never called you that. It was your brothers. You had…"

"Buck teeth." She reached back and brushed her hair back with the tips of her fingers. "Dentists today can do wonderful things." She smiled broadly and tapped the front of her teeth, showing him. They were perfect.

Daniel looked at her teeth and then at her eyes. He couldn't stop staring. She met his. "So, cousin Daniel. Come here often?"

"You know," he said, "the word *cousin* doesn't have quite the ring it used to." He took a deep breath and stepped back. "Yes," he said, "as a matter of fact, I do come here often. I've been all over this town—all over this club." He gazed out the windows.

She followed his gaze. "I was so surprised when Mom and Dad told me we were coming here." She turned back to him. "The history of this place—how Uncle Brent came here to meet his friends—well…it's fascinating to me."

Jason came up behind Daniel and folded one arm gently around his neck, as though he were capturing him. “Can I take him for just a moment?” Jason said to Kate. “We’ve got a little catching up to do.”

I looked at my watch. It was well past dinner, and I was starving. I had mistakenly thought the reunion was going to include dinner. Close by was a table laden with delicious Malaysian snacks. I headed for the scores of chicken and beef portions that had been placed on a stick and were roasting on a grill. I placed a few pieces of the chicken on my plate and then topped them with the spicy peanut sauce.

Across the table, another very familiar face caught my eye.

A young man was very much captured in an intense conversation in which he was clearly taking little part. Lest he escape, I noticed that two of Nicole’s young nieces were actually holding on to parts of the young man’s dinner jacket while they spoke in rapid-fire, staccato conversation, interrupted only by sudden bursts of giggles.

No doubt, I thought, *that the numbers for my birthday party have been increased three-fold due to the knowledge that this very famous man would be here.* I had seen nieces and cousins of my own here that I barely knew. Word got around fast when Rod Chambers was coming to town.

I felt myself being poked in the back.

“You cheapskate,” Jason said in mock exasperation.

“Guilty,” I said, nibbling a piece of the chicken off the stick. “But what did I not buy this time?”

“You flew your family here coach class.” Jason swung his arms in mock exasperation. “It’s a thirty-hour trip.”

Daniel stepped in between us. “We fly coach class everywhere.” Daniel tapped Jason lightly on the shoulder with his forefinger. “Dad uses the money he could spend on business class to help bring Mom and me with him.”

"Cheapskate," Jason teased, but then Julie beckoned him, and he flew to her side.

Daniel remained. He stuck his finger in my plate and scooped up a generous portion of the peanut sauce. He licked it clean and then leaned closer, speaking in a low voice, "Do you remember my cousin Kate?"

I looked over at the young woman, occasionally glancing in Daniel's direction. She was standing alone next to one of the white columns in the room. "Of course I do," I said.

He looked back toward her and shook his head. "Dad," he spoke in mournful tones, "this is awful."

I watched my son watch Kate. "She's beautiful, isn't she?"

"She's beautiful. She's smart… Who would have thought?" Kate caught us looking at her, and we both turned away. "What is this cousin prohibition about anyway?" he said, almost sharply, to me.

"Well," I said, "the theory goes that it's genetics. If people intermarry too closely to family lines, they're more likely to pass on undesirable traits."

"I don't think she has any undesirable traits, Dad." He scooped more sauce off my plate.

"Okay," I said, "let's think through this. You know that she is Uncle Roy and Aunt Ginny's daughter."

Daniel's face was serious. "I know. And Uncle Roy is Mom's brother."

"That would make her your cousin then, wouldn't it?"

Daniel looked down at his hands and popped his thumb knuckle. He said nothing.

"But what you didn't know…" I set down his plate and reached over to clasp Daniel's tie, sticking my finger firmly in his tie knot while giving it a twist and giving it a perfect dimple. "And what we probably never told you…is that Uncle Roy is Aunt Ginny's second husband."

Daniel looked up at me. His eyes widened.

"And you didn't know that Kate came from Aunt Ginny's first marriage."

He got the message. A smile slowly came across his face. He turned and looked at Kate, who was staring at a spot on the white column. "Thanks, Dad," he said without looking at me, and he was gone.

I turned and was about to approach Rod but saw that he was in the process of autographing the light-blue birthday party invitations of the two girls. He handed them back to them and then gently and expertly removed their hands, which he held for a while as the breathless girls stared deeply into his eyes. Finally, he slowly and firmly lowered their hands to their sides and then stepped back. He was free.

His eyes scanned the room until they stopped, and I saw him smile. Rod stepped forward.

The chatter of long-lost friends and family filled the room. But yet, amid the clatter, I could somehow hear Rod's clothes rustle as he passed through it all. As he touched some, they turned to him and were startled. Their faces filled with surprised laughter. He nodded and smiled. Sally Mannings, Nicole's sixty-eight-year-old great aunt, was talking to Nicole when he brushed up against her. She turned and found her face eight inches from the man whom the Academy of Fine Arts had awarded the Best Actor Oscar only last year. She nearly cried. In one very natural movement, he smiled and with both hands pulled her firmly close to him, kissing her softly on the forehead. He moved her head back and stared at her. They never spoke.

Nicole had covered her lower lip with her finger, an endearing gesture to me. She turned and looked directly at me. I mouthed the words, *I love you.*

Nicole smiled and walked to me, taking my arm. Together, we watched Rod release a flushed and now limp Aunt Manning and step forward again. He walked past the piano player, moved past the dance floor, and past the central white pillar of the great hall.

Outside, a sudden uproar from the crowds caused the conversations inside to be interrupted as many rushed to the large framed windows. Someone shut off the room lights, which made the outside appear to light up like Madison Square Garden. All heads were facing north, toward the outdoor television screen.

Rod, undistracted by the noise, had reached the center of the room.

This time, even the crystal glasses and chandelier shook. Malaysia had scored again, and they were now in a tie. With only seconds left in the game, the near-hysterical announcer declared that the new world champion badminton player would make the next point.

No one spoke. The casually acquainted in the room unconsciously placed their hands on each other's shoulders. The Americans, now caught up in the excitement, came close. The pianist had long stopped playing; the waiters had stopped serving. Someone far away cleared his throat.

And then the clamor hammered the night so loudly that I thought the crystal glasses might break. The shouts were followed by exaltations of joy, the lights from the giant TV blinking on and off in thousands of colors. All those in the room, Malaysians and Americans, silhouetted by the bright lights, celebrated with tears and hugs. Dato could be seen in the midst of them all, receiving congratulations from the Americans as though he himself had scored the final point.

The attention was off Rod, who continued his slow vigil.

Darkness would have hid him, I thought, *had it not been for his regal profile and long, loping stride as he moved at last toward an area to the right.*

His destination was someone standing near the doorway. The man held a soda in one hand and a tray filled with carrots in the other. A Malaysian couple next to him was clearly enthralled by whatever story he was telling.

I marveled how, in spite of the seven years in prison that had preceded this day, Charles still retained that all-American, boyish look. "Out early for exemplary behavior," the papers had said. Probably the only convict released who was met at the outside gate by seven prison guards, the librarian, and assistant warden. They gave him flowers.

There had been someone else waiting for him outside, I remembered. Someone who had flown to the prison the first Saturday of each month without fail. At first, Charles told me, they hadn't known what to say to each other, so they just played cards. Then they began to discuss books and movies. During the last few years, they talked about each other, and the four-hour afternoons flew by.

Without a sound or a change of expression, Rod entered Charles's group and laid his hand gently on Charles's shoulder, as though he were resting it there. Charles never stopped his story but turned slowly and stared momentarily at his son. No word was spoken between them, and without missing a beat, Charles was now back in his story. Rod listened to the story and lifted a carrot from Charles's plate, biting the end of it and chewing loudly.

"If Somerset Maugham could have been here," I said, putting my hand over Nicole's, "he would have written about Rod."

"That would be a good story," she said. "But I think Somerset would have liked your story better."

"My story?" I turned my head toward the window as more cheers filled the outside air.

"Because your story is more complete. And it has its own sequel—Kate's story."

"Kate?" I looked back at her. "What on earth are you talking about?"

"The lovely, fulfilled, balanced life Kate will have."

"Kate?" I repeated.

"Or whoever Daniel chooses to love someday. And for all the love he can give." Nicole stepped directly in front of me. "And she'll have you to thank for it."

I cocked my head to one side and deepened my voice. "You speaking woman-talk now. Me no understand."

Nicole laughed, patted me, and walked back toward her aunt.

I felt another pat on my shoulder.

"Will you be needing me for a little while?" This time it was a grinning Daniel standing at eye level to me.

"What's up?" I asked.

"I'd like to take Kate around the club, show her the place." Daniel's eyebrows danced as he spoke. "After all, this is my fourth time here. I know it pretty well."

"I think that's a nice thing to do," I said. "I'm sure Kate will be impressed."

Daniel looked toward Kate and smiled.

I saw the expectation in my son's eyes. It was clear he was fighting to keep himself from just laughing out loud so great was his joy. Kate was not far away and stood with the straight posture of a lady, arms folded above her tight, narrow waist. She seemed to be staring at the piano, located to my back.

"It's great, isn't it, Dad?" Daniel said, grinning with double dimples that shot almost up to his eyes. "I mean, we're not really cousins, are we?"

I almost laughed, and in the same moment, I knew I was in trouble. My hands began to shake. I held them in front of me and stared.

Daniel grabbed them and held them tight. "Dad? What is it?"

I pulled them away and held them to my side. "It's nothing, son, just jet lag. You go on."

Daniel watched me cautiously for a moment. I could feel my face flush, and beads of sweat appeared on my forehead. "Dad, you need to sit." He took me firmly by the arm and led me to a small sofa.

I nervously looked around. No one seemed to be watching me. "Please go ahead, son. I'm okay," I said, and I clenched my teeth to keep them from chattering.

The room became hushed as the sounds of a band began to play outside. Dato appeared at my side, totally oblivious to my condition. Dato leaned over as though he were about to whisper but, unable to suppress his glee about the recent Malaysian victory, shouted directly into my ear. "They're getting ready to pass on the trophy. Come, come. Let's look through the window." He ran to another group of people, taking them by the arm and leading them.

Kate's eyes followed Dato and then looked toward Daniel. He held up five fingers and mouthed, "Five minutes. Give me five minutes." Daniel turned his eyes toward me. "You're having a spell, aren't you? Never mind. Don't answer. I'll just sit here with you until it passes."

I felt a chill at my neck that moved slowly down the small of my back.

Daniel cocked his head to one side and smiled. The applause again thundered through the room. Shouts were heard outside of the club. All across the city, horns began to blare.

Kate, a slight distance from us, smiled.

I remember Kate's parents telling me how she had dreaded this trip. Malaysia was so far away, and she had never even been to Mexico. She had heard there was a jungle, and the thought of it frightened her. When she first came in the room, she had looked doubtful, tired. But things change fast.

Kate stared at Daniel for a moment and then turned away, running her hands through her hair. She looked out through the darkened room, over the deep-green lawn of the Royal Selangor Club, and down the long path that led to the blue-and-red colored fountain.

I knew that this was not what she expected—not what anyone would expect. If one had ever imagined such things, they would have been painted in pastel watercolors—the cover of a children's book, indistinct shapes in the midst of soft, swirling motions. Nondescript couples, painted with no more than six brushstrokes, moving in an absence of pattern toward a billowing cloud of floating mist. If she had imagined it at all, it would have been a dreamscape.

But this was not a dream. This was a young woman who would fulfill dreams she never knew she had. She would learn the rules of badminton. She would try it on the manicured grass in the front. She would absorb and reflect Daniel's every word as she walked around the club and through the hallways, peering into each room. Within a week, if Daniel encouraged her, she would probably find herself in the jungle.

Now she was daydreaming. Judging from the smile on her lips, I guessed she was planning on what she would say to Daniel, perhaps how he would react to her new tropical dress, and how she hoped this night would go on for a long, long time.

Daniel leaned against the back of the sofa and took my hand firmly in his. "You feel cold," he said, frowning. "But the color in your face is looking better." Daniel crossed his legs and waited.

I also leaned against the sofa, facing Daniel. I took a deep breath and felt the shaking subside.

Kate stole another glance at Daniel. Daniel caught her eye as well but held up five fingers again. "Five more minutes," he mouthed silently.

No doubt he wanted to take her through the Royal Selangor Club immediately and show her everything. But he stayed with me. Now he was the father, and I was the son, and I was the one in need. And he stayed. He sat with me patiently, smiling and full of hope, glowing with the determination and strength that comes from being loved and having a limitless supply of love to give back.

What you follow follows you, I thought, and then I smiled.

And Kate watched patiently and waited. Waiting for the moment when she could step forward and somehow be included in the life of this amazing man whom I called my son. A man whose future success had been tied, in more ways than she would ever know, to a chain reaction sacrifice that Charles began with his own son. And I understood Nicole's words—that Kate, or the woman Daniel chose to love some day, would receive its fruit. There would be no bursts of uncontrolled anger from this man, no demons to exhort, no bouts of unexplained depression to be shrouded by alcohol, and no futile searches for meaning to his life. Because of the full measure of love he received from Nicole and I, there would be no empty cavity in his soul. There would be no bottom to his heart.

"Take your time," I saw Kate whisper toward Daniel, and I thought, *No...five minutes, five years, wouldn't be too long to wait.*

Not for a man like this.

Acknowledgments

I wish to thank several people. I would like to thank my beautiful wife, Jan, for her love, support, and patience during the years it has taken me to finish this book. I would also like to thank my big brother, Tom, who is also my biggest fan in all things. After I heard Pastor and friend Craig Groeschel's message entitled, "What You Follow, Follows You," I knew how to approach this sensitive subject, so I am very grateful to him for that. I also want to express special appreciation to my best friend, Kyle Dillingham, who has heard many of these stories firsthand, over and over again.